I0643335

George C Graham

Graham's School Dialogues for Young People

George C Graham

Graham's School Dialogues for Young People

ISBN/EAN: 9783337334895

Printed in Europe, USA, Canada, Australia, Japan

Cover: Foto ©Andreas Hilbeck / pixelio.de

More available books at **www.hansebooks.com**

PREFACE.

In offering this collection of Dialogues to the public, the author aims at giving to advanced scholars an opportunity for the display of some dramatic power and ingenuity. They are not intended to be instructive, as he believes there are ample facilities for conveying information in all well regulated schools, and that serious and instructive dialogues are a sort of sugar-coated pill to most young folks. Hoping, therefore, that amusement, merriment and fun will not be considered objectionable by the professors, and certain of the full sympathy of the boys and girls, the author has written this little volume for the hours of relaxation from graver and more important studies.

The majority of the dialogues are humorous, but an opportunity has also been afforded for the introduction of some good recitations, and ample scope for the display of dramatic talent.

CONTENTS.

GRAHAM'S
SCHOOL DIALOGUES
FOR YOUNG PEOPLE.

THE EMPTY HOUSE.

Characters.

MR. LETTUM—*Owner of the empty house.*

MR. TAKUM—*Tenant of the empty house.*

MRS. TAKUM—*A very timid lady, afraid of burglars.*

PAT,
JERRY, } *Two ragged, barefooted Irish Newsboys.*

POLICEMAN.

SCENE.—*A Room, with a large open closet, and a window in back-ground. No furniture excepting one very shabby chair and an empty packing-box.*

Enter MR. LETTUM *and* MR. TAKUM, *conversing.* MR. LETTUM *carries a large bunch of keys.*

MR. LETTUM. Yes, sir, I can truly say the house is in perfect order throughout, papered and painted since the last tenants left.

MR. TAKUM. Modern improvements?

MR. LETTUM. Everything, sir. Stationary washstands, mirrors

in each front room, stationary wash-tubs in laundry, wardrobes in sleeping rooms, and every convenience.

MR. TAKUM. Any protection against burglary?

MR. LETTUM. I'm glad you spoke of that, for there is *every* protection—chains on every outside door, double back-action catches on every window, electric bells on each floor, and two very loud burglar alarms, one front and one back, steel traps on the cellar windows, and a patent alarm mat at the gate.

MR. TAKUM. You really rejoice me! Mrs. Takum is so excessively timid!

MR. LETTUM. H'm, yes! ladies are, as a rule.

MR. TAKUM. My wife is afraid of her own shadow if she sees it unexpectedly, faints at the sight of a cockroach, and has hysterics if a board creaks in the night. I am sure the sight of a burglar would kill her outright.

MR. LETTUM. Wife of my last tenant was just so! Dear me! her husband was always running to me for some addition to the protection of the property; so that I think I may safely assert that there is not a house in town that is so perfectly burglar-proof as this one. It is barricaded—positively barricaded—with bolts, spring locks, and contrivances to prevent felonious entrance.

MR. TAKUM. (*Aside.*) What a paradise for my dear Maria! I really must take the house. (*Aloud.*) Can I have immediate possession, Mr. Lettum? I believe we agreed upon the rent up-stairs?

MR. LETTUM. Yes, sir. I can leave the keys with you to-night, if you wish. The house has been cleaned within a week, so you can move in at once, if you wish.

MR. TAKUM. I will take it, then, for one year.

MR. LETTUM. I am sure you will continue a tenant much longer. You cannot desire a better property.

MR. TAKUM. I will be a better judge of that at the end of the year.

MR. LETTUM. Just so! You will take the keys?

MR. TAKUM. Yes. I'll call at your office in the morning and sign the lease. (*Takes keys from* MR. LETTUM.)

MR. LETTUM. Quite satisfactory, sir. Good afternoon!

MR. TAKUM. Good afternoon! (*Exit* MR. LETTUM.)

MR. TAKUM. (*Looking at his watch.*) Now I'll just step round and get Maria! Five o'clock! Plenty of time to cook a chop, and put up the furniture of one room. I'll go at once! It is scarcely worth while to lock up for a few minutes, particularly as there is nothing in the house to tempt a burglar. (*Exit* MR. TAKUM.)

After a moment, enter JERRY *and* PAT. *During the conversation between the boys the light must be gradually lowered, as if daylight was fading, till the stage is in the dimmest light; and this light must not be raised again, the candle giving light after it is introduced.*

JERRY. Was there iver sich iligant luck, Pat?

PAT. (*Laughing.*) Niver, me boy. (*Both stamp their feet and blow on their fingers, as if cold.*)

JERRY. Jist as I see the snow a-comin' down, an' was a-thinkin' how cowld the ould barril we've been slaping in would be the night, out comes the gint—

PAT. (*Laughing, and slapping his knees.*) An' clane forgot to lock the door! And, see the lovely closet, Jerry! We'll be warmer'n toost in there, sure!

JERRY. And the beautiful box! (*Peeping in.*) And by all good luck, Pat, there's an iligant layer of straw in the bottom.

PAT. A regular fither bed, be jabers!

JERRY. It's nearly dark, Pat. (*Yawns.*)

PAT. An' we've sold the last paper.

JERRY. Suppose we have a bit o' supper? (*Takes paper out of his hat.*) Here's an iligant bit of chase. (*Unfolds paper.*)

PAT. (*Takes paper out of his hat.*) And didn't I git two doughnuts for a cint because they was baked yisterday? (*Unfolds his paper.*)

JERRY. (*Taking paper from pocket.*) An' I found this bit o' cowld mate.

PAT. (*Taking paper from his pocket.*) Didn't an ould gint ating his luncheon chuck this out the windy? An iligant chicken bone, Jerry, me boy, with lashin's o' mate on it.

JERRY. Och, ain't it foine? (*Sits on end of box.*) Draw up the chair, Pat. (*They begin to eat.*)

PAT. Where's your tin cup, Jerry?

JERRY. (*Taking a small cup out of his pocket.*) Here.

PAT. I'll be huntin' some warther. (*Exit* PAT, *with cup.*)

JERRY. An' I'll put a taste more of the chase on his doughnut, and a thrifle more o' the mate over his way. Pat's bigger'n me, and it stands to rayson he'll ate more. Be jabers ! whativer is that? (*Bells ring, burglar alarms go off—in fact, all the noise that can be made back of stage.*) Powers alive! the b'y 'll be kilt.

PAT. (*Rushing in, his hair sticking up in terror.*) Arrah, Jerry, did iver ye hear the loikes o' that? (*Noise gradually dies away.*)

JERRY. Are ye hurted, Pat?

PAT. Niver a bit. But iverything I touched wint off, like fire-works on the Foorth o' July. There's bells on all the doors, an' rattles on the windys.

JERRY. Them's burglar things. I wonder if the police'll come in?

PAT. It's too early. We can slape in security, me boy. If thaves come into this house we'll hear thim sure. (*Both eat remainder of food.*)

JERRY. (*Anxiously.*) Are you sure the newspaper money's all right for the mornin', Pat?

PAT. (*Striking his breast.*) Niver you frit about that, Jerry, me boy. I've got it sewed up in me coat. An' who iver gits that's got to foight Pat Malone.

JERRY. An' can't he foight like a hyena, jist! Can we go to bed, Pat?

PAT. Whiniver ye like.

JERRY. I'll slape in the closet.

PAT. Sure the box is aisier, with the beautiful straw in it.

JERRY. (*Aside.*) So it is, and he'll slape like an angel in it. (*Aloud.*) But I'll fale safer in the closet, Pat, if you're outside here in the box. (*Creeps into closet, and lies down.*) It's just beautiful here. (*Sleepily.*)

PAT. (*Sighing.*) I could ate another supper if I had it, Jerry.

JERRY. Don't ye be a nepicure at your time of loife, Patrick Malone. It's ashamed of yes I am.

PAT. Small chance of it, Jerry. Are yes comfortable in there?

JERRY. Is it comfortable? Sure the President himself won't slape better than I will the night. (*Yawns.*) It's dark intirely, Pat. We won't touch nothink in the house, Pat.

PAT. (*Scornfully.*) What is there to touch, barrin' the thraps for thaves?

JERRY. But we wouldn't touch nothink, Pat, if there was piles o' goold.

PAT. Niver, Jerry. It's not thaves we are, only two poor Irish boys that's like to fraze an's cript in out of the snow. Good night, Jerry.

JERRY. (*Drowsily.*) Good night. (JERRY *sleeps. Stage almost dark.*)

PAT. (*Closing the closet door, till nearly shut.*) It'll be warmer for him with the door shut. Poor boy, he's clane tired out. An' I'll crape around the house a little to be sure there's no burglars. Whativer would we do if we lost the newspaper money again, as we did when a thafe of the world stole Jerry's hat with forty-siven çints in it? We failed intirely and had to buy on cridit, and we'll niver git that chance again. (*Exit* PAT.)

After a moment's pause, enter MR. *and* MRS. TAKUM, *with baskets and bundles, and a tin candlestick with a candle in it, lighted.*

MR. TAKUM. There, my dear, there is a chair, you see, so you can be quite comfortable while I go out to get something for supper, and hurry up one van of furniture. (*Puts candlestick on box.*)

MRS. TAKUM. Comfortable! Do light the gas, John, all over the house, before you go.

MR. TAKUM. Gas is turned off, my dear. I'll see to it the first thing in the morning.

MRS. TAKUM. Oh, I shall die of fright in a strange house with no gas!

MR. TAKUM. Pooh, pooh! I shan't be gone five minutes, and I'll bring a whole box of candles, if you wish. (*Exit* MR. TAKUM.)

MRS. TAKUM. I shall die of terror, I know I shall! (JERRY *moves in closet.*) Oh, what was that? (*Sinks into chair.*) It must have been a rat. (*Looks timidly around.*) Dear me! I thought the landlord said the house had been cleaned, (*looking at papers left by* JERRY *and* PAT) and here is a perfectly disgusting mess of cheese. Ugh! how it smells! and bones! (*Pushes aside the papers, and upsets candlestick, putting out the candle—this can easily be blown out first.*) Oh, oh! what shall I do? John has all the matches in his pocket. I wonder if I can find *one* in some of the baskets! (*Gropes about for the basket.*)

JERRY. (*Very sleepily.*) What are you making such a hullaba-loo about, Pat?

MRS. TAKUM. Oh, somebody spoke! Oh, there's somebody in

the room! He'll murder me! (*Leans against the box, as if faint with fright.*)

JERRY. (*Pushing open the closet door.*) Whativer are you doing?

MRS. TAKUM. (*Creeping away from door towards chair.*) Oh, where is the door? I'd rather wait for John on the pavement, than stay in this room another minute.

Enter PAT, *stepping softly.*

PAT. Whist, Jerry!

MRS. TAKUM. (*Sinking into chair.*) There is another! Oh, John, John! (*sobbing softly*) how could you leave me here alone to be murdered! (*The chair must be pushed by the boys to the foreground, facing audience, when they have done eating, so that they will be behind it in this scene.*)

JERRY. (*Whispering.*) Oh, Pat, what are you doing?

PAT. Whist, Jerry, there's people come in! (JERRY *creeps out of closet.*)

MRS. TAKUM. Oh, they are whispering together. I'll be murdered. I feel a knife at my throat already, and I dare not scream! Oh, John, John, where are you?

PAT. Can't you creep over to me, Jerry?

JERRY. It's thrying to foind yes I am.

PAT. Aisy! Don't be spaking so loud.

JERRY. We'll have to get out o' this. Bad luck to thim! Why couldn't they lave us in pace till morning?

MRS. TAKUM. (*Standing up.*) I can't sit here and be murdered in cold blood!

PAT. (*Groping about and moving gradually towards* MRS. TAKUM.) If yes 'll take hoold o' me hand, I'll take you out, Jerry!

JERRY. (*Groping away from* PAT, *towards window.*) I'm thrying to find yes.

MRS. TAKUM. Oh, what shall I do! I must get out! I wonder if I can find one of the alarms John says are all over the house! (MRS. TAKUM *and* PAT *grope towards each other, with their arms extended, until they run into each other's arms,* MRS. TAKUM *screaming.*) Oh! oh!

PAT. Whist! Whatever are yes screaming that way for!

MRS. TAKUM. (*Grasping* PAT.) I've got you! Thieves! murder!

PAT. (*Struggling.*) Oh, be jabers, it's not Jerry at all, at all!

MRS. TAKUM. Police! police!!

JERRY. Oh, Pat! Pat! is it murthered ye are?

MRS. TAKUM. (*Dropping* PAT.) There's another of them! (*Staggers back to chair, as if fainting.*)

PAT. (*Staggering back from the sudden release.*) Oh, Jerry, where are yes, me boy?

JERRY. (*At window.*) Come this way, Pat. (PAT, *groping towards* JERRY, *knocks over the baskets and bundles on the floor;* JERRY *opens window and starts an alarm;* PAT *falls over packing box;* MRS. TAKUM *sits upright and screams.*)

JERRY. Hurry up, Pat! We can get out of the windy!

MRS. TAKUM. John! John! Help! murder! police!!

PAT. Oh, I'm kilt entirely! (*Gets up limping.*)

MRS. TAKUM. John! John! Oh, there must be an army of men, to dare make so much noise. (*Gets up and runs about as if frantic with terror.*) John! murder! murder!

Enter POLICEMAN.

POLICEMAN. What is all this noise about?

PAT. Oh, we're kilt now. (JERRY *and* PAT *crouch under the window. When they speak it must be in a low tone, as if afraid.*)

JERRY. Are you here, Pat?

PAT. Whist, Jerry! We'll be craping out. It's the perlice.

JERRY. Oh, Pat! Have you the newspaper money safe?

PAT. Yis. Watch a chance to bolt out o' the windy. (POLICEMAN *and* MRS. TAKUM, *during this conversation, grope about in foreground until they meet.*)

POLICEMAN. (*Seizing* MRS. TAKUM.) Ah! I've got you, have I?

MRS. TAKUM. Oh, let me go! I'll give you my watch and all my money.

POLICEMAN. (*Shaking her.*) Want to bribe an officer in discharge of his duty, do you?

MRS. TAKUM. (*Trembling violently and sobbing.*) Oh, let me go! Let me go!

POLICEMAN. (*Sarcastically.*) Oh, I'll let you go! You're a nice one, ain't you, coming into vacant houses at this time o' night to steal the lead pipes. I've caught you at it before.

MRS. TAKUM. Oh, if you'll only not murder me!

PAT. (*Softly.*) Can't you try the windy now, Jerry?

JERRY. (*Climbing up.*) Will you come too?

PAT. Av coorse I will.

POLICEMAN. (*Listening.*) So there's more of them. (*Takes hold of* MRS. TAKUM *with left hand, and gets a rattle out of his pocket.*)

MRS. TAKUM. (*As if fainting.*) Oh, John! John!

POLICEMAN. Here, stand up. None of that. I believe there's a whole nest of them. (*Springs his rattle.*)

PAT. Quick, Jerry. (JERRY *gets on window seat, and starts a bell ringing.*)

POLICEMAN. Stop, or I'll fire!

JERRY. Will ye? (*Drops out of window.*)

MRS. TAKUM. Oh, if he fires, there's no knowing who will be hit. Where can John be? (*Struggles.*)

POLICEMAN. Bother the woman! they'll all get away while I'm holding her. Be quiet, will you, or I'll knock you over the head with a club. (PAT *stands up before window, as if to climb out.*) Shut that window, or I'll fire. (PAT *creeps on hands and knees towards door. All this time* MRS. TAKUM *must scream and struggle.*)

MRS. TAKUM. Oh, let me go! Oh, good burglar, let me go!

POLICEMAN. How many of you are there? (PAT *reaches door and tries to crawl out. Just at the doorway* MR. TAKUM *rushes in, slams the door, and falls over* PAT, *who lies motionless, as if stunned.*)

MR. TAKUM. What is the matter, Maria?

MRS. TAKUM. Oh, John! John! the house is full of burglars.

POLICEMAN. Another one.

MR. TAKUM. I'll start the alarms. (POLICEMAN *springs rattle,* MRS. TAKUM *screams violently,* MR. TAKUM *rushes about the room, opens and shuts the window, slams the door. Behind the scenes have all the noise possible—bells ringing, burglar alarms going off, rattles, gongs, and, if practicable, a dog or two yelping.*)

MR. TAKUM. Great heavens! What can this all be? Where is the light gone to? Stop! I've got some matches, and I'll strike one. (*Strikes a match, and finds the candle, which he lights. Stage lights must be raised a little, and noises cease.*) What! Maria struggling with a policeman! (*To* POLICEMAN.) What do you want in here? How dare you assault my wife?

POLICEMAN. (*Advancing toward* MR. TAKUM.) What do I want, hey? I'll let you know that fast enough. Just you two pack along with me, and you'll have an opportunity to-morrow morning to explain in court what you are doing here after dark in an empty house. (PAT *rouses himself, looks around bewildered, and listens.*)

MRS. TAKUM. Oh, John! what *does* the man mean? I shall die if I am locked up in a cell—I know I shall.

POLICEMAN. Die? I guess you'll survive it. Come along, come. Do you suppose I'm going to wait all night for you? (*Takes out a pair of hand-cuffs.*)

MRS. TAKUM. (*Screams and runs behind* MR. TAKUM.) John, you can't allow this! Can't you—

MR. TAKUM. (*Getting composed.*) Calm yourself, Maria; I begin to see it all now. (*To* POLICEMAN.) Have the kindness to clear out instantly; this is my house, and I have the right to occupy it without your interference.

POLICEMAN. (*Sarcastically.*) That's very neat, indeed. Very cool. This house has been long empty, and I shall need more than your word to convince me that you have any right here at all.

MRS. TAKUM. (*Trembling, but calmer. To* MR. TAKUM.) Can't you satisfy this terrible man that we have taken this house? Oh! if Mr. Lettum were only here.

POLICEMAN. Mr. Lettum! why, that's the owner.

MR. TAKUM. Ah, you know him, then? Well, just go to him and fetch him here, and we will soon end all this nonsense.

POLICEMAN. Very neat indeed. Why, where would *you* be when I got back? Too thin! Come, you had better come along— willingly if you please, forcibly if you won't. Hullo! What boy is that? Come here, you young rascal. There were two of you; where's the other?

MR. TAKUM. Here, boy. (*Aside.*) How fortunate he's here. (*To* PAT.) Here, take this card (*writes on a card*) to Mr. Lettum, and wait for an answer. (*To* POLICEMAN.) Now just wait a minute until he gets back, and see what Mr. Lettum says about it. (*To* PAT.) Run, boy, and I'll give you a quarter when you get back. (*Exit* PAT. *To* POLICEMAN.) Now, if you please, I wish to repeat to you that we have taken this house, and Mr. Lettum will be here in a few moments to confirm what I say.

POLICEMAN. Well, I'll give you five minutes, and then you march with me. (*Looks at his watch.* MR. TAKUM *soothes* MRS. TAKUM, *and appears to talk to her, and she to him, for a few moments.* POLICEMAN *again looks at his watch.*) Only one minute more. You'd better be getting these bracelets on. (*Holds out hand-cuffs.*)

Enter MR. LETTUM, *hurriedly.*

MR. LETTUM. Bless my soul! what's the matter, Mr. Takum?

MR. TAKUM. Why, we had just got in here, in advance of our first load of furniture, and I had stepped out to get some provisions, leaving Mrs. Takum here alone for a few minutes. When I returned, I found my wife struggling to free herself from the grasp of that officious policeman. He ridiculed the idea of our being the rightful tenants, and would have locked us up as burglars if you had not arrived so quickly. (*To* POLICEMAN.) Now, are you satisfied?

POLICEMAN. (*To* MR. LETTUM.) Is this all right?

MR. LETTUM. Why, of course. Mr. Takum has rented this house of me, and now I think you had better relieve them of your presence.

POLICEMAN. Certainly. I hope, however, you will perceive that I did my duty in protecting your property. When people leave the front door open, it is my duty to see whether everything is right inside.

MR. TAKUM. Well, I suppose that's so. It seems to be a mistake all round. I wonder, though, what that boy wanted in here, and how he got in. He can't be very bad, or he would have run off as soon as he got out, instead of delivering my message. I suppose he's too scared to claim his quarter. (*To* MRS. TAKUM.) Now, my dear, how do you like your first evening in an EMPTY HOUSE?

CURTAIN.

BILLY. Elegant order, sir. Ground this morning, an' I only sawed a little wood with it since.

JOHN. Knife sharp?

BILLY. Sharp as a razor. Tried it on the corks yesterday.

PAT. Oh, the murthering pair of thim!

TEDDY. Aisy now, Pat. Ye'll not be wanting a dull knife, sure!

JOHN. Now, my good fellow, (*fusses over table with instruments*) we'll have you all right inside of ten minutes. Billy!

BILLY. Yessir.

JOHN. Help him on the table.

BILLY. Yessir. (BILLY *and* TEDDY *stretch* PAT *on table.* PAT *groans and howls all the time.*)

JOHN. (*To* TEDDY.) You hold his arms.

TEDDY. I'll do that same, sir! (*Holds* PAT's *arms.*)

JOHN. Billy!

BILLY. Yessir.

JOHN. Hold the other leg.

BILLY. Yessir.

JOHN. (*Taking up a long knife.*) Now then. (*Motions as if cutting.*)

PAT. Oh, it's killing me entirely ye are this toime. Oh, murther! (*Groans.*)

TEDDY. Aisy now, Pat. It'll soon be over!

JOHN. Billy!

BILLY. Yessir.

JOHN. Pass me the saw. (BILLY *takes knife and passes saw.* JOHN *saws like a carpenter.*) So. It is almost off.

PAT. I'm a dead man! Oh, murther an' Irish, that iver I come to this. (*Howls and groans.*)

TEDDY. Och, it's faling sick I am mesilf.

JOHN. (*Holding up a leg, hidden on table.*) A beautiful operation!

PAT. Is it beautiful? Be jabers, I wish it was both your own legs!

JOHN. Billy!

BILLY. Yessir.

JOHN. Bandages!

BILLY. Here, sir. (*Passes bandages.*)

JOHN. (*Bandaging* PAT's *legs together with great show and flourish.*) You see, my good fellow, there is nothing like tending to these little matters in good time.

PAT. (*Groaning.*) Little matters, indade! There's impudince for you.

TEDDY. Sure, Pat, you'll not be blackguarding the docther whin he's savin' yer life.

JOHN. Just so, my good fellow. And I'm going to do this very cheap, very. (*Bandages* PAT'S *legs still.*) Billy!

BILLY. Yessir!

JOHN. Help to put the patient in the chair. (BILLY, TEDDY *and* JOHN *place* PAT *in a chair.*) More bandages.

BILLY. Yessir.

JOHN. It is very important to bandage well, to prevent hemorrhage.

TEDDY. Indade it is, sur. (JOHN *bandages* PAT'S *body, holding his arms down.*)

JOHN. Billy!

BILLY. Yessir.

JOHN. Mix a dose of the Universal Cure.

BILLY. Yessir. (*Pours out of bottle into tumbler.*)

JOHN. There, my good man, drink that! (PAT *swallows one mouthful, and begins to spit and make faces.*)

TEDDY. Oh, ye babby, drink the medicine!

PAT. (*Choking.*) Oh, it's poison! It's fire and murther mixed! (*Struggles.*) Oh, I'm being kilt amongst yes! Untie me hands, an' I'll fight the three of yes with one leg!

TEDDY. Aisy now, Pat, or you'll bust the bandages.

PAT. I'll bust everything in the place. (*Struggling.*) Give me my leg, ye thafe o' the world!

JOHN. (*Coolly.*) He is a little feverish and light-headed. Don't mind him.

PAT. Ye'd better moind me, thin, if ye know what's good for you!

JOHN. Billy!

BILLY. Yessir.

JOHN. Go hire a cart, and have this man carried home at once.

BILLY. Yessir. (*Exit* BILLY.)

JOHN. Now, my good fellow, I'll take my fee.

PAT. Fee, is it? Jist untie my hands, an' I'll give it to you right between the eyes.

TEDDY. Oh, docther, now, he's not maning any harrum, poor fellow !

JOHN. (*Very coolly.*) Certainly not. He is a little delirious.

TEDDY. And he's a poor man, docther; so you will not be hard on him about the fee.

JOHN. Oh, no. I'll only charge him fifty dollars.

PAT. Fifty dollars ! Tare an' ages ! wheriver do you suppose I'm going to get fifty dollars ?

TEDDY. (*Feeling in his pockets.*) I'm thinking, docther, fifty cints will be nearer.

JOHN. (*Grandly.*) Fifty dollars is only half my usual fee.

PAT. Hear that, now ! I'd do it mesllf for a quarther.

BILLY. (*Rushing in.*) Cart's here, and about fifty men to help Pat !

PAT. Bring 'em all in ! I'll see if I can't be avin wid ye, if I am tied up.

JOHN. No, no ! Keep them out, Billy !

TEDDY. We'll stand by ye, Pat ! Hey ! Is it fifty dollars for killing a dacint man ?

PAT. (*Calling.*) Come in, the whole of yes ! Here, Murphy ! Flaherty ! O'Sullivan ! Come in !

JOHN. (*Going to back of stage.*) Only one door. They'll murder me for certain !

PAT. Come in ! Hey ! I've got fifty pairs of arms and legs, if I am tied up ! Come in, all of yes !

CURTAIN.

STRATEGY.

Characters.

JENNIE, } *Two School-girls.*
MOLLIE, }

MISS AMANDA FIDGET—*Their Aunt.*

LIZZIE—*The Servant Girl.*

SCENE.—*A handsome Parlor. Open piano, centre of background.* LIZZIE *dusting;* JENNIE *sewing;* MOLLIE *walking up and down.*

MOLLIE. It is downright tyranny, and I will not submit to it!

LIZZIE. (*Aside.*) She's said that fifty times in as many minutes.

JENNIE. What's the use of making a fuss, Mollie? You know if Aunt Amanda says you can't go, you will have to stay here.

MOLLIE. I won't, then! I would run away, only I can't take my trunk if I do that, and I don't want to go to Mulberry Hall without every one of my new dresses.

LIZZIE. There, this room is dusted; I'll go and get dinner. (*Exit* LIZZIE.)

JENNIE. Do sit down, Mollie. I don't wonder Aunt Amanda says your restless ways nearly tire her to death.

MOLLIE. Did she say that?

JENNIE. Yes. Hasn't she said so to you?

MOLLIE. No, but she will! She's dreadfully particular—isn't she, Jennie?

JENNIE. Dreadfully! When I first came here I was all the time in trouble. But I learned to keep quiet, to let all her pet things alone—

MOLLIE. (*Impatiently.*) I know. You are no more like the bright, gay Jennie of two years ago, than I am like Aunt Amanda. But you want to stay here?

JENNIE. I have no other home. Common gratitude would make me careful to respect all Aunt Amanda's wishes.

MOLLIE. But I don't want to stay. You have no idea what a

glorious time we have at Mulberry Hall. All the girls expect me to spend a month at least in vacation.

JENNIE. And Aunt Amanda objects to your going? It does seem too bad!

MOLLIE. Too bad! It is outrageous. But I am going.

JENNIE. You won't run away?

MOLLIE. No, but I will be sent away! Let me see, where shall I begin? Oh, I know! (*Sits down at piano and plays a very loud accompaniment to* "Rory O'More.")

JENNIE. (*Smiling.*) I really believe she will be sent away if she makes as much noise as that often.

MOLLIE. (*Singing loudly.*)

  Oh, Rory O'More courted Kathleen Bawn;
   He was bold as—as—

(*Speaking.*) Bless me, Jennie, I've forgotten the words! My brain must be softening. (*Bangs another loud accompaniment to* "A Life on the Ocean Wave." *Sings very loudly.*)

  "A life on the ocean wave,
   A home on the rolling deep,
  Where the scattered waters rave,
   And the winds their revel keep.

(*Speaking.*) Aunt Amanda must be dead if this don't bring her down-stairs.

JENNIE. You'll break a blood-vessel, Mollie, if you scream in that way.

MOLLIE. I hear a footstep. (*Sings.*)

  "Like an eagle caged I pine,
   On this dull, unchanging shore;
  Oh, give me the flashing brine,

Enter MISS AMANDA.

MOLLIE. (*Singing.*)

  The spray and the tempest's roar.

MISS AMANDA. Mary! Mary!

MOLLIE. (*Not heeding.*)

  "Once more on the deck I stand

MISS AMANDA. Mary!

MOLLIE.   Of my own swift gliding craft;
   Set sail; farewell to the land,
   · The gale follows far abaft."

JENNIE. (*Aside.*) She will split her throat.

MISS AMANDA. (*Shaking* MOLLIE.) Stop that noise.

MOLLIE. (*Dropping both hands on piano with a crash.*) Oh, how you startled me!

MISS AMANDA. Startled you! What do you mean by making such a din?

MOLLY. (*Innocently.*) Din! Why, Auntie, I heard you telling Mr. Softum you *adored* music.

MISS AMANDA. Music! I abominate noise.

MOLLIE. But everybody says I sing splendidly. I will sing "Wait for the Wagon!"

MISS AMANDA. I forbid you to shriek another word. Mercy on me! My nerves won't recover their tranquillity for a week.

MOLLIE. They won't if I can prevent it. (*Leaves the piano and goes to window.*)

JENNIE. (*Holding up sewing.*) Does this embroidery suit you, Auntie?

MISS AMANDA. Perfectly, my dear.

MOLLY. Oh, come here! come here! both of you. (*Pulls* JENNIE *toward window.*) Oh, see the dog chasing a cat up the tree! (*Shouting.*) Hi, hi! At her! (*Claps her hands.*) Sh, hi! Oh, what fun!

MISS AMANDA. Mary, are you not ashamed!

MOLLIE. (*Innocently.*) Ashamed! of what?

MISS AMANDA. (*Severely.*) Of behaving like a boy, and an exceedingly ill-bred boy, too. (*Aside.*) She was quiet enough yesterday.

MOLLIE. I can't help it. When I feel happy and at home I'm always lively. Oh, what a pretty rose! (*Smells flower in vase.*) I do love roses. I'm going to put this in my hair. (*Jerks flower and upsets vase.*) Oh, dear! there goes all the water on the table-cloth.

MISS AMANDA. My embroidered stand-cover. (*Hastens to table.*) Ring the bell for Lizzie.

MOLLIE. Oh, I'm awfully sorry! (*Rings a hand-bell very violently.*)

MISS AMANDA. Stop! stop!

Enter LIZZIE.

LIZZIE. (*Panting.*) Oh, my! I thought the house was on fire.

MISS AMANDA. Take that table-cloth to the fire to dry, and clear up that mess on the table.

LIZZIE. (*Clearing table.*) I'm afraid it will stain. What a pity! (*Exit* LIZZIE, *with cloth.*)

MISS AMANDA. I wish you would sit down, Mary. You set all my nerves in a quiver, (*severely*) and I think you have done mischief enough for one day.

MOLLIE. (*Aside.*) I don't. (*Aloud.*) But, Auntie, it is vacation. Nobody *can* keep still in vacation. At Mulberry Hall we play croquet and dance, and we have charades, tableaux, all sorts of things. You ought to see me play lawn tennis—this way. (*Taking a book for a bat to toss a small basket in the air.*)

MISS AMANDA. My shell basket! It must be ruined.

MOLLIE. (*Picking up basket.*) Oh, no! it's only bent a little, and some of the shells are broken.

MISS AMANDA. Dear, dear! I value that basket immensely. Captain Jenkins brought it from the Bahamas expressly for me. Mary, I desire you to sit down!

MOLLIE. (*Bouncing into a chair.*) Yes, ma'am! (*Kicks her feet.*)

MISS AMANDA. And keep still.

MOLLIE. (*Fidgeting.*) Oh, I can't.

MISS AMANDA. Take some sewing, as Jennie does.

MOLLIE. Oh, yes! (*Takes a work-basket from table.*) I'll embroider. (*Pulls needles out of a piece of knitting.*)

MISS AMANDA. Oh, you've ruined my collar!

MOLLIE. Why, your collar looks all right.

MISS AMANDA. The one I am knitting. (*Takes it up.*) I shall never get these stitches back.

MOLLIE. I wonder if these scissors are sharp? (*Cuts a tidy on back of chair.*)

MISS AMANDA. You'll spoil everything in the room! Stop cutting my tidy!

MOLLIE. Yes, ma'am.

JENNIE. (*Aside.*) Auntie will have hysterics in five minutes more. (*Aloud.*) Let me teach you this new embroidery stitch, Mollie.

MOLLIE. Oh, yes, do! (*Jumps up, letting work-basket fall.*) Oh, my gracious, there go all the sewing things! (*Stoops, and upsets a chair.*)

MISS AMANDA. I do believe the girl will drive me frantic!

MOLLIE. I'll pick them all up. (*Scrambles about on the floor, scattering the things about as fast as she takes them up.*)

MISS AMANDA. Oh, let them alone! Lizzie will be here presently, and will pick them up.

MOLLIE. Yes, ma'am. (*Drops all she has.*) Oh, oh! I see a kitten! (*Rushes out of the room.*)

MISS AMANDA. Jennie!

JENNIE. Yes, dear Auntie.

MISS AMANDA. (*Sinking into a chair.*) She will kill me! What a voice! Do you think she ever cried catfish? What a manner! Or what an entire absence of manner! No repose.

JENNIE. She is just released from the restraints of school, Auntie. If she *lived* here—

MISS AMANDA. I can never be too thankful she does not!

JENNIE. In a day or two this excitement will be over, I am sure, and she will be all you wish.

MOLLIE. (*Outside.*) Oh, oh, oh! (*Enters, sobbing loudly.*)

JENNIE. What is the matter?

MOLLIE. Oh, my finger! my finger!

MISS AMANDA. Stop that noise! A child of two years old would not make more noise over a hurt.

MOLLIE. Oh, Jennie, get some arnica—bind it up.

JENNIE. (*Looking at finger.*) Why, what ails it? (*Aside.*) I can't see anything.

MOLLIE. (*Aside.*) Well, you needn't say so. (*Aloud.*) I was chasing the dear, darling little kitten—by the way, Auntie, I upset the flower-stand in the hall.

MISS AMANDA. My Japan lilies!

MOLLIE. John is picking them up. But the dear little kitten ran out on the porch, and up and down, and I couldn't catch her. So I just went up to the parrot's cage, and said, "Pretty Polly!" and the horrid thing bit my finger.

MISS AMANDA. And served you right.

MOLLIE. Well, she won't bite any more fingers in this house!

MISS AMANDA. What do you mean?

MOLLIE. I just opened the cage door, and away she went.

MISS AMANDA. Oh, you dreadful girl! (*Going out.*)

JENNIE. Oh, Mollie, that really was too bad. Auntie values the bird so much.

MOLLIE. She is in the luncheon-basket in my room. You can bring her down after I go to Mulberry Hall. (*Sits down by* JENNIE.)

JENNIE. Did she bite you?

MOLLIE. Of course not.

Enter MISS AMANDA.

MISS AMANDA. I have sent all the servants into the garden to search for my dear parrot. I would not have taken a hundred dollars for the bird! She converses like a rational being. My poor Polly! (*Sits down, sadly.*)

MOLLIE. (*Jumping up suddenly.*) Oh, there's a mouse!

MISS AMANDA. (*Nervously.*) Where! I—are you sure?

MOLLIE. (*Jumping on sofa.*) I saw it under the table. Oh, oh! Kill it! Oh, I'm so afraid of a mouse!

MISS AMANDA. (*Sitting down and drawing up her feet.*) I never saw a mouse in the house.

JENNIE. (*Stooping under table.*) I think it is only your emery cushion that has rolled under the table, Auntie.

MOLLIE. (*Jumping down.*) Why, so it is! I was sure it was a mouse!

MISS AMANDA. (*Fanning herself.*) Jennie, get my vinaigrette. I am actually faint with all this confusion!

MOLLIE. I'll get it! (*Rushes out of room, upsetting a small table on her way.*)

MISS AMANDA. My Japanese stand!

JENNIE. (*Picking up table.*) It is not broken, Auntie.

MISS AMANDA. But everything in the house will be broken if this girl stays here. I really am inclined to let her go to Mulberry Hall, after all.

Enter MOLLIE, *unperceived by the others.*

JENNIE. She is very anxious to go, Auntie.

MISS AMANDA. But it is really encouraging her in her boydenish manners. She needs the quieting influence of a refined home.

JENNIE. But you are not strong, Auntie, and it must be very trying to your nerves to have so much noise.

MOLLIE. (*Aside.*) I'll bring Jennie the prettiest present my pocket money will buy for that.

MISS AMANDA. My poor nerves! I do not know, indeed, if I shall not be *obliged* to send Mary to her friends.

MOLLIE. (*Rushing forward.*) Here are the salts, Auntie. I had an awful time finding them. I tossed over all the bureau drawers, and upset your work-box, and broke a Cologne bottle and everything trying to find them!

MISS AMANDA. (*Leaning back.*) She will kill me!

MOLLIE. Oh, she is going to faint! (*Fans* MISS AMANDA *vigorously.*) Oh, Jennie, run for some wine! (*Takes a glass of water and dips her handkerchief in it.*) Oh, Auntie, don't faint! (*Dabs the wet handkerchief in her face.*)

MISS AMANDA. (*Sitting up suddenly.*) You are too much! I am drenched! Go away!

MOLLIE. (*Sobbing.*) I'm sure I thought people always had water in their faces when they were faint.

JENNIE. (*Fanning* MISS AMANDA *gently.*) Do you feel better?

MISS AMANDA. Yes.

MOLLIE. Oh, oh, there is a wasp on your cap! Oh, it will sting you!

MISS AMANDA. Where? Take it off!

MOLLIE. (*Flapping the wet handkerchief about.*) Sho! sho! Oh, see, it will sting you!

MISS AMANDA. (*Nervously.*) Oh, where is it?

JENNIE. I don't see it, Mollie.

MOLLIE. It just flew out of the window. Oh, I am all out of breath! (*Drops in a chair.*) I am so afraid of a wasp.

JESSIE. (*Aside to* MOLLIE.) You are really too bad.

MISS AMANDA. (*Faintly.*) Where are my salts?

MOLLIE. (*Jumping up.*) Now, where did I put that bottle? (*Tosses everything about.*) I must have put it down here somewhere. Jennie, didn't I give it to you?

JENNIE. Look in your pocket.

MOLLIE. (*Putting her hand in her pocket.*) Why, here it is! Here, Auntie. (*Pokes the bottle under* MISS AMANDA'S *nose.*)

MISS AMANDA. (*As if choking.*) Bless me, Mary, you will strangle me. Oh! (*Takes the bottle.*) Go away! Go up-stairs, do.

MOLLIE. (*Pouting.*) Of course I will, if you don't want me here. (*Exit* MOLLIE.)

JENNIE. Vacation seems to excite her.

MISS AMANDA. It has driven her crazy. (*An accordeon behind the scenes drawn in and out without any tune.*)

JENNIE. (*Aside.*) She will never stop.

MISS AMANDA. Mary has got that horrible accordeon again!

MOLLIE. (*Singing loudly, and pulling accordeon to and fro.*)
"If a body meet a body,
    Comin' thro' the rye,
If a body kiss a body,
    Need a body cry?
Every lassie has her laddie,
    None, they say, ha'e I;
Yet a' the lads they smile at me,
    When comin' thro' the rye."

(*While* MOLLIE *sings,* MISS AMANDA *presses her hands over her ears and grimaces.*)

MISS AMANDA. Go stop that noise, Jennie! (*Exit* JENNIE.) I cannot endure this another hour. If she can make her friends at Mulberry Hall give her house room, I'll send her off to-morrow.

Enter MOLLIE *and* JENNIE.

MOLLIE. Can't I play the accordeon, Auntie?

MISS AMANDA. You may play what you like when you leave here. Pack up your trunk, and put the accordeon in. You will take the first train to Mulberry Hall to-morrow! If your friends there can live under the same roof with you, it is more than I can. (*Exit* MISS AMANDA.)

MOLLIE. (*Dancing about.*) Hurrah! Who says that a little strategy is not a good thing? Come, Jennie, help me pack. (*Twirls* JENNIE *round in a waltz.*)

CURTAIN.

THE PICNIC PARTY.

Characters.

JOHN—*Laid up with a lame foot.*
MARY—*His Cousin.*
HOWARD—*A City Boy.*
GERALD—*A Country Boy.*
LAURA—*A very affected City Girl.*
SARAH—*An uneducated Girl.*

SCENE.—*A Sitting-room.* JOHN *seated in an arm-chair, with his foot upon a hassock.* MARY *seated near him, sewing.*

JOHN. It must be nearly time for them to be home from the picnic.

MARY. Quite time.

JOHN. It was more than good-natured of you, Mollie, to stay at home with me.

MARY. I should not have enjoyed myself, knowing you were here alone. And (*laughing*) I am afraid Gerald would have quite neglected me. He has eyes and ears for no one else, since Laura came.

JOHN. I can understand that—for Laura is very pretty, if she is affected. But how her brother can fancy Sarah puzzles me. She never would study, and her English is something horrible to hear.

MARY. I suppose Howard admires her because she is such a contrast to Laura. But he is as affected in his way as she is.

JOHN. But does not use up the dictionary quite so effectually.

MARY. I hear quite a bustle in the entry. They must be here.

Enter GERALD, *with* LAURA *leaning on his arm.* HOWARD *escorting* SARAH. *All wear out-door dress, and carry baskets, fans, shawls and sun-umbrellas.*

GERALD. Do sit down. You must be quite tired out.

LAURA. (*Sinking languidly into a chair.*) I am utterly exhausted.

HOWARD. Are you very weary, Miss Sarah?

SARAH. Not a bit of it. I ain't never tired when I'm having a good time. I'm sorry you didn't go, Mollie—we had a scrumptious time.

LAURA. You are to be congratulated, John, upon the vicissitude that necessitated your absence from this so-called pleasure party. (*Shudders.*)

GERALD. I am sorry you do not enjoy our rural pleasures, Miss Laura.

MARY. Our picnics are usually very pleasant.

JOHN. Were you crowded, Howard?

HOWARD. Well, yes. There were not cars enough.

LAURA. The multitude of people was overpowering. I was actually faint with the oppressive atmosphere in the steam-car.

SARAH. There was rather a jam, to be sure. But that ain't nothing, for such a short ride. I say, the more the merrier!

GERALD. I was positively ashamed of you, Sarah. You acted more like a boy than a young lady.

JOHN. (*To* MARY.) Gerald never discovered *that* before.

MARY. (*To* JOHN.) No; he rather admired Sarah's love of fun and frolic.

JOHN. Do tell us something about the picnic.

LAURA. I presume one of these boisterous assemblages of the vulgar multitude is the counterpart of another. We were called upon to admire a lot of trees and fences, water and hill, called scenery.

MARY. The view from where you were is generally considered very fine.

LAURA. The aborigines may admire it. *I* have been abroad!

JOHN. Aborigines! That's cool.

GERALD. It must be very inferior to the scenery in Europe.

SARAH. Wall, that 'ere tarnal idiot of an Englishman that was here last summer pretty near went into fits over it. Said it beat Europe all hollow.

HOWARD. I thought it very fine.

LAURA. Oh, Howard, when you have seen Italy! The soft azure of Italian skies, the vivid glow of her sunshine, the ethereal loveliness of her landscapes, quite spoil one for these American views.

SARAH. Well, if traveling makes a body turn up her nose at her own country, I'll stay to home!

HOWARD. I applaud your patriotism.

MARY. But you were surely not all day admiring the view?

GERALD. Oh, no, indeed! We had a delightful row upon the lake.

LAURA. (*Shuddering.*) Delightful!

SARAH. Tip-top! I row better and better every day, Mollie.

LAURA. For my part, I have no sympathy with these modern innovations upon the delicate refinements formerly considered appropriate to the education of a lady. Rowing appears to me a most masculine pursuit.

HOWARD. Awfully hard work, I call it!

GERALD. Most inappropriate for a lady.

SARAH. Good gracious me! Why, you didn't let me have no rest nor peace till you'd learned me all about it.

MARY. (*Aside to* JOHN.) That is true.

JOHN. (*Aside to* MARY.) And she rows better than her teacher to-day.

LAURA. I suffered the most excruciating terrors on the water. My dread of the treacherous wave is constitutional.

SARAH. What did you go for, then? Nobody made you.

LAURA. I yielded to the solicitations of your cousin.

GERALD. I should never have urged the point, I assure you, had I supposed you would suffer.

SARAH. (*To* HOWARD.) Don't you like rowing?

HOWARD. (*To* SARAH.) With you for a companion.

SARAH. Pooh! Don't be soft! You're too young!

HOWARD. (*Stiffly.*) Pardon me!

SARAH. Oh, you needn't be uppish, neither!

MARY. Did you play lawn tennis or croquet?

GERALD. Of course we did. But Miss Laura found it fatiguing.

LAURA. (*Languidly.*) In the extreme. It wearied me to watch such boisterous games, for I certainly would never attempt to participate in them.

SARAH. You'd oughter seen Laura, Mollie, when we met a drove of pigs!

LAURA. (*Shuddering, and covering her face.*) How can you recall that horror! It was unendurable! The dreadful animals ran hither and thither, with the most appalling cries. I was in agonies of terror, lest one should touch me. I am sure I should have fainted.

GERALD. They are disgusting creatures to a person of refinement.

SARAH. Sakes alive, Jerry! Why, you was as fond of that hog you riz for the agricultural fair as if it had been a kitten! Why, he'd poke out his snout when he seen you comin' with a bucket o' corn and milk as if he was a human critter! I'm sure you most cried when he was took to market after the fair.

HOWARD. One becomes attached to any pet.

LAURA. The idea of a pet *pig*!

MARY. I do not wonder at some surprise. But it was more pride than affection Gerald felt, I imagine, as his hog took the prize.

HOWARD. I am sure, Laura, your nerves were not more powerfully affected than mine. I was escorting Miss Sarah to a favorite spot, when we encountered a horrible savage animal.

SARAH. The mildest cow in the county!

HOWARD. Miss Sarah bore up with heroic fortitude, but I was really quite overcome.

MARY. Poor fellow! Was your basket well supplied, Sarah?

SARAH. Enough for a regiment.

LAURA. But nothing tempting. I was quite faint, I assure you, until Gerald procured me a glass of iced lemonade.

MARY. I thought the sandwiches were very delicate.

HOWARD. And the cold chicken was delightful.

LAURA. But one cannot enjoy even the most delicate viands, without the elegancies of a well-appointed table. Imagine, I saw *girls*— I *cannot* call them young ladies—with chicken in their fingers! actually eating the meat off the bone! It was shocking!

SARAH. But awfully good! For my part, being as hungry as a bear, I found everything splendid. I ate a whole chicken, I am sure.

HOWARD. (*Aside.*) I think she did. Her appetite was something appalling!

SARAH. Nine sandwiches!

LAURA. Horror! Half a one would suffice me for an entire day.

SARAH. Six hard-boiled eggs.

GERALD. Sarah, do spare us the further recital of such horrible gluttony.

SARAH. I've seen the time when you could eat your allowance at a picnic, Mr. Jerry, if you are so finiky all of a sudden. You didn't make nothing of a whole apple-pie last year, after nearly emptying a basket of substantials.

JOHN. Out-door exercise gives everybody an appetite. I can eat my share at a picnic, I assure you!

LAURA. But there were no goblets, no sauce-plates, no silver, no finger-glasses!

GERALD. It was very rough.

SARAH. We will pack all the table appointments next year, Jerry, and let *you* carry them!

GERALD. You are really too good! Probably I shall decline assisting at these festivities again.

MARY. That will be too bad. You are generally the life of the party!

SARAH. But he wasn't to-day—not a bit of it. He was a-languishing about as lackadaisical as could be, and never doing nothing all day to help be jolly. Why, he wouldn't even swing Laura, when I give up my place to her.

GERALD. Miss Laura declined the recreation.

LAURA. Oh, it would utterly prostrate me! I never could imagine the pleasure of swinging.

SARAH. And you wouldn't see-saw, neither!

LAURA. Most assuredly not!

HOWARD. I had no idea it was such fun, Laura! Miss Sarah showed me quite a number of entirely new pleasures to-day.

SARAH. But you can't climb a tree, Howard. I thought I should a' died laughing when you stood lookin' at the tree I asked you to climb for those great yellow pears, as if it was Mount Vociferous! Now, Jerry, he'll go up a tree like lightning. He got me lots of those pears last summer; but I don't suppose he could a' climbed a tree to-day to save his life!

JOHN. (*To* GERALD.) Your tastes seem to have undergone a great change, Gerald.

GERALD. (*Loftily.*) I am no longer a boy, and do not care to scramble up trees like a monkey!

JOHN. Seventeen! Don't renounce your boyhood too early. You may wish it back some day.

MARY. Was the band there?

SARAH. Oh, yes! And the platform for dancing.

LAURA. Dancing? I assure you the poetry of motion was utterly annihilated, Mary, in the boisterous hopping about we witnessed to-day. I actually saw some of the gentlemen take off their coats, and dance with them over their arms!

SARAH. That's the way to dance—with your heart in your toes!

HOWARD. The dancing was enjoyable, compared to the music!

LAURA. Each instrument played in a different key. The discord was appalling.

MARY. That is very singular. Our band is generally considered to be a very fine one.

SARAH. So it is!

GERALD. It probably appears fine to our uncultivated ears; but you forget Miss Laura has heard music abroad.

LAURA. (*Affectedly.*) Italian opera rather unfits one for rustic fiddling.

JOHN. But Italian opera would be rather difficult music to dance quadrilles to.

HOWARD. But we have heard Strauss' waltzes in Paris! Oh, Miss Sarah, if you could only see Paris!

SARAH. But I can't speak no French.

HOWARD. You would soon acquire the language.

GERALD. (*Aside to* MARY.) She had better acquire her native language first. It makes me shudder to listen to her.

MARY. (*Drily.*) You endured it very philosophically until your fine city friends came to visit you.

GERALD. It does make one fastidious to meet with such refinement as Miss Laura's.

MARY. But it should not make you neglect old friends.

SARAH. Oh, Molly! Bobby Bates has come home from college, and was to the picnic. I wish you'd a' been there and seen him. (*Imitating dandy airs.*) How d'ye do, Miss Saraw! Foine day! He was all dressed in store clothes, as fine as a fiddle—white waistcoat, shiny boots, silk hat, and he was afraid to move for fear he'd spoil them, so he just stood up against a tree, and sucked the top of a little cane, as if it was sugar candy. I nearly died a-laughing. "Ain't you a-going to dance?" sez I. (*Imitating.*) "I nevaw dance," says he. "Won't you row on the lake?" says I. "I nevaw wow"—he said *wow*, Mollie! And he had a fan, a little fan in his pocket; and when he got tired of sucking the little cane, he fanned himself—this way. (*Imitates.*)

LAURA. I am sure, Sarah, Mr. Bates was the most perfect gentleman at the picnic.

JOHN. (*Aside.*) How will Gerald like that?

GERALD. (*Aside.*) Insufferable puppy!

SARAH. Oh, oh! There's manners, when there's three of them here. You'd oughter say, "Present company always excepted!"

LAURA. (*Pettishly.*) I shall certainly not come to you, Sarah, to be taught etiquette. (*Rising.*) I am going to my room to change my dress. I am sure it is all dust and mud with this disgusting picnic.

GERALD. Allow me to carry your shawl and parasol up-stairs. (GERALD *and* LAURA *go out.*)

HOWARD. I believe I will follow Laura's example. (*Exit* HOWARD.)

MARY. I am afraid you did not have a very nice time, Sarah.

SARAH. Oh, but I did! It was the best of fun to watch Jerry and Laura; Jerry tried to imitate all Howard's airs; and Laura—you'd oughter seen her! If there was a wasp flew within forty feet of her, she'd screech as if it was a hyena, and she nearly had hysterics over a stray goose that poked its head over her shoulder while she was eating some ice cream. Dear creature! that was all Jerry could find she could eat! (*Imitating.*) "My appetite is so fastidious!" and keeping Jerry fanning her, and holding up her parasol! She wouldn't dance, and she made such a fuss in the boat, you'd a' thought we was drowning all the time!

JOHN. Gently, gently, Sarah! She is our guest, remember.

SARAH. True, true, bless ye! (*Imitating.*) Well, I think I also will retire to my room, to remove the dust and mud of this disgusting picnic.

CURTAIN.

AN ASPIRANT FOR FAME.

Characters.

MR. STEPHEN CRITICAL—*An Editor.*
RICHARD ROVER—*A Young Writer.*
BOB—*The Office Boy.*

SCENE.—*An Editor's Office. Large table, covered with papers, books, manuscript, pen and ink, and other literary matters.* MR. CRITICAL *looking over the mail.*

MR. CRITICAL. Thirteen, fourteen, fifteen, seventeen—seventeen more manuscripts! The world has gone mad on manuscript-writing! (*Opens letter.*) H'm—genius on the rampage. (*Reads.*) "Dear Sir: I wonder you are not ashamed of the paltry sum offered in your letter for my sonnet on sunrise. Please return the manuscript at your earliest convenience. John Jenkinson"—with a fearful black dash under earliest. Now there's gratitude! The man wrote such a pitiful letter—starving and freezing, apparently —that I concluded to send him five dollars in pure charity! Well, I'm just five dollars richer, and he is one page of fearful trash in hand. Bob!

Enter BOB, *in shirt sleeves, very much begrimed with printer's ink.*

BOB. Did you call, sir?
MR. CRITICAL. Any callers while I was out?
BOB. Yes, sir; Miss Araminta Pinkerton.
MR. CRITICAL. (*Shuddering.*) What did you tell her?
BOB. Said you'd gone to California, sir, and that we didn't hope to see you for three months.
MR. CRITICAL. Bob, remind me to add a quarter to your week's salary.
BOB. Thank ye, sir.
MR. CRITICAL. Anybody else called?
BOB. Yes, sir; the man with the coal bill.

MR. CRITICAL. Well?

BOB. Said you was out, sir; and didn't know as you'd be back to-day.

MR. CRITICAL. All right. Anybody else?

BOB. Party from the country, sir, with carpet-bag. Wasn't sure about him, and he said that he would call again.

MR. CRITICAL. All right, Bob. It may be my uncle. Anybody else?

BOB. No, sir. Shall I show the country party in if he calls again?

MR. CRITICAL. Yes, and you can wait, Bob, and see if it is my uncle. If it is anybody else, give him ten minutes, and then come in and say I'm wanted, as usual.

BOB. Yes, sir. (*Tapping noise outside.*) Somebody at the counter now, sir. (*Exit* BOB.)

MR. CRITICAL. I hope it was Uncle John. I'd like to run down to the farm with him for a week.

Enter RICHARD ROVER, *with a huge old-fashioned carpet-bag.*

RICHARD. Good morning, sir!

MR. CRITICAL. Good morning!

RICHARD. Mr. Critical?

MR. CRITICAL. That is my name, sir.

RICHARD. Editor of the Smokingtown "Spread Eagle"?

MR. CRITICAL. Yes, sir.

RICHARD. (*Sitting down.*) I called to see about some contributions to your paper. (*Opening bag and taking out a folded manuscript.*) I've only lately taken to literature, and really, money is not so much of an object to me, as a desire to substitute something good for the horrible trash now printed.

MR. CRITICAL. (*Drily.*) Very benevolent!

RICHARD. Now I have a story here—you see, sir, I don't bother about inspiration or anything of that sort; I write upon a *plan* —a plan, sir. To be sure it is somewhat confusing at times to get your characters out of a snarl, though very easy to get them in. I am sure sometimes the heroine herself has not been more puzzled about her escape from her difficulties. Indeed, she has the consolation of knowing she must get out somehow; but I have to devise ways and means.

MR. CRITICAL. Really, sir, my time will not admit of my listening to—

RICHARD. (*Interrupting.*) No, no, of course not. *This* story in
my hand, sir, is in the modern sensational style—without proba-
bility, possibility—

MR. CRITICAL. Has it *ability* of any kind?

RICHARD. (*Laughing.*) Very good, very good. Nothing, sir,
can be more complete than this story. My plot is all double knots
and intricacies that are nicely drawn out and wound off in
even threads into neat little balls of explanation at the end. It is
called, "Ernestine, the Paper Collar Girl; or, The Mysteries of the
Fifth Floor Parlor." (*Speaking rapidly.*) The heroine, a pure
blonde, of course, of the most fragile description, with azure eyes
that make the sky mud-color by comparison, goes through adventures that would kill a circus acrobat in six days. She dares the
raging storm, the earthquake, is saturated and stunned, faints in
all the proper places, recovers in the nick of time; is thrown from
her horse, drowned in a river, plunged in dungeons for months
without change of raiment, and comes forth as fresh as a daisy;
lives in a cave and never heard of influenza; brought up on a desolate sea-coast, she enters society with all the accomplishments of
a modern governess; is snubbed, scolded, persecuted, driven from
palace to cave, from dungeon to desert island, from cottage to
storm-driven mountains; elopes in the dead hours of the night
with the wrong man, who stabs her lover just as the heroine springs
from the turret chamber window into his arms; escapes from a
villain by a series of most heart-rending adventures, and appears
at the end of the story, beautiful as a dream, having carried her
harp, preserved her snowy muslin unspotted, and kept fresh flowers in her hair throughout.

MR. CRITICAL. I am afraid, sir, your story will be too sensational for our columns.

RICHARD. Oh, no! you must become acquainted with my hero.
He has not his equal—a Spanish cloak and jetty curls—always on
hand, like patent blacking, to catch the heroine as she falls fainting from her horse, to steady the rope ladder for her fairy foot-
steps, to accompany her sweet voice in dulcet songs. Strong
as Hercules, beautiful as Apollo, he defies tyrants, bursts bonds,
recovers from fatal wounds, discovers poisoned bowls, evades assas-

sins, and finally—still in the Spanish cloak—dashes in when the heroine is being forced to marry the villain, denounces the perpetrators of this hideous sacrifice, and carries off his Angeline—no, Ernestine—in triumph. There are, of course, the usual accessories —nuns, monks, daggers, concealed doors, secret staircases, dimly-burning lamps, mysterious noises, poison, shrouds, skeletons, ghosts, bats, smugglers—all the paraphernalia complete.

MR. CRITICAL. Rather too thrilling, I am afraid, sir.

Enter BOB.

BOB. Gentleman waiting to see you, sir.

MR. CRITICAL. In one moment. (*Exit* BOB.)

RICHARD. (*Plunging into carpet-bag and finding another manuscript.*) Well, here is a society novel.

MR. CRITICAL. Really, Mr.—

RICHARD. Rover, sir; Richard Rover.

MR. CRITICAL. There is some one waiting for me, and—

RICHARD. Won't keep you five minutes. Just give you an idea of this. (*Speaking rapidly.*) As I said, society novel—heroine born in lap of luxury, reared in Oriental splendor, beautiful as Venus, accomplished as all the Nine Muses, and two or three more thrown in; wears No. 5 gloves and No. 1 boots, jewels enough for a king's ransom, Parisian costumes—

MR. CRITICAL. Really, Mr. Rover—

RICHARD. Stern papa, fashionable mamma. Only child, of course—who ever bothers heroines with brothers and sisters ? Lover —lover is scorned by her mother, insulted by her father—poor, of course—equally, of course, adored by heroine—heir, really, to some three or four millions—will lost or stolen—proves to be in hidden drawer. By the way, Mr. Critical, I wonder it never occurs to heroes, in these circumstances, to smash all the furniture in the house ; it would be certain to pay.

MR. CRITICAL. Very likely; but if you will excuse me, Mr. Rover —

RICHARD. Just one moment, sir. The hero is an artist—gives his betrothed a huge diamond, small private fortune in itself—leaves her fainting on the floor, and goes to Italy—

MR. CRITICAL. Yes, I see—but my time—

RICHARD. Of course the heroine is orphaned, and plunged into

the depths of poverty; learns to sew, cook, scour, scrub, wash and
bake, preserving her dainty costume and milk-white hands, however; goes out as a governess, slandered, and finally falls fainting
in the street, from starvation, just as her lover passes and recog-
nizes the huge diamond, already mentioned, flashing upon her
finger.

MR. CRITICAL. Very fine, no doubt; but really we are crowded
with society novels. If you will excuse me—

RICHARD. (*Replacing manuscript in bag, and taking out
another.*) I have a domestic romance here. There is a blue-eyed
bread-and-butter heroine, and a great whole-souled woman who is
scorned for the baby-faced idiot. There is a rival, a villain—mild,
of course, as the novel is domestic—a jockey, a spy; brain fever,
recovery, dying confession of villain—a hero, of course.

MR. CRITICAL. But, really, Mr. Rover—

RICHARD. (*Putting manuscript back and taking another.*) Perhaps this will suit you better; this is really thrilling : heroine stolen
in infancy, elopes in youth, innocently marries two men, supposing
herself a widow; tried for bigamy—

MR. CRITICAL. I am afraid, Mr. Rover, that want of room will
compel me to decline.

Enter BOB.

BOB. Gentleman's in a hurry, sir. (*Exit* BOB.)

MR. CRITICAL. I really must ask you to excuse me, Mr. Rover.

RICHARD. Certainly, certainly; just one moment more. This is
a military and nautical romance—splendid thing, sir, suit the boys.
Full of slang, military movements and ship yarns. The heroes
are twins. Sailor, tortured by a brutal guardian, runs away to
sea—

MR. CRITICAL. I am sorry to interrupt you, sir; but really I
must ask you—

RICHARD. Bundle—three cents—aquiline nose, raven curls—
brutal captain, pirates, lovely maiden to rescue, triumphant career
—while the soldier pursues equally wonderful adventures on
land; camp life, fight with Indians, scalped, tied to a stake to
be burned, rescued by White Fawn, who proves to be an heiress
captured by Indians in infancy, and adopted by them—

MR. CRITICAL. Really, Mr. Rover, I am afraid we cannot use
your articles.

RICHARD. Do you prefer poetry? I have seventy-nine odes, forty-six sonnets, twenty-three short poems, one epic, and a tip-top tragedy in five acts.

Enter BOB.

BOB. I'm afraid that gentleman will go, Mr. Critical, and he says his business is of the utmost importance. (*Exit* BOB.)

MR. CRITICAL. You see, sir, I cannot spare another moment.

RICHARD. Well, be quick, then. I'll wait until you come back.

MR. CRITICAL. (*Aside.*) Well, of all the sublime impudence! (*Aloud.*) I am afraid, Mr. Rover, I cannot converse with you any further to-day.

RICHARD. But you have not told me which of my stories you prefer?

MR. CRITICAL. Well, to be frank with you, Mr. Rover, I do not think any of them will suit us.

RICHARD. Oh, but I must *publish* something, after spending so much time over them!

MR. CRITICAL. I am afraid you will find most of the periodicals are fully supplied.

RICHARD. But I will publish. I will see " Ernestine, the Paper Collar Girl," in print, if I pay for it as an advertisement.

MR. CRITICAL. (*Very drily.*) Twenty cents a line.

RICHARD. There are about three hundred thousand lines, more or less. I'll figure it up.

MR. CRITICAL. You will find it rather expensive, I fear, Mr. Rover.

RICHARD. (*Dramatically.*) What is money to fame!

MR. CRITICAL. Very true.

RICHARD. (*Very tragically.*) What are base mercenary calculations, when your soul is in arms!

MR. CRITICAL. Just so.

RICHARD. (*Flourishing carpet-bag.*) I scorn such paltry considerations. I'll print or die! (*Exit* RICHARD.)

MR. CRITICAL. (*Falling back in his chair.*) I'll have a chain put on the door! I'll buy a revolver! Jupiter, what a man! Bob!

Enter BOB.

Bob, you young rascal, *does* anybody want to see me?

BOB. No, sir; but I thought you was being bored, sir.

Mr. Critical. (*Groaning.*) Bored!

Bob. And so I come in, sir. The editor of the "Speaking Trumpet" *was* in, sir.

Mr. Critical. Ah!

Bob. And I told him that you were engaged with Mr. Wilkie Collins, who'd come over from England a-purpose to see about writing a story for the "Spread Eagle." You should a' seen him, sir; he just turned green.

Mr. Critical. Bob, Bob! I am afraid your morals are becoming perverted.

Bob. If that country party should come back, Mr. Critical?

Mr. Critical. (*Jumping up.*) Barricade the door! Tell him I've gone to Europe!

Enter Richard.

Richard. I just called in to say there was one of those stories I didn't mention. (*Opening bag. Exit* Bob.) It is something entirely original. I'll read you a little extract.

Mr. Critical. (*Running his hands over his hair.*) Confusion and lunacy! is there no way to get rid of this man?

Enter Bob, *with every appearance of terror.*

Bob. Fire! The whole back office is afire!

Mr. Critical. Run for the fire-engines! (*Exit* Mr. Critical, *hastily.*)

Richard. (*Following him.*) We can just step outside, and you can hear this on the pavement while they are putting out the fire. (*Exit* Richard.)

Bob. Well, I *am* beat! I'll run around the back way, and tell Mr. Critical there ain't no fire.

CURTAIN.

THE NEW BOY.

Characters.

HORACE—*The new Boy, just arrived at school.*
STEPHEN,
ALFRED, } *Boys already in the school.*
THEODORE,

SCENE.—*A Bed-room. Small bed, with white spread; bureau, washstand, table and trunk. Closet in background.* HORACE *kneeling before trunk.*

HORACE. Heigho! I wonder how I shall like boarding-school! It won't be much use to get homesick while father and mother are in Europe! (*Takes a coat out of trunk.*) There! this coat is the last thing I'll unpack! I think I have all my things nicely arranged now, and this I will hang in the closet. (*Goes to closet and enters, nearly closing the door.*)

STEPHEN. (*Outside.*) Coast clear?

ALFRED. (*Outside.*) Clear.

THEODORE. (*Outside.*) Don't miss our chance, then.

Enter STEPHEN, ALFRED *and* THEODORE, *treading very softly.*

STEPHEN. I was afraid we wouldn't get in here before bed-time, and it's half the fun to set the traps.

ALFRED. And he's really green—never was away from his dear mammy before!

THEODORE. Dear little baby! We'll make him a nice little apple-pie bed, so we will! (*They make up the bed, doubling one sheet, to appear at the top like two.*)

STEPHEN. I've got a little tar to put on the pillow, so that when we come in to tie his legs to the bed-post, he can't lift his head up. (*Smears tar on pillow.*)

THEODORE. And I've got some wax to put in his boots. Where are they? He had on his slippers at tea-time.

ALFRED. (*Finding boots beside bed.*) Here, give me the wax. (*Drops some lumps in boots.*)

STEPHEN. Where is the tin basin of water?

THEODORE. At the door.

ALFRED. (*Getting a chair.*) I'll put it on the door. (*Goes out side.*)

THEODORE. Get it on, so that we can go out.

ALFRED. (*Outside.*) All right! But he will give the door a push, of course.

STEPHEN. And he won't get wet—oh, no!

ALFRED. (*Entering.*) That's all right. We can get in and out easily, but the least touch will topple the basin over, and drench whoever is coming in.

THEODORE. That is about all we can do *now!*

STEPHEN. But we must understand fully our plan of action.

THEODORE. At nine o'clock the gas will be turned out, as usual, in the cellar. As soon as the house is dark, I will give a low whistle.

STEPHEN. Let us hear. (THEODORE *whistles one low note.*)

ALFRED. All right!

THEODORE. None of us will undress, just taking off our coats and boots. When I whistle, you two rise softly, and follow me. Steve, you will bring the ink-bottle to grease his hair with.

STEPHEN. All right!

THEODORE. And you, Al, will bring a nice dose of castor oil to give him, for fear he should be ill.

ALFRED. Correct!

THEODORE. And I have the rope to tie his hands and feet, so the pretty dear can take his medicine and have his hair oiled nicely, without making any fuss. (*Bell rings.*)

STEPHEN. Bless me! there's the retiring-bell. (*All three run out.*)

HORACE. (*Coming forward.*) I begin to think that my being excused to-night from any of the evening exercises, on account of the fatigue of traveling, was more of a favor than I had imagined. So that is the initiation, is it? Perhaps, my very dear young friends, you may not have quite so much fun as you anticipate. (*Opens trunk.*) I wonder where I put that package of red pepper and strong snuff mother gave me to sprinkle on my overcoat in the spring. Oh, here it is! (*Takes small package from trunk, and sprinkles contents upon the bed.*) Phew! how strong it is! Oh, the wax! I must shake that out of my boots before I put them on again, or I might want two boot-jacks and a darky to get them off. (*Shakes wax out of boots beside the bed, and crosses floor to entrance.*) And while I am about it, where is my box of beans for my shooter? I had it a little while ago. Oh, here it is on the table. (*Sprinkles hard white beans all over the floor.*) I fancy, as my slippers are thick, and my visitors leave their boots behind them, I'll have the best of my carpet. And I'm to be drenched, too. (*Fills basin on washstand with water, and stands it on the floor beside the bed.*) There, my dears; if the beans make your dear little toes feverish, you can cool them off in that! Is that all? Oh, oh! (*Dances about.*) I forgot my pumpkin! What fun! I thought it would do for charades or something, but this is lots better. (*Goes to his trunk again.*) Come here, my beauty! (*Takes out a hollow pumpkin, with a hideous grinning face cut on one side, and a candle behind the face.*) Have I got a match to light you up by and by? Where's your wig? (*Takes a lot of black wool, made in a wig, out of trunk, and puts it on pumpkin.*) And there is a broom in the closet. (*Gets broom, and fastens pumpkin upon it.*) Ah! as my bed is made with only *one* sheet, here is the other, as handy as possible. (*Drapes sheet over broom and stick.*) Oh, you sweet little dear, won't you be handsome when I light you up! (*Puts broom in closet.*) As I don't care about sticking to the pillow, being tied to the bed, dosed and inked, I guess I will not go to bed! (*Draws chair to closet.*) I can sit here very comfortably; and if I am besieged, there is a catch *inside* the closet, so that I can fasten myself in, and only a lock outside, of which I will take the key, so I cannot be *fastened* in. (*Takes key of closet, and pockets it.*) Now, young gentlemen, whenever you are ready, so am I. (*Sits down near the closet.*) But don't hurry on my account. (*Clock strikes nine.*) "'Tis now the very witching time of night!" (*Lights lowered suddenly, leaving stage almost dark.*) I hear a stealthy stir in the next room. (*Low whistle outside.*) That is the signal—now for the advance! (*A moment of silence, then a crash, splash and exclamation.*) My ducking, gentlemen; but you are quite welcome to it!

Enter STEPHEN, ALFRED *and* THEODORE, *shaking their heads, and wringing their sleeves as if wet. They wear no coats or boots, and stop near entrance to listen.*

ALFRED. Goodness—I am drenched!

THEODORE. I am saturated.

STEPHEN. (*Softly.*) Now how in the world could he get in without upsetting that basin? (HORACE *snores, but not loudly.*)

ALFRED. I wonder if the noise wakened him? (ALL *listen.* HORACE *continues to snore very faintly. All the conversation must be in low tones.*)

STEPHEN. No, I can hear him breathe.

THEODORE. I suppose he's awfully tired, traveling all day. Now, boys, follow me! (*Steps forward and back hastily.*)

STEPHEN. What's the matter?

THEODORE. I stepped on something hard. Gracious, how it hurt!

ALFRED. (*Going forward.*) Oh, come on! (*Limps.*) Oh!

STEPHEN. (*Going forward.*) What ails you two fellows? (*Limps.*) Why, the floor's all over pebbles! (*All three stop and rub their feet. Then they grope forward, limping and jerking as if walking on the beans, and twitching their feet as if treading on the wax and sticking.*)

STEPHEN. What on earth has he spilled all over the floor?

HORACE. (*Aside.*) Don't you wish you knew!

THEODORE. I am perfectly crippled. Feels like shot.

ALFRED. (*Going to bed.*) You fellows make an awful noise! (*Falls over basin.*) Goodness!

THEODORE. What is that?

ALFRED. Basin of water. I am drenched now.

STEPHEN. Must have been soaking his feet.

THEODORE. Hush! (ALL *listen.* HORACE *continues to snore.*)

STEPHEN. He's surely the eighth sleeper, if he is not one of the seven. (ALFRED *sneezes violently. All the boys lean over the bed and sneeze.*)

STEPHEN. (*Feeling pillow.*) He's not here! (HORACE *dodges into closet, and a click is heard.*)

THEODORE. Not here! (ALL *grope about, pitching on the beans, falling over the furniture, and feeling about.*)

STEPHEN. He's in the closet!

ALFRED. (*Pulling closet door.*) No, he's not—it's locked!

THEODORE. I'll bet Mrs. Mason has taken him to her room for some supper. She often does ask the new boys. (*Sits down on bed, and jumps up, sneezing violently.*)

ALFRED. What a fraud!

STEPHEN. What is to be done? Oh, bother those hard things on the floor! (*All three come forward.*)

HORACE. (*Softly opens closet door and steals to entrance.*) I'll lock them in here and have *my* fun. (*Appears to go to door and return.*) Prisoners not recommended to mercy. (*Steals softly back to closet.*)

THEODORE. Shall we go back to bed, or wait here till he comes up?

ALFRED. Let's go back.

STEPHEN. Oh, pshaw! Let's wait here!

ALFRED. What for? He may bring a lamp. (HORACE *gives an awful groan.*)

THEODORE. What was that!

STEPHEN. Come, no tricks on each other!

ALFRED. It was at the other end of the room. (HORACE *groans again. The boys huddle close together.*)

ALFRED. I'm going to bed! (*Goes towards door.*)

THEODORE. (*Following him.*) So am I.

STEPHEN. Well, I'm not going to stay here alone. (HORACE *groans again.*)

THEODORE. Come on! (ALL *go to door and rattle the lock.*)

STEPHEN. The door is locked. (ALL *come to front of stage.*)

ALFRED. There will be a pretty fuss in the morning, if we are not in our room. (HORACE *opens closet door, and comes slowly forward, covered with sheet, holding the pumpkin head above his own; the candle lighted.*)

THEODORE. (*Looking round.*) Oh! (*All three look around, and scream, as if terrified.*)

ALFRED. Oh, what is that? (*All three huddle together.* HORACE *stands still, centre of stage.*)

THEODORE. Oh, if we were only in our own room!

HORACE. (*In a hollow voice.*) What do you here?

ALFRED. It is somebody dressed up.

HORACE. (*Naturally.*) You don't say so! (*Turns the broom, so that the candle shows, and the lights are raised.*)

STEPHEN. I do believe it is the new boy!

HORACE. (*Putting the broom against the wall and coming forward.*) You do! Well, I am of the same opinion myself. Now, gentlemen, you can commence these little tricks you proposed whenever you like. Only I give you fair warning, before you touch me, that I am stuck full of pins, and have both hands full of red pepper and snuff.

THEODORE. (*Laughing.*) I guess you've been at boarding-school before!

STEPHEN. Of course he has.

HORACE. Allow me to remark that you are entirely mistaken. I never saw the inside of a boarding-school until this evening.

STEPHEN. Well, I guess we are quits; for if we intended to bother you, you succeeded in bothering us. I shall be lame for a month!

THEODORE. And we are all drenched.

HORACE. (*Politely.*) If you would like to retire, here is the key of the door. (*Gives key to* ALFRED.)

ALFRED. (*Very politely.*) Thanks.

HORACE. Good evening, gentlemen. Allow me to light you across the hall. (*Takes broom up to light them. Exeunt* STEPHEN, THEODORE *and* ALFRED, *all four boys making exaggerated bows, and saying* Good evening, *as they go out.*)

CURTAIN.

WHICH WAS THE HERO?

ℭ h a ꞯ a ꞓ ꞇ e ꞯ s.

GILBERT.   FRANK.

HOWARD.

During the whole of the conversation the manner of the boys must be very strongly contrasted, HOWARD speaking dramatically, with much gesticulation, FRANK in a slow, drawling tone and lounging attitude.

SCENE.—*A Sitting-room, with a large window centre of background. GILBERT sitting near the window, reading. FRANK and HOWARD in the foreground, playing chess.*

FRANK. Check!

HOWARD. (*Moving.*) I see!

FRANK. (*Frowning.*) H'm! Yes! I did not notice that knight! (*Moves.*) You've certainly got me in a tight place now.

HOWARD. (*Conceitedly.*) If there's anything I can do well, it is to play chess.

FRANK. (*Studying the board.*) Yes! H'm! That castle covers this bishop, and the pawn—h'm!—yes— (*Suddenly.*) Checkmate!

HOWARD. Impossible! Why, so it is! Nearly an hour playing, and beaten at last. (*Rising.*) We will not play any more now; I am tired. (*Pushes the board aside.*)

FRANK. (*Yawning.*) So am I. What are you reading, Gilbert?

GILBERT. Scott! "The Lady of the Lake."

HOWARD. (*Dramatically.*) Ah! those were grand scenes and times! (*Reciting, with much gesture.*)

> " Fitz-James was brave: Though to his heart
> The life-blood thrilled with sudden start,
> He mann'd himself with dauntless air,
> Returned the chief his haughty stare;
> His back against a rock he bore,
> And firmly placed his foot before

'Come one, come all! This rock shall fly
From its firm base as soon as I!'"

FRANK. That's a good climax!—I mean a good place to stop
shouting.

HOWARD. Frank, you are as tame as a cat. Nothing rouses you.
Now reading Scott makes me discontented.

FRANK. Don't read him, then.

HOWARD. Everything seems so tame and commonplace after
reading "Marmion" and "Ivanhoe." If only I had lived in those
days!

FRANK. These days are decidedly more comfortable.

HOWARD. (*Contemptuously.*) Comfortable! As if a hero cared
for comfort. If I could only be a knight, to don my armor, and
go out upon a mail-clad charger (*dramatically*) to conquer or to
die!

FRANK. (*Lazily.*) Or fight wind-mills.

GILBERT. Like Don Quixote.

FRANK. Precisely. I am not devoted to mail-clad chargers myself, and imagine armor must have been decidedly awkward.

HOWARD. But how grand to be the champion of a good cause,
and ride forth under the smiles of fair ladies, like the knights of
Christendom! I'd like to be a soldier, anyhow. Fancy fighting
six or eight of the enemy single-handed, (*striking an attitude, and
gesticulating as if flourishing a sword*) cutting down your foes
right and left till they lay slain around you!

FRANK. But suppose they cut you down!

HOWARD. Never! Heroes are fearless, and courage conquers!
Only cowards are ever defeated.

GILBERT. I say, I thought you fellows were going to play chess.
Nobody can read if you're going to be chattering like two insane
parrots.

HOWARD. Oh, we're tired of chess!

GILBERT. I'll go into the reading-room, then. (GILBERT *goes out.*)

HOWARD. Gilbert's a regular book-worm. For my part, I get
enough of reading in school-time.

FRANK. Do you? I read lots in the holidays.

HOWARD. So do I, about giants and ogres.

FRANK. Stuff and nonsense!

HOWARD. I don't agree with you. I think it makes a fellow

brave to read of desperate battles with monsters nine feet high, and two-headed magicians.

FRANK. Read history, then. You can find plenty of desperate encounters there.

HOWARD. I mean to be a soldier when I leave school, to do something grand, and leave a glory of fame upon my name.

FRANK. (*Stretching himself lazily.*) Well, I mean to be a merchant. I have no taste for blood and thunder. I very much think if I were to find myself in a battle I should make tracks for the rear in a great hurry.

HOWARD. Be a coward! I would not! I would face the enemy, sword in hand, cheering on my men to victory, flinging fear to the winds. I would never be a coward!

FRANK. I hope there will not be any war in your life or mine to test your courage.

HOWARD. Still one may be a hero even in time of peace. The doctor who visits plague-stricken houses, risks contagion and dares his life every hour, is a hero.

FRANK. Yes—I should not care to be a doctor.

HOWARD. The sailor who leaves home and friends to dare the stormy ocean, to ride over the swelling wave, is a hero.

FRANK. Yes—I shall respectfully decline being a sailor.

HOWARD. (*Contemptuously.*) I declare, Frank, if I was a coward I would keep it to myself.

FRANK. (*Indifferently.*) Would you?

HOWARD. Yes, I would. Why, all the boys are talking about it.

FRANK. About what?

HOWARD. Your—your—

FRANK. Oh, my cowardice!

HOWARD. Well, you know it did look like that, when you refused to fight George Bates last week, and you are bigger than he is, too!

FRANK. Decidedly! So I am a coward because I won't fight a smaller boy. Is that it?

HOWARD. Why, of course it is! It is bad enough to be afraid of a boy your own size or bigger; but to let a little fellow like George Bates scare you, did look queer.

FRANK. Very queer.

HOWARD. And you wouldn't come down in the woods to try Tom Harding's revolver.

FRANK. Because I was afraid ?

HOWARD. Well, all the boys said so.

FRANK. Revolvers being a plaything of which Professor Davis entirely approves.

HOWARD. Well, of course we had to try it on the sly, but none of us were *afraid* of it.

FRANK. Nor afraid of breaking the strictest rule of the school—a rule established for the protection of the scholars entirely.

HOWARD. What a set of milksops we would all grow up to be, if we knew nothing of the use of firearms.

FRANK. Certainly. By all means practice with cheap, ill-made revolvers and ignorant fingers, even if you do risk your own life and that of your companions. Indeed, I think a murder would be a grand commencement for a hero.

HOWARD. A murder !

FRANK. Exactly. What else is it, if, through your disobedience, you shoot another boy ? I have told Tom that unless the revolver is out of the school to-night, I shall inform Professor Davis of its whereabouts to-morrow.

HOWARD. You wouldn't be such a sneak as to tell !

FRANK. (*Coolly.*) Dreadful, isn't it? Perhaps if some of you had come home minus a finger or two, you might have wished I had told sooner.

HOWARD. (*Excitedly.*) Well, I wouldn't be a coward and a sneak for anything !

Enter GILBERT, *hurriedly.*

GILBERT. Oh, Frank ! Howard ! Nero has broken his chain, and they think he is mad.

HOWARD. Shut the door ! (*Runs to shut it.*) Where is he ?

GILBERT. He is running all round the house, and nobody dares go near him. James is afraid he will go to the woods !

FRANK. (*Springing to his feet.*) The woods ! Why, all the little fellows are down there, nutting !

GILBERT. Yes, the whole primary class.

FRANK. Horrible ! (*Goes out, hurriedly.*)

HOWARD. Shut the door ! (*Shuts door.*) I've half a mind to lock it. Suppose Nero should get in here ! (*Trembling violently.*) He is as big as a colt.

GILBERT. But gentle as a lamb, generally.

HOWARD. (*Still trembling.*) Who said he was mad ?

GILBERT. James. He says he snapped his chain, and rushed into the house with his tongue hanging out and his mouth all frothy. I wonder if Professor Davis would scold, if we got Tom's revolver and shot him ?

HOWARD. But it might go off and not hit him !

GILBERT. (*Going to a window.*) Where is Frank going ?

HOWARD. Frank ! He is hiding under the bed somewhere, I bet ! Why, he is afraid of his own shadow, much more of a mad dog !

GILBERT. But he is out here (*looking from the window*) in his shirt sleeves, and with the heaviest poker in the kitchen. He is going to the woods. No, he has turned round to— Oh, Howard ! Nero is rushing right at him ! He will tear him to pieces !

HOWARD. (*Sinking, trembling, into chair.*) Is he all alone ?

GILBERT. All alone ! He has struck Nero twice with the poker, but Nero has sprung on him ! Oh, see, Howard ! He is struggling with Nero, and calling to the children to keep back. All the little fellows are coming out of the woods. "Keep back !" Don't you hear him ?

HOWARD. (*Shuddering, and hiding his face.*) Oh, it is dreadful !

GILBERT. The men are coming up from the farm. Hurrah ! They've got Nero now with a rope round his neck ! Hurrah ! (GILBERT *runs out.*)

HOWARD. Oh, how deathly sick I feel ! I wonder if they have got Nero safely, and will kill him ? How could he break his chain ? Professor Davis has no business to keep him, even if he does need a watch-dog. I am as cold as ice ! Who would have thought Frank would dare face a mad dog !

Enter GILBERT, *supporting* FRANK, *who has one arm bound up.*

GILBERT. Get a chair, Howard.

HOWARD. (*Pushing chair forward.*) Oh, Frank, are you hurt ?

FRANK. (*Faintly.*) It is nothing much. (*Leans his head against* GILBERT, *who fans him with his handkerchief.*) But I was afraid Nero might get amongst the little fellows.

HOWARD. Oh, Gilbert, he is fainting ! Was he bitten ?

GILBERT. Yes, on the arm, and he marched right into the kitchen and put a hot poker on the place, himself.

HOWARD. Oh, Frank, can you ever forgive me for calling you a coward ?

FRANK. No harm done ! Better be called a coward than to be one.

GILBERT. Here, Howard, hold his head while I go and see if the doctor is coming. (HOWARD *takes* GILBERT'S *place*. GILBERT *goes out.*)

HOWARD. Are you better ?

FRANK. Oh, I'm all right ! My arm aches some, and you may laugh at me if you choose, Howard ; I am faint with fright, now it is all over. I feel sick when I think of all those little boys, if that great dog had got to the woods.

HOWARD. As he would have done, but for you.

FRANK. Yes, I thank my Heavenly Father that he let me hold him.

Enter GILBERT.

GILBERT. Oh, Howard, Frank, I have good news ! Nero is not mad. He was stung by some hornets and frantic with pain, but he is not mad, and Frank need not be afraid of hydrophobia.

HOWARD. I don't believe Frank is *afraid* of anything.

FRANK. (*Brightly.*) Halloo ! That's not the tune you were singing this morning.

GILBERT. But Nero is to be shot ! Professor Davis says he will not have any more such risk.

FRANK. Poor Nero !

HOWARD. I am glad, for I am afraid of him now, if you are not. But I guess, Frank I won't brag any more about being heroic.

CURTAIN.

ASTONISHING THE NATIVES.

ℭ𝔥𝔞𝔯𝔞𝔠𝔱𝔢𝔯𝔰.

ELOISE GRANDALL—*A recent Graduate of a Seminary.*
HESTER LORING—*Her intimate Friend.*
SUSY—*The Servant Girl.*

SCENE.—*A Modern Sitting-room. Open piano, with music upon it. An aquarium, fernery, cabinet with drawers, stand of flowers, and a table, with a few books scattered upon it.* SUSY *dusting the furniture.*

SUSY. Well, I do be kept busy, to be sure, now Miss Eliza—Oh, gracious! I forgot—Miss Eloise has come back from the grand school where she got such a pile of learning. Why, the parson himself can't beat her on the big words! And she's always a-going off with clompy boots and a big shade hat, a-digging for worms, and a-scooping fishes out of the creek, and catching bugs and butterflies in little nets; and when she is at home dressed to kill! (*Dusts the aquarium.*) Here's her aquarium, all full of stones and shells and little bobbity bits of fishes. How they wriggle! Poor things! I think it's a shame to take them out of the cool, shady creek, and keep them in glass cases.

Enter ELOISE, *very elaborately dressed.*

ELOISE. Susan!
SUSY. Yes, Miss Eliz—Eloise!
ELOISE. Does my skirt hang gracefully?
SUSY. Beautifully, miss!
ELOISE. Is the flounce on my overskirt looped in the proper manner?
SUSY. It couldn't be better, miss.
ELOISE. (*Walking slowly across stage.*) Does my train follow my movement in a delicate curve?
SUSY. (*Looking bewildered.*) I—think—it—does.

ELOISE. Think! Can't you *see?*

SUSY. Yes, miss. It is splendid!

ELOISE. How does the dress fit me?

SUSY. Magnificent, miss!

ELOISE. Does it not wrinkle on the shoulders?

SUSY. Not a wrinkle as big as a hair anywhere about it, miss! And all the crinkle-crankleums on it is lovely. I never saw such sweet silk!

ELOISE. Is my collar straight?

SUSY. Couldn't be straighter.

ELOISE. One might as well be buried at once, as to live in a house without a full-length mirror. I am quite resolved not to let papa have one moment's peace until he puts one in my room. I always feel half dressed, if I cannot see the sweep of my skirts or the fall of my cloak.

SUSY. Well, you're elegant to-day, miss! Do you expect visitors, miss?

ELOISE. Miss Hester Loring is coming to see me.

SUSY. My! won't you be glad to see her? You was never apart before you went away last year, and I know she has been awfully lonesome since you left. (*Aside.*) But she won't dress up like that, I know, to see you.

ELOISE. Is my hair all right at the back?

SUSY. Lovely, miss.

ELOISE. (*Sitting down.*) Bring me a footstool.

SUSY. Yes, miss. (*Brings footstool.*)

ELOISE. Hand me a book from the table.

SUSY. Which one, miss?

ELOISE. Any one. (SUSY *hands book.*) You may go now, Susy. When Miss Hester comes, show her in here.

SUSY. Yes, miss. (*Exit* SUSY.)

ELOISE. I wonder if my skirt is draped gracefully over the footstool, so as to show the rosette upon my new slippers! Hester is so primitive, and her education has been so shockingly deficient, that I consider it a positive duty to show her the advantages *I* have gained by a year in Mrs. Stickumup's Seminary. Indeed, I calculate that now I shall in every way—dress, deportment and accomplishments, astonish the natives. (*Bell rings.*) That must be Hester. (*Appears absorbed in reading.*)

Enter HESTER, *very quietly dressed.*

HESTER. Oh, dear Eliza— (*stops confused, as* ELOISE *does not seem to see her.*) Good morning!

ELOISE. (*Looking up.*) Oh, pardon me! I was so interested in this new work upon botany, I did not hear you enter. (*Rising gracefully.*) I am delighted to see you.

HESTER. I—why, Eliza, you don't seem to be a bit delighted. (*Aside.*) A year ago she would have kissed me twenty times, if we had been separated for one day.

ELOISE. Dear Hester, would you mind calling me Eloise? Eliza is such a very common name.

HESTER. Not at all. Is it the fashion nowadays to change your name?

ELOISE. I know nothing about fashion, my dear friend. My mind is so absorbed in the pursuit of knowledge, that I care nothing for such frivolities as fashion demands of her votaries.

HESTER. Oh, I beg your pardon, I am sure! But your dress—

ELOISE. A fancy of my dressmaker's. She knows I care nothing for such things, and exercises her own discretion. Let me take your hat and shawl. You have come to spend the day?

HESTER. I did intend to do so, but perhaps you have renounced friendship, with other frivolities. (*Aside.*) She shall not see how much she wounds me by her coldness.

ELOISE. (*Clasping her hands.*) I renounce friendship! How little you know me.

"Friendship above all ties doth bind the heart;
And faith in friendship is the noblest part!"

I could not live without friendship! (*As if affected.*)

HESTER. I did not mean to wound you. (*Aside.*) I had rather have one of her old warm kisses than all her protestations!

ELOISE. (*Removing* HESTER's *hat and shawl.*) You must stay all day. I have a thousand things to show you.

HESTER. Thanks! I suppose you brought a great many new things from the city? Oh, you have an aquarium! (*Goes to aquarium.*)

ELOISE. Yes, a trifle to amuse leisure hours, when my brain wearies of study. That is a very fine specimen of the *Dyticus Marginalis.* You recognize it, of course?

HESTER. It is difficult to tell one of the water beetles from another, they dart about so quickly. But I see you have a *Hydrophilus piceous!* (*Aside.*) She will find two can play at that game.

ELOISE. (*Aside.*) Now who would imagine she knew the Latin names for those horrid little beetles! (*Aloud.*) Oh, I am so glad, dear Hester, that you share my enthusiasm for this fascinating pursuit. I spent the entire day yesterday at the creek. I obtained a *Helophorus aquaticus* and an *Acilius sulcatus*, but looked in vain for a *Colymbetes.*

HESTER. (*Aside.*) It is too funny that Bob should have just taught me all the Latin names of the contents of an aquarium! I'll just air a little of *my* learning. (*Aloud, very gravely.*) I think, my beloved Eloise, that we have ever been in sympathy in our pursuits. Pardon me, therefore, if I presume to criticise your aquarium. I find therein a deficiency of *Algæ*, most necessary for the health of your aquatic pets. We can easily procure a supply, however. Let me recommend, my charming friend, some of the *Cladophora Arcta*, a little of the *Enteromorpha*, which is, however, so common, that I would use it sparingly, a few specimens of the *Porphyra laciniata*, or *Ulva latissima*, whichever you prefer. Both are effective.

ELOISE. (*Aside.*) I guess I will show her something else. (*Aloud.*) You are very kind, dear, to make any suggestion. This anemone is very rare ; did you notice it ?

HESTER. I did. You must really come over and see my collection.

ELOISE. Have you a *Goniodoris nodosa ?*

HESTER. Two, my love, and a perfect *Gemellaria loricata*. My *Scrupocellaria scruposa* has been very much admired.

ELOISE. I have a *Patella pellucida*—a very fine specimen.

HESTER. Indeed! Have you an *Aspidophorus Europæus ?*

ELOISE. (*Aside.*) Now isn't she provoking! (*Aloud.*) Are you fond of ferns, Hester ? (*Going to fernery.*)

HESTER. I do not care to keep them in the house. They grow so luxuriantly near here that one can admire their beauty in every walk.

ELOISE. But mine are all English ferns.

HESTER. Indeed! (*Examines ferns.*)

ELOISE. I gave quite a small fortune for some of the specimens.

(*Aside.*) I will amaze her now. (*Aloud, very rapidly, as if fearing interruption.*) This one is the *Asplenium adiantum nigrum*, this the *Lastica dilatata*, this the *Polystichum aculeatum*, and this the *Scolopendrium;* but the treasure of all is this lovely, lovely *Polystichum lonchites.*

HESTER. (*Coolly.*) They are very pretty ; but I think our American ferns are quite as graceful.

ELOISE. If you will excuse me a moment, I will find my portfolio of dried specimens to show you. (*Aside.*) I am sure my hair is coming down. (*Exit* ELOISE.)

HESTER. A year ago she would have put her arm around my waist, and said, " Come, Hettie, to my room, and see my ferns!" Well, (*sighing*) I hope her affectations make her happy.

Enter SUSY.

SUSY. Oh, Miss Hettie, ain't our Miss Eliza got a heap o' learning in that cemetery she's been to?

HESTER. (*Smiling.*) It seems so, Susy.

SUSY. She studied up a whole pile o' furrin' talk about the fishes and the ferns yesterday. I was listening to her going it all over—all about the polly-stick-um and the goney on nosa and screw-pole in air, and screw-pole on nosa, and salt-cellar beetles !

HESTER. Those are the Latin names, Susy, for very common little fishes and beetles.

SUSY. Do tell ! But I s'pect they must be, for she calls the soap a slaponoseous compound.

HESTER. Indeed !

SUSY. And how was I to know she wanted the bread, when she asked for flarinaceous food ?

HESTER. What is butter ?

SUSY. She ain't got to the butter yet. But the pickles are all con—con—

HESTER. Condiments !

SUSY. Now, Miss Hettie, don't you go at it too, or I'll never be able to wait on the table. I'm so flustercated now, I expect I'll give her red pepper for pudding-sauce, and sugar to put on her meat.

HESTER. (*Laughing.*) No fear of that ! You are far too handy !

SUSY. But I came in to see if I was to put on a plate for you at dinner.

HESTER. Yes, Susy, I shall stay to-day. (*Exit* SUSY.) But I shall not repeat my visit very soon. The fun of fighting Miss Eloise with her own weapons sadly needs an audience! If only Bob were here, now!

Enter ELOISE.

ELOISE. I find my portfolio is in one of my trunks at Aunt Miriam's, where I promised to return in a few days. I am anxious to spend a little more time in the city, to add to my collection of shells. Are you fond of conchology?

HESTER. Only to admire. I have not studied it.

ELOISE. It is most absorbing. (*Opens cabinet drawer.*) My collection is very limited, as you see; but I have some rare specimens.

HESTER. (*Pointing.*) That is a pretty *Trochus ziziphinus.*

ELOISE. But not so fine as this *Littorina littoralis.*

HESTER. Still, periwinkles are so common.

ELOISE. (*Pettishly.*) I assure you there is nothing *common* in the collection.

HESTER. I had no intention of offending you, Eliza.

ELOISE. I wish you would call me Eloise.

HESTER. Pardon me! (*Going to piano.*) Have you brought home any new music?

ELOISE. (*Aside.*) Now I *will* astonish her. (*Aloud.*) Oh, you know I adore music! Shall I play for you the last trifle I learned?

HESTER. I shall be delighted to hear it. (ELOISE *plays a very showy, sky-rocketty piece of instrumental music, often blundering, often striking a false note. It should be very short, but played with all the affected airs and graces possible to assume.*)

ELOISE. Do you not admire that?

HESTER. It appears to be difficult.

ELOISE. Not at all; a mere trifle!

HESTER. (*Aside.*) It was a pity, then, not to learn to play it correctly.

ELOISE. Will you not sing for me? I believe you do sing?

HESTER. You have heard me hundreds of times, and I have learned nothing very new.

ELOISE. But do sing!

HESTER. Certainly, if you wish it. (HESTER *sings some simple ballad, well, but without any affectations. The contrast in the musical performances must be very marked.*)

ELOISE. Thanks! But you really should learn something less old-fashioned.

HESTER. Such as this. (*Sings a brilliant variation.*)

ELOISE. (*Amazed.*) Where did you learn that?

HESTER. Of Professor Squallum, of course. But I do not care to sing in that style, as I cannot rival professional performers, and prefer to confine my efforts to what pleases my friends.

ELOISE. (*Coming forward.*) This is very fatiguing weather. (*Sinks into a chair.*)

HESTER. Very! (*Sinks into another chair.*)

ELOISE. The heat quite prostrates a delicate person. (*Fans herself languidly.*)

HESTER. It is almost insupportable! (*Fans herself with the same air of languor.*)

ELOISE. I think it is quite an error to suppose country air cooler than that in the city. The sea breezes are the only real relief.

HESTER. Or mountain air. I sigh for the summit of Mont Blanc!

ELOISE. (*Very sentimentally.*)

"I love to stand on some high beetling rock,
    Or dusky brow of savage promontory,
    Watching the waves, with all their white crests dancing,
    Come, like thick plum'd squadrons, to the shore
    Gallantly bounding!"

HESTER. (*Still more sentimentally.*) I love the mountain air!
"The mountain wind! most spiritual of all
    The wide earth knows—when, in the sultry time,
    He stoops him from his vast cerulean hall,
    He seems the breath of a celestial clime,
    As if from heaven's wide open gates did flow
    Health and refreshment on the world below!"

ELOISE. (*Aside.*) I don't seem to have made much impression upon her. (*Aloud.*) Are you still fond of long walks, Hester? You were untiring last year.

HESTER. Last year! Oh, one really cannot be expected to retain any favorite taste for such an age!

ELOISE. How do you amuse yourself in this dull little place?

HESTER. We continue to exist, with lawn tennis, croquet, outdoor concerts, charades, tableaux, music and picnics. All vulgar pursuits to a mind of such exquisite refinement as yours, I do not doubt; but the aborigines of these parts manage to live!

ELOISE. I am weary of all such trifling pursuits, and pass my time in study. As Cicero says: *"Animæ cultus quasi quidam humanitatis cibus."**

HESTER. And yet Seneca remarks: *"Interdum et insanire jucundum est."†*

ELOISE. (*Suddenly springing up.*) A truce, Hetty!

HESTER. (*Also springing up.*) With all my heart, dear Lida!

ELOISE. (*Embracing* HESTER.) I think I have played the fool quite enough for one day. We will go to my room and you shall tell me all your year's experiences. You have kept pace with me, at any rate.

HESTER. (*Laughing.*) Well, I understood you promised, upon your return home, to astonish the natives, and being one of them— (ELOISE *kisses her.*)

ELOISE. Not another word. Since we have become such good Latin scholars, let me remark, *" Amicum perdere est damnorum maximum."**

HESTER. I was very much afraid I was losing my old friend, but I resolved to make a bold stand.

ELOISE. And you have fairly beaten her with her own weapons.

HESTER. There is one old Italian proverb that says, *"Al finir del gioco, si vede che ha guadagnato."*

ELOISE. Translate, my dear, for the benefit of the country members.

HESTER. At the end of the game one may see who has won. (*They go out arm in arm.*)

CURTAIN.

---

* Cultivation is as necessary to the mind as food is to the body.
† It is sometimes pleasant to play the fool.
* To lose a friend is the greatest of losses.

THE CRITICS.

𝕮𝖍𝖆𝖗𝖆𝖈𝖙𝖊𝖗𝖘.

GEORGE.	FRANK.
HERBERT.	WILFRED.
LAWRENCE.	JAMES.

SCENE.—*A Stage, with curtains draped at each side.* HERBERT *is seated in the audience, left of foreground ;* LAWRENCE *in the audience, right of foreground ;* FRANK *in the audience, in one of the rear seats.* WILFRED *on the stage, left, concealed by curtain.* JAMES *on the stage, right, concealed by curtain.*

To be effective, this dialogue must be rehearsed until every boy is prompt and perfect in his part, as any hesitation will ruin the fun.

GEORGE. (*Advancing to front of stage, and speaking very slowly and dramatically.*) " On Linden, when the sun was low "—

HERBERT. Oh, oh!

GEORGE. (*Looking indignantly at* HERBERT.) You had better go home, boy !

LAWRENCE. Oh, come, speak your piece.   Never mind him.

GEORGE. " On Linden, when the sun was low "—

HERBERT. You said that once !

GEORGE. Really, if I am to be constantly interrupted in this silly manner—

LAWRENCE. Oh, go ahead !   We did not come here to hear you two quarrel.   Go on about the sun.

HERBERT. Yes.   (*Imitating.*) " On Linden, when the sun was high !"

LAWRENCE. Come, you shut up !

FRANK. (*Gruffly.*) Can't you boys in the front there be quiet ? We'd like to hear the recitation.

GEORGE. (*As if confused.*)
>"On Linden, when the sun was low,
>   All bloodless lay the untrodden snow."

HERBERT. You'd better get some more of your voice up from down cellar!

GEORGE. (*Loftily.*) Perhaps you can say it better?

HERBERT. Perhaps? Of course I can!

GEORGE. (*Bowing with great ceremony.*) You had better take my place then.

HERBERT. All right! (*Gets upon stage.*) Now *I* will show you some elocution! (*In a very high voice.*)

"On Linden, when the sun was low."

LAWRENCE. Punch and Judy! How are you, Mr. Punch?

HERBERT. (*Angrily.*) Who asked your opinion?

LAWRENCE. Oh, if it comes to that, who asked yours?

FRANK. This is a pretty way for you boys to go on, now, isn't it? Sit down, and don't interrupt George again.

HERBERT. Just as you say. (*Sits down on stage.*)

GEORGE. (*Coming forward.*) "On Linden, when the sun was low"—

HERBERT. That's four times we've had that line!

GEORGE. (*Pettishly.*) And you'll have it fifty, if you won't allow me to begin!

HERBERT. Oh, you're first rate at *beginning;* the trouble seems to be to go on!

LAWRENCE. You'll find yourself put out if you do not keep still.

HERBERT. I won't be half as much *put out* as you appear to be, if you send me home!

FRANK. I'll put you both out, if you don't keep quiet.

GEORGE. I might as well retire. I hope, ladies and gentlemen, you will not attribute this most unwarrantable confusion to me.

LAWRENCE. Oh, go ahead! If he bothers you again, we'll just give him a standing seat outside.

GEORGE. (*Clearing his throat.*) On Linden—ahem.

HERBERT. He don't know it!

GEORGE. "On Linden, when the sun was low"—

HERBERT. That's five times.

GEORGE. "All bloodless lay th' untrodden snow,
            And dark as winter was the flow
            Of Iser, rolling rapidly.

        But Linden"—(*hesitates.*)

HERBERT. I knew he didn't know it.

GEORGE. (*Aside.*) Why don't you prompt?

WILFRED. (*Concealed.*) Saw another sight!

HERBERT. That's it. Go ahead now! Saw another sight.

GEORGE. "But Linden saw another sight,
When the drum beat, at dead of night,
Commanding"— (*Hesitates.*)

WILFRED. (*In a loud whisper.*) Fires of death!

GEORGE. "Commanding fires of death to—" (*Hesitates.*)

WILFRED. (*In a loud whisper.*) Light!

GEORGE. "Fires of death to light."

HERBERT. (*Imitating.*) Fires of death to— (*whispers*) light. (*Aloud.*) Fires of death to light. Don't you think the fellow with the book, behind there, had better speak the piece?

GEORGE. I would like to hear anybody recite with such provoking interruptions. It is just because you are too stupid to learn a piece yourself that you are trying to spoil mine!

HERBERT. I can recite "Hohenlinden" anyhow! I knew that old stuff in my cradle.

GEORGE. Recite it, then! I'll not speak another word to-night! (*Goes to back of stage sulkily.*)

HERBERT. (*With a low bow.*) Ladies and gentlemen, owing to the extreme indisposition of the boy whose name is upon the programme—

GEORGE I am as well as you are!

HERBERT. Just so, but you said you were indisposed to speak.

LAWRENCE. If you climbed up there to make wretched puns, you had better climb down again.

HERBERT. In a few minutes, my dear friend, I will avail myself of your polite suggestion, but not until I have taken George's place for a sufficient length of time to show this aristocratic and intelligent audience how "Hohenlinden" should be recited.

FRANK. Puppy!

HERBERT. Pardon me! Did some gentleman in the rear call you, Lawrence?

GEORGE. I thought you were going to recite "Hohenlinden"!

LAWRENCE. He can't! He don't know how!

HERBERT. That is slander! (*Strikes an attitude.*)
"On Linden, when the sun was low"—

LAWRENCE. I thought *you* mentioned that we had already heard that line five times !

HERBERT. You dry up, will you !

"On Linden, when the sun was low "—

LAWRENCE. Is that seven times or eight ? I've lost the count.

FRANK. Can't you boys up there behave yourselves ? You are a disgrace to the Institution !

HERBERT. You're pretty safe, back there. Come up here and say that !

FRANK. I flatter myself I know better than to encourage the disturbance you are making.

LAWRENCE. It is too bad. Go ahead, one of you. I'll be as silent as a gravestone !

HERBERT. (*Coming to front of stage.*)

"On Linden, when the sun was low,
  All stainless—"

GEORGE. Hadn't you better learn the words ?

HERBERT. I had the words right.

GEORGE. You didn't ! (*Emphatically.*)

"All *bloodless* lay the untrodden snow."

HERBERT. It is all the same, anyhow.

GEORGE. A pretty mess you'd make of poetry !

HERBERT. "All *bloodless*, then, lay the untrodden snow,
  And dark as winter was the flow
    Of—of—" (*Aside.*) Why don't you prompt ?

WILFRED. (*Coming forward with a book.*) I didn't undertake to prompt *you.*

LAWRENCE. Of course not. He was so perfect that he did not secure the services of a prompter. Why, he knew that old stuff in his cradle !

WILFRED. I think you both had better have stayed at home, for my part. I won't prompt either of you.

LAWRENCE. Nobody asked you. If I didn't know my part well enough to speak it alone, I would not attempt it.

HERBERT. Oh, you are very smart, ain't you ? Come up here and say it.

LAWRENCE. If I do, I won't growl like a bear or squeak like a Punch and Judy show.

GEORGE. Recitations ought to be made in a deep voice, if the subject is solemn.

HERBERT. Since you are so *very* fine an elocutionist, suppose you just step up here to show us how "Hohenlinden" should be read.

WILFRED. Really, these proceedings are very irregular.

FRANK. Irregular! They are perfectly outrageous.

HERBERT. You can keep *your* opinion until it is called for.

FRANK. As you did yours.

LAWRENCE. Had you there, Master Herbert!

GEORGE. I think we might as well all retire for the next recitation. I don't suppose we amuse the audience very much.

HERBERT. Hold on! We want that super-excellent recitation of "Hohenlinden," by Professor Lawrence.

LAWRENCE. (*Climbing on stage.*) If the audience will kindly excuse a total want of preparation—

FRANK. We'll excuse anything if you will go on with the performances.

LAWRENCE. And overlook the deficiencies arising from an absence of rehearsals—

HERBERT. Never mind any more apology.

LAWRENCE. And take into consideration my extreme youth and constitutional bashfulness—

GEORGE. Bashfulness!

LAWRENCE. And kindly allow for the impromptu character of the recitation, I will endeavor to recite "Hohenlinden!" (*Recites with most exaggerated gesture and strained voice.*)

> "On Linden, when the sun was low,
> All bloodless lay th' untrodden snow,
> And dark as winter was the flow
> Of Iser, rolling rapidly."

GEORGE. (*To* HERBERT.) He commenced at the climax!

HERBERT. Yes! He will fly to pieces if he piles any more agony on that.

LAWRENCE. "By torch and trumpet"—

GEORGE. Hold on! That's the *third* verse!

LAWRENCE. Oh, yes! I wish, however, you would not bother me. It breaks the thread of inspiration!

HERBERT. He'll break a blood-vessel if he's not careful!

FRANK. Are you at it again?

LAWRENCE. You needn't interfere, if we are! (*Reciting as before.*) " But Linden saw another sight,
When the drum beat, at dead of night,
Commanding fires of death to light
(*Drops voice suddenly.*)
The darkness of her scenery."

HERBERT. "Oh, what a fall was there, my countrymen!"

GEORGE. He couldn't get up any higher, and he had to do something!

LAWRENCE. (*Contemptuously.*) You boys know nothing whatever of dramatic effect! Who ever heard any great speaker keep his voice at one pitch all the time!

GEORGE. Who ever heard any great speaker *start* at the pitch of his lungs?

WILFRED. It is my opinion you don't any of you know what you are talking about.

GEORGE. (*Sarcastically.*) Oh, here is another full-blown critic!

WILFRED. I have no desire to interrupt or criticise you; but the absurd way in which you are all acting calls forth remark from anybody.

GEORGE. Who commenced the fuss? I am sure I was doing exactly what was on the programme for me to do.

WILFRED. (*Looking at programme.*) Here! You are down to recite "Hohenlinden"!

GEORGE. Well, it is not my fault that I did *not* recite "Hohenden." I came here ready—

HERBERT. Ready! Why, you bungled over the very first verse —had to be prompted!

GEORGE. Anybody would get confused, badgered as I was.

FRANK. I'm going out to ask for my money at the door. We came here to listen to recitations and music, and we have had nothing but a schoolboy squabble, as uninteresting as it is disgraceful!

LAWRENCE. Your growling has been as much of a disturbance as anything!

HERBERT. Yes, and you're very safe back there making a fuss!

WILFRED. Come, come! We've had about enough of this for one evening. You boys get down, and see if you can't keep your mouths shut while George recites "Hohenlinden."

GEORGE. Oh, we've had about enough " Hohenlinden" for one evening.

WILFRED. But it is on the programme.

HERBERT. I'll get down, and I'll not speak a word, even if George gets his voice down into his boots. (*Gets down and resumes his place in the audience.*)

LAWRENCE. I won't interrupt you; you may be sure of that. (*Gets down and resumes seat.*)

WILFRED. I will prompt you, if all this disturbance has confused you. (*Retires behind curtain.*)

FRANK. I do hope now we are to have a *little* order and quiet!

HERBERT. We will if you'll stop growling!

LAWRENCE. And you'll dry up!

GEORGE. (*Coming forward.*)

"On Linden, when the sun was low—"

Enter JAMES.

JAMES. Professor Johnson* sent me to say that the time for "Hohenlinden" is up, and they are waiting for the next recitation!

CURTAIN.

THE EXPECTED VISITORS.

Characters.

DELIA.	BESSIE.
SADIE.	CORNELIA.
NETTIE.	EVANGELINE.

SCENE.—*A Prettily-furnished Sitting-room, with muslin curtains, matting and summer surroundings, as if at a country-seat.* SADIE *arranging some flowers in a vase;* BESSIE *at the window, draping the curtains.*

BESSIE. What a fuss Delia makes about this visit! After all, Cornelia and Evangeline Stuart are only girls like ourselves.

---

* Name the Principal of the school.

SADIE. But they were very polite to Delia when she was in the city last winter.

BESSIE. I know that; but when we are receiving our own friends, and even papa's and mamma's, without any fuss, I can't see why the whole house should be turned upside down for two girls.

Enter NETTIE, *laughing.*

NETTIE. Oh, girls, such fun!

BESSIE. What is it?

NETTIE. I went into the dressing-room, and the door leading into mamma's room was open. Of course I don't listen; but I couldn't help hearing Delia. (*Laughs.*)

SADIE. Does she want mamma to send to Paris for a new cap before these wonderful guests of hers come?

NETTIE. No; but she asked mamma's permission to give us a few hints about deportment.

BESSIE. As if we did not know how to behave ourselves!

SADIE. (*Indignantly.*) I think mamma taught us to " make our manners," as the old nurses say, a long time ago!

BESSIE. What did mamma say?

NETTIE. She said she had no objection, if we had none.

SADIE. Well, I have! I have no desire to be such a piece of affectation as Delia has been since she came home from Aunt May's.

BESSIE. Oh, never mind, Sadie! Don't let her know we care! As Nettie says, it will be fun to see how far she will go!

SADIE. Oh, very well!

Enter DELIA.

DELIA. (*Whose manner and voice must be very affected and artificial.*) Oh, my dear sisters, I am so glad you are all here!

SADIE. (*Drily.*) It must be a source of deep delight. It is about an hour since we were *all* at the breakfast-table!

BESSIE. Make some allowance for Delia's absence for six weeks, which has doubtless increased her sisterly affection!

DELIA. (*Aside.*) Are they making fun of me? No, they are all as grave as owls! (*Aloud.*) Mamma told me I might give you a few hints about city etiquette, before my friends come.

NETTIE. (*Very gravely.*) You are exceedingly kind!

BESSIE. (*Very gravely.*) It will be an inestimable advantage to such rustics as we are, to have the benefit of your experience and observation.

SADIE. (*Very gravely.*) As you expect your friends very early, there seems to be no time to lose.

DELIA. (*Aside.*) I thought they would be vexed, but they probably see their own deficiencies since I returned. (*Aloud.*) You know, girls, the Stuarts move in the very *best* society, and they are accustomed to meet only refined people. (*During the entire scene the faces of* NETTIE, BESSIE *and* SADIE *must be grave to solemnity, and they must appear to give scrupulous attention to* DELIA, *and to be really trying to follow her directions.*)

BESSIE. We understand !

SADIE. You don't want us to wipe our fingers on the table-cloth.

NETTIE. Or pick our teeth with the forks !

BESSIE. Or tilt our chairs on two legs !

DELIA. Of course I am not afraid of your doing anything *rude !*

BESSIE. Oh, we thought that was the trouble !

DELIA. It was only some little points.

SADIE. Such as—

DELIA. Well, you know you all have a fashion of rushing out to the porch and welcoming people as if—as if—

NETTIE. We were glad to see them !

SADIE. But cordial welcoming of guests may not be the fashion.

DELIA. If you will let me receive them at the door, and bring them in here, I will introduce you each in turn, and then if you will each say something different—you, Bessie, say : I am pleased to welcome you to Bay Ridge !

BESSIE. (*Making a very stiff, ceremonious bow.*) I am pleased to welcome you to Bay Ridge !

DELIA. And you, Nettie, might say : You have had a lovely day for a drive.

NETTIE. (*In a simpering voice.*) You have had a lovely day for your ride !

DELIA. Drive—they will not come on horseback.

NETTIE. Oh, I will remember.

DELIA. And Sadie ?

SADIE. (*Imitating* BESSIE.) I will say : We shall be most truly rejoiced to see you *drive* home again.

DELIA. (*Piteously.*) Now, Sadie!

SADIE. Oh, you are to tell us *exactly* what to say!

DELIA. Won't you say: We have looked forward with great pleasure to the prospect of this visit?

SADIE. Certainly. (*Very primly.*) We have looked forward with great pleasure to the prospect of this visit.

DELIA. And, girls, would you mind sinking into your seats gracefully? You all bounce so!

BESSIE. (*Rising.*) This way? (*Slowly sinks into a chair, holding out her skirts daintily.*)

DELIA. Yes! I am sure that is more graceful than just bumping down anyhow.

NETTIE. Let me try. (*Spreads her skirts and sinks down languidly, as if fainting.*)

SADIE. Something in this style? (*Imitates* BESSIE, *but very stiffly, her elbows pointing out and all her fingers straight.*)

DELIA. And would you mind calling me Cordelia, just for to-day?

SADIE. Certainly; anything to oblige, *Cordelia!* I believe my baptismal appellation is Sarah.

BESSIE. And mine Elizabeth.

DELIA. Nettie has the sweetest name, Antoinette. And the Stuart girls have lovely names, Evangeline and Cornelia.

SADIE. I think, my dear sisters, as Cordelia has made so elaborate a toilette, we had better follow her example.

BESSIE. (*Jumping up.*) Oh, yes!

SADIE. Gently, Elizabeth. Don't bounce, my beloved sister! Sail gracefully from the apartment, as I do. (SADIE *walks with an exaggeration of languid grace to the door,* NETTIE *and* BESSIE *following her with exact imitation of her movements. The* GIRLS *must all wear pretty summer dresses, except* DELIA, *who should wear a very showy dress, much too fine for a morning in the country. When* BESSIE, NETTIE *and* SADIE *return, they must have added bows of ribbon, jewelry, any finery available, to their dresses, but in absurd profusion. Wreaths of artificial flowers have a good effect, or any other finery entirely inappropriate to the time and occasion.*)

DELIA. There! Mamma said they would laugh at me! Now I am sure they do appreciate the improvement in my deportment,

and are anxious to become lady-like and graceful. They are rather
stiff, I must confess; but one cannot effect too much at once.
(*Bell rings.*)   Oh, there are the Stuart girls! (*Exit* DELIA.)

BESSIE. (*Outside.*) Shall we appear singly or in force?

SADIE. (*Outside.*) Singly.

Enter DELIA, *with* CORNELIA *and* EVANGELINE, *who are dressed
with elegant simplicity, without any jewelry or finery of any
kind.*

DELIA. (*Affectedly.*) It is so very kind of you to come to this
dull place!

EVANGELINE. (*Cordially.*) Oh, we enjoy a day in the country
above all things—don't we, Neal?

CORNELIA. (*Laughing.*) You would not know Eva, Delia, at
our country-seat.   She is a perfect tomboy.

EVANGELINE. I hope I am not quite a savage ; but it is so delightful to move and act with perfect freedom, to dress in easy garments, and thoroughly *enjoy* Nature.

Enter BESSIE, *fanning herself languidly with an enormous fan.*

DELIA. (*Aside.*) Oh, what did possess Bessie to put on that
wreath!   *Aloud.*)   Miss Stuart, my sister, Elizabeth—Miss Evangeline Stuart, Elizabeth.

BESSIE. (*Very stiffly.*) I am pleased to welcome you to Bay
Ridge, Miss Stuart, and Miss Evangeline Stuart.

EVANGELINE. You are very kind! (*Aside.*)   I wonder if she is
insane !

CORNELIA. Thank you! (*Aside.*)   What a queer-acting girl!
(BESSIE *sinks into a chair, still fanning herself.*)

DELIA. (*Aside to* BESSIE.) I do believe you mean to mortify me.

BESSIE. (*Aside to* DELIA.) Why, I thought I was doing exactly
as you asked me ! (CORNELIA *and* EVANGELINE *stand right of
foreground, as if embarrassed.   DELIA centre of stage, confused.
ALL stiff, and as if doubtful what to do.*)

CORNELIA. (*Aside to* EVANGELINE.) Did you ever hear she had
a crazy sister ?

EVANGELINE. Never!   Oh, there are two !

Enter SADIE, *smelling at a vinaigrette, and walking stiffly.*

DELIA. (*Aside.*) Oh, this is dreadful ! (*Aloud.*) My sister Sarah
—Miss Stuart, Miss Evangeline Stuart.

SADIE. (*With a profound courtesy.*) We have looked forward with great pleasure to the prospect of this visit, Miss Stuart, and Miss Evangeline Stuart.

EVANGELINE. (*Nervously.*) Thank you! (*Aside to* CORNELIA.) I wish we had not come, Neal. (SADIE *sinks into a chair, smelling the vinaigrette, while* BESSIE *continues to use her fan.*)

DELIA. Would you not like to go up-stairs and take off your hats?

CORNELIA. Thank you! I— (*Aside.*) Oh, if we had only kept the carriage!

Enter NETTIE, *with an exceedingly small fan, which she uses very slowly and with a great sweep of her arm.*

EVANGELINE. Oh, Neal, I am afraid of them. They can't be right in their minds!

DELIA. My sister Antoinette—Miss Stuart, Miss Evangeline Stuart.

NETTIE. (*With great ceremony.*) Much pleased to meet you, Miss Stuart. I hope you enjoyed your drive from the city, Miss Evangeline Stuart.

EVANGELINE. Very much, thank you! (NETTIE *seats herself and sits very stiffly.*)

DELIA. (*Aside.*) I wish I had let them alone. (*Aloud.*) Was it very warm driving?

CORNELIA. Not uncomfortably!

DELIA. Warm weather is so oppressive.

EVANGELINE. But this has been a delightful summer, I think!

DELIA. Very. (*Solemn pause.*) Are you fond of music?

EVANGELINE. Very.

DELIA. Do you play croquet?

CORNELIA. Sometimes.

DELIA. (*Aside to* BESSIE.) Why don't you say something?

BESSIE. (*Aside to* DELIA.) You didn't teach us any more, you know!

DELIA. (*Rising.*) Do come up-stairs and take off your hats.

CORNELIA. Thanks! (*Exeunt* DELIA, CORNELIA *and* EVANGELINE.)

BESSIE. Oh! (*laughing violently.*) I couldn't have kept a straight face two minutes longer.

NETTIE. (*Laughing.*) Poor *Cor*delia!

SADIE. And the poor Stuarts. I think they were half afraid of us.

BESSIE. They look like sweet, unaffected girls.

NETTIE. None of Delia's absurd airs!

SADIE. And no finery. (*Taking off bows, flowers and jewelry.*) I'll run up and join them. I can drop all this stuff in my room as I pass.

NETTIE. I will tell Betty to hurry luncheon a little, for it is a long drive. (*Exit* NETTIE.)

SADIE. I guess Delia has had enough airs for one day. (*Exit* SADIE.)

BESSIE. There will have to be some sort of explanation! I don't know, though—perhaps they won't recognize us minus all our finery and affectations.

Enter NETTIE *and* SADIE, *divested of all their finery.*

NETTIE. Oh, Bessie, Delia is furious! She says we behaved ridiculously, and exaggerated her instructions on purpose to mortify her. She says she won't come back among us, and that we must shift for ourselves without her.

BESSIE. Well, we can do that. We will rather imitate our visitors, and behave naturally, as they do. I will run and get rid of my trumpery, and then bring our visitors down with me. (*Exit* BESSIE.)

SADIE. It certainly is rather embarrassing, but it serves Delia right.

NETTIE. Mortify her, indeed! She ought not to have assumed any superiority over us. I am sorry for her, but pride is apt to have a fall.

Enter BESSIE, *without her finery, having one of her visitors on each arm.* SADIE *and* NETTIE *hasten to meet and shake hands with* CORNELIA *and* EVANGELINE.

CORNELIA. Why, this is as it should be! What was the matter with you when we arrived? You all appeared as if you were preparing a high comedy.

NETTIE. Indeed we were! Delia thought that our simple manners would entirely shock high-toned city folks, and—— But how absurd it must have appeared! (*Laughs.*)

BESSIE. Come, now—as the ice is so successfully broken, what do you say to a game of croquet? (*To* CORNELIA.) Or perhaps you would prefer to rest awhile after your drive? (*Bell rings.*) Ah! there is the bell for luncheon; let's all go, and then we can arrange for our amusements afterwards. (*As they all move off, the curtain falls.*)

A NIGHTMARE OF INDIA.

Characters.

KARL—*Who has recently been in India.*
JOHN—*Who has remained at home.*
JACK—*A Chimpanzee Monkey.*
ROYAL BENGAL TIGER.
LION.
RHINOCEROS.
ELEPHANT.—(*Only a head.*)

SCENE.—*A Sitting-room. Centre of background a wide lounge, with pillows and a high back. Behind this a platform, a little lower than the back of the lounge. Between lounge and platform a black curtain, that can be raised and lowered very quickly. It falls, hiding the platform, when scene opens.*

[The introduction of the ANIMALS may at first seem an insurmountable difficulty; but a little ingenuity and patience only are needed to conquer it. The more absurd and grotesque the imitations are, the better; and robes of fur, pasteboard heads, tails of mamma's fur boas, a boy's arm for an elephant's trunk, and some rehearsals, are all that are needed. The boy taking the part of JACK had better have a complete costume, easily hired, or made of rough brown cloth, with a monkey mask.]

KARL *and* JOHN *discovered, seated, as if conversing.*

JOHN. Why, my dear fellow, Gordon Cummings must have been a mere baby, compared to you!

KARL. Oh, I have told you very little!

JOHN. But a lion—an actual roaring lion—conquered alone, without arms!

KARL. You see, I never anticipated meeting him, and left my rifle under a tree, where I had been sleeping.

JOHN. And you strangled him with your hands alone?

KARL. Pooh! Why will you consider that such an astounding feat?

JOHN. I never heard anything so amazing in my life! It quite takes my breath away.

KARL. A mere nothing! But it was vexatious to lose my rifle, which must have been stolen whilst I was fighting the king of the forest.

JOHN. You say you have his head?

KARL. No, I did have it; but my uncle, in Calcutta, insisted upon retaining it.

JOHN. A very natural desire on his part. But you must have many other curiosities.

KARL. A great variety. I will present to you the tusks of a wild elephant I trapped and killed.

JOHN. Oh, thank you! I shall value them highly.

KARL. I suppose you never witnessed a tiger hunt?

JOHN. Well, no. I have had no experience in that way, I confess.

KARL. That really is exciting. The last one in which I took part, I forbade the natives to fire. I was anxious to kill the monster with my own hand, and I had a tough fight, I assure you. Again and again I fired; but the tiger clung to *Tootoo*, the elephant, until he mounted to the head, where the mahout (the driver) was seated, and tore the faithful fellow badly, before I succeeded in dispatching him with my hunting-knife.

JOHN. Dispatching the mahout?

KARL. No, no! the tiger! I have his skin in my trunk!

JOHN. I should like to see that!

KARL. Certainly! My large trunks are still in the city—will be sent on here. You never hunted the rhinoceros, I think you told me?

JOHN. (*Drily.*) Well, no! They do not frequent the vicinity of Toodleville.

KARL. True! true! I am such a cosmopolitan that I forget localities. You really should hunt a rhinoceros.

JOHN. I will at the first opportunity that offers itself.

KARL. Poor Tootoo—we were obliged to shoot him after the tiger hunt! He was so wounded, it was a cruelty to let his suffering be prolonged. I felt his loss very keenly, as he was my pet elephant. But my greatest pet was Jack, a Chimpanzee that I caught myself and tamed perfectly. I wished to bring him home, but was assured that the climate would kill him; so I most reluctantly left him in Calcutta!

JOHN. (*Rising.*) I should like to sit here all night to hear your adventures; but it is getting late. Will you come up-stairs?

KARL. Not just yet. I will soon follow you.

JOHN. Good-night, then!

KARL. Good-night! (*Exit JOHN.*)

KARL. (*Moves about the room restlessly.*) I cannot think what makes me feel so exceedingly uncomfortable! I didn't eat but two plates of lobster salad, and three saucers of peaches and cream, and a slice of plum-cake, and a few raisins. To be sure, there was the cheese and coffee and hot cakes; but nothing to make anybody feel as if he had been eating cobble-stones, as I do. I'll lie down here a little while. (*Lies down on lounge.*) This is very comfortable —very! I'll have a tiger-skin covering for this, (*yawns*) and some softer pillows, (*very drowsily*) and it will not make a bad bed, on a pinch—(*sleepily*) better than—a—hammock (*yawning*) in—a bung—a—low—much better. (*Sleeps. After a moment moves restlessly, muttering, and turns over to lie flat upon his back. When speaking afterwards must speak as if choked and in a nightmare. Curtain behind lounge draws up, and shows a jungle, either a painted scene or a few tall plants in pots. The* CHIMPANZEE *monkey comes forward, chattering, and leans over* KARL.) Go away! Mercy on me! Who are you?

CHIMPANZEE. I am Jack! I've heard of your great hunting expeditions, and I have come (*in a terrible voice*) to avenge my friends of the jungle!

KARL. Go away! Monkeys don't talk! You're a fraud.

CHIMPANZEE. Don't talk! You'll find we all talk. (*Leans over* KARL, *chattering and grinning.*)

KARL. (*Moving restlessly.*) I don't know what you mean. Who's Jack?

CHIMPANZEE. The dear little pet you left in Calcutta. But

(*jumps over lounge to floor*) you shall see the rest of your friends from India. (*A great growling behind the scenes.*)

Enter the BENGAL TIGER, *lashing his tail and roaring.*

KARL. Dear me! Who can this be?

TIGER. (*In a hollow voice.*) You don't know me! I am the ghost of the tiger you murdered in India. I have come to look upon the mighty warrior who conquered the prince of the jungle. (*Roars.*) Before I go I'll crunch your head in my jaws.

KARL. (*Trying to get up.*) I'll not stay here!

CHIMPANZEE. (*Sitting on lounge, but appearing to sit upon* KARL'S *chest.*) Lie still, my friend—we are not half done yet. (*Picks his teeth with his tail.*)

TIGER. In my jungle I had a home—a home of domestic bliss! There my beautiful wife, my innocent babes, wait my return, hungering for a fat negro for their breakfast. They wait in vain! Never again will my familiar roar waken the echoes of my native jungle. (*Wipes his eyes with his tail.*) My widowed wife, my fatherless babes, in vain call upon me. And thou—(*in a roaring voice*) thou hast made them desolate! (*Puts his head over the back of the lounge, close to* KARL'S *face.*)

KARL. Oh, you are smothering me!

TIGER. Did you not shoot me?

KARL. Never! I never even saw you before! (*Moves uneasily, and* TIGER *draws back.* Oh! (*As if getting breath.*)

CHIMPANZEE. Lie still, my friend! there's more to come. (*Tickles* KARL'S *nose.*)

KARL. Couldn't you find a chair somewhere? You are really very heavy to sit on one's beast-bone.

CHIMPANZEE. I am quite comfortable! (ELEPHANT'S *head rises slowly from behind lounge, the trunk waving to and fro.*)

KARL. What is that?

CHIMPANZEE. Speak for yourself, Tootoo!

ELEPHANT. (*The effect of whose voice should be heightened by speaking through a paper tube.*) I am Tootoo! Tootoo! Tootoo!

KARL. What do you want?

ELEPHANT. The blood of an enemy—Tootoo!

KARL. But there is no one here!

ELEPHANT. He is here who caused my death! He is here who let the great Bengal tiger—

TIGER. (*Roaring.*) That's me!

ELEPHANT. You climbed up my legs, over my chest, tearing my skin, lacerating my flesh. That was your business; I've no spite against you. But I seek the wretch who fondled and petted me until I was his willing slave, and then doomed me to a cruel death, murdered me when I was the bleeding victim of his cruelty and vanity. I come for vengeance! I—Tootoo! Tootoo! Tootoo!

KARL. (*Struggling.*) Get off my breast! Let me get up!

TIGER. Hold him down! hold him down! (*Leans over* KARL.)

ELEPHANT. Crush him! smother him! (*Waves his trunk over* KARL's *face.*)

KARL. (*Struggling.*) I never heard of any of you! This is some horrible conspiracy!

Enter RHINOCEROS, *on platform.*

CHIMPANZEE. Come here, my friend, and tell your woes—woes —(*louder*) woes!

ALL. (*In a roaring noise.*) Woes—woes—woes!

RHINOCEROS. Who came in the night to my pool of mud, where I lay in the shade of a rock—who!

ALL. Who—who—who!

RHINOCEROS. And waited until I slept and was helpless, to give me a coward's blow!

ALL. Oh—oh—oh!

RHINOCEROS. Who knew he could never conquer me in a fair battle, but waited until I lay low.

ALL. Oh—oh!

RHINOCEROS. But my ghost seeks revenge!

ALL. Our ghosts seek revenge!

RHINOCEROS. You see, my fellow-sufferers, I depended upon my thick skin to save my bacon. I laugh at bullets!

ALL. Ha, ha, ha!

RHINOCEROS. Knives are the best of jokes to me!

ALL. Ho, ho, ho!

RHINOCEROS. Spears fly from me like straws. But where force would have failed, treachery gained the day. There are vulnerable spots, if my foe can approach me closely enough to thrust in his blade; and I had supped well, quenched my thirst, and slept.

KARL. (*Struggling.*) It is all a base fabrication! I never even saw a sleeping rhinoceros.

CHIMPANZEE. Easy, now! Don't interrupt the speaker! (*Presses his arms on* KARL, *to keep him down.*)

ELEPHANT. Shall I come and stand on him, and relieve you? (*Waves his trunk.*)

CHIMPANZEE. Thank you, no! I'll keep him quiet, (*grinning in* KARL's *face*) or I'll bite him!

KARL. Oh! let me get up and I'll fight the whole of you! (*Struggles.*)

TIGER. What is he doing?

RHINOCEROS. Where is the great Indian hunter? We will hunt him!

ALL. We will hunt him! (RHINOCEROS *and* TIGER *prowl around platform; the* ELEPHANT *waving his trunk, as if feeling about;* CHIMPANZEE *chatters and grins.*)

RHINOCEROS. (*Putting one foot over back of lounge, upon* KARL's *legs.*) I have found our foe!

ALL. Oh, oh, oh!

RHINOCEROS. Prostrate and low!

ALL. Oh, oh!

CHIMPANZEE. Yes; we have him here, prostrate, and at our mercy. What shall we do to him? (KARL *must not speak, but mutter and groan, move uneasily, and jerk like a person in a nightmare, during all the conversation amongst the animals.*)

ELEPHANT. I will walk over him, crushing all his bones—his bones!

ALL. His bones! his bones!

TIGER. I will take his head in my jaws, and grind his skull to powder! (ALL *make a crunching noise.*)

RHINOCEROS. I will take my horn and rip him to pieces! Ha, ha!

ALL. Ha, ha!

TIGER. (*Sings—Tune, " Dixie's Land."*)
    We'll grind his bones to powder fine!

ALL. Oh, ho! Oh, ho!

TIGER. We'll smash him up to powder fine!
    And eat him without curry!

ALL. Oh, ho! Oh, ho! We'll eat him without curry!
    Oh, ho! Oh, ho! We'll eat him without curry!

ELEPHANT. You quite forget I don't eat meat! How am I to be avenged?

CHIMPANZEE. That is really a difficult question. We ought to allow you to toss him about awhile in your trunk, walk over him a few times, and trumpet in his ears.

ELEPHANT. Tootoo! Tootoo! Tootoo!

RHINOCEROS. But my claim is as good, and I cannot eat the nasty little wretch, either. I can only gore him with my horn, pin him to a tree.

CHIMPANZEE. Really, I think our friend the tiger ought to resign all claim while he is alive, since he only can make a dinner off him when dead. (*Horrible roaring outside.*)

Enter LION, *in a rage.*

LION. Why am I left out of this meeting, I should like to know?

CHIMPANZEE. Now here's a pretty mess!

LION. Who has a stronger claim upon upon this miserable carcass than I have?

RHINOCEROS. Your majesty must forgive us!

TIGER. We left you sleeping!

LION. And made enough noise to rouse an entire forest. Let me see this vile slayer of lions.

CHIMPANZEE. (*Hopping up.*) This way, your majesty—this way.

LION. (*Coming close to* KARL.) So! so! This is the great hunter! This is the mighty Nimrod of India! A dainty titbit he will make for my wife and babies, whom he brags he has left without a protector. (*Roars.*)

TIGER. I claim half the meat, after the elephant and rhinoceros have finished him.

LION. Half!

TIGER. Half, cut lengthwise! My wife is especially fond of the right arm.

LION. Do you presume to dictate to me?

TIGER. I have the best claim. He killed me first.

CHIMPANZEE. Don't quarrel, gentlemen. You can draw lots for the choice of pieces!

LION. I claim the head. I like brain sauce!

ELEPHANT. I think it is time we commenced.

CHIMPANZEE. (*Jumping on platform.*) Take your turns! (ALL *advance, roaring, growling and angrily, to the back of lounge.*)

KARL. Help! help! murder! (*Springs to middle of the floor. Curtain behind lounge drops and conceals background.* KARL *pants.*) Go away! murder! (*Looking around fearfully.*) Bless me! I must have had the nightmare!

CURTAIN.

• • •

AN INDIAN RAID.

Characters.

TOM DICKSON—*A Western boy.*
BOB DICKSON—*His brother.*
SUSY DICKSON }
DAISY DICKSON } *Sisters of* BOB *and* TOM.
DICK WETHERILL—*Their cousin, from New York.*

SCENE—*A Room, furnished rather roughly, as if in a new settlement. The table and chairs of plain pine wood and the floor without carpet. In the background a large closet.* SUSY *sewing;* DAISY *playing with a doll.*

SUSY. (*Aside.*) I am half sorry I consented to Tom's mischievous plan for testing our city cousin's courage! It does not seem exactly hospitable, especially while father and mother are both away. And yet Dick is certainly provoking, coming here from the city, to teach the frontier boys how to manage Indians and hunt. Papa had hard work not to laugh yesterday, when he said he could stand erect if a herd of buffaloes went past him, and shoot them as they passed. And as for Indians—why, he can fight an entire tribe single-handed! Tom fairly choked when he said the proper way to (*imitates*) treat the red man is to annihilate the race, never to conciliate one man! Dear! dear!

DAISY. Susy, I'm not going to be afraid of the naughty Indians any more!

SUSY. Are you not, darling?

DAISY. No; because Cousin Dick says he can kill ever, ever so many—forty-'leven nineteen, if they come.

SUSY. Indeed!

DAISY. Ain't he brave, Susy? He swells all up big when he talks about Indians.

SUSY. Exactly. (*Aside.*) I wonder if he would strut about so fiercely if he saw one.

DAISY. He says he hopes they will come here! I—*think* I won't be afraid.

SUSY. (*Aside.*) I think I had better send her away. She is such a timid little darling. (*Aloud.*) Daisy!

DAISY. Yes, Susy.

SUSY. Won't you run over to Mrs. Green's, and ask her to lend me the pattern she promised me. You may stay and play with Mamie a little while.

DAISY. Yes, I will go. Come, Dolly, you and I will go see Mamie. (*Exit* DAISY.)

SUSY. It is just as well to be on the safe side.

Enter DICK, *very much dressed, and carrying a very showy rifle.*

DICK. Good morning, cousin! (*Puts rifle down.*)

SUSY. Good morning! Are you going out?

DICK. I think I will take a tramp over the hills, as soon as Tom and Bob come.

SUSY. They will soon be here. Will you not sit down? (*Aside.*) I hope Tom remembered to draw the charge in that rifle.

DICK. We are going deer-stalking.

SUSY. I hope you will not meet any Indians.

DICK. Pooh! Who cares for an Indian!

SUSY. But several of them together are no joke, I assure you!

DICK. I'm not afraid!

SUSY. Well, one need not be exactly *afraid*, you know, but common prudence suggests caution.

DICK. Brave men despise caution.

SUSY. That is a new maxim. We at the West think the bravest men are the most prudent. But if you should meet a party of Indians, you may safely trust to Bob. He can speak with them, and conciliate them.

DICK. I would never stoop to conciliate one. If they were insolent, I should shoot them down.

SUSY. And have the whole tribe upon you for vengeance. That would be poor policy, unless you had an army to support you!

DICK. I do not believe in timidity and coaxing. Show an Indian a brave, defiant front, and he will flee away.

Enter DAISY.

DAISY. Oh, Susy! I started to go see Mamie, and, oh, Susy! Susy! I *am* afraid!

SUSY. What is the matter with my pet? (*Aside.*) I did not bargain to have Daisy frightened.

DAISY. Oh, Susy, there are two big Indians at the back door, and they want the city chap!

DICK. (*Trembling violently.*) The city chap!

DAISY. They say there is a boy here who wants all the Indians killed, and they want him. If he doesn't go with them, they'll set the house a-fire.

DICK. (*Dreadfully terrified.*) Oh, Susy, say I am out!

SUSY. Nonsense. Go to them boldly, and tell them to go about their business—or shoot them!

DICK. And have the whole tribe here after me?

SUSY. Well, show them a defiant front! (*Outside a great jabbering, in guttural voices.*)

DICK. They are coming! they are coming! Oh, Susy, where can I hide? (*Runs into closet, and holds door.*)

SUSY. (*Aside.*) Tom was right. He is a coward!

Enter TOM *and* BOB, *painted and dressed as Indians, flourishing tomahawks and making guttural noises.* DAISY *runs out.*

TOM. Ou—ou—ah—hoo—yah!

BOB. Hoo—hoo—ya—yam!

SUSY. (*Standing up.*) What do you want? (*During the following conversation* SUSY *must stand between* DICK *and the Indians, who stand so as not to see the closet when* DICK *speaks. In speaking* DICK *must put out his head, and draw it in again as if fearful of discovery.*)

TOM. Wantee white boy!

DICK. Oh, Susy, say I went home to-day!

SUSY. But we have more than one white boy here.

BOB. (*Fiercely.*) Wantee city boy!

SUSY. What do you want of him?

TOM. Wantee kill him!

BOB. (*Savagely.*) Wantee scalp him!

TOM. Wantee burn at stake!

BOB. Wantee shoot arrow in he!

SUSY. Why, what has he done?

DICK. Oh, Susy, Susy, protect me!

TOM. Talkee bad.

BOB. Very bad.

TOM. 'Bout Injun. Say Injun snake!

BOB. Say he *dog!*

TOM. Say killee—killee all Injun!

BOB. Injun killee he! Ugh—ugh! Injun killee he—burnee! shootee! scalpee!

DICK. Oh, Susy, can't you send them away?

SUSY. But we cannot give up our guest to be scalped and shot!

TOM. (*Fiercely.*) Burnee house down!

SUSY. Are you not Shoot-'em-in-eye?

TOM. Ugh! Ugh! Me Shoot-'em-in-eye!

SUSY. Don't you remember coming here half starved, and being fed?

TOM. Ugh! Ugh! Give me bake beans—wantee more bake beans!

SUSY. But I'm not going to feed you now.

DICK. Oh, Susy, give him the beans. Give him anything!

TOM. Bakee white boy!

BOB. Like bakee white boy better than bean!

TOM. Better than bakee dog!

SUSY. But we will not give you the white boy to bake. You had better go away. If you commit any violence, the whole settlement will turn out to follow you.

DICK. That's right, Susy, scare them away!

TOM. Not settlement boy! Wantee city boy. Settlement boy no talkee bad 'bout Injun.

BOB. City boy want all Injun killee!

SUSY. But he is only a boy. He could not hurt you if he tried!

TOM. Got shootee gun, killee long way off!

Bob. Got shootee pistol, shootee fivee, sixee Injun—pop—pop—pop—never stopped!

Susy. It is a pity you bragged so much about your rifle and revolver.

Dick. Tell them they can have both if they will only go away. (Tom *and* Bob *prowl about the room, as if looking for* Dick.)

Tom. Where he hidee?

Bob. He hidee! Injun findee!

Susy. I don't know what I can do!

Dick. Coax them into the kitchen! Give them my rifle, my pistol—anything!

Tom. Give Injun something eatee?

Dick. Oh, Susy, do—feed them into good temper!

Susy. But that is conciliation.

Dick. Oh, get them away! I'll go home to-morrow if I escape now.

Bob. Got whisky?

Susy. No.

Bob. Wantee eatee! wantee drinkee!

Tom. Findee beans! (*Both rush at closet and pull out* Dick.)

Dick. (*Falling on his knees.*) Mercy! mercy! Oh, good Indians, let me go! I'll give you my watch!

Tom. Lookee watchee! (*Holds out his hand.*)

Dick. Take it! I'll give you everything I've got! My money! (*Gives* Tom *watch.*)

Bob. Lookee money! (*Holds out his hand.*)

Dick. (*Pulling out his purse.*) Here! here!

Susy. But, Dick, this is worse than conciliation—it is downright bribery.

Dick. Oh, Susy, I can't help it! See how fierce they look!

Susy. I'll get your rifle.

Dick. (*In an agony of terror.*) Not for the world! If I hurt one, the other would murder me outright. (Tom *and* Bob *come forward, as if examining money and watch.*)

Tom. Ugh! ugh! gotee watchee! (*Strings it to belt.*) Tickee! tickee! (*Aside to* Bob.) I guess he will not have so much to say about Indians to-morrow.

Bob. Gotee money, (*flourishes tomahawk*) wantee scalp!

Dick. Oh, what can I give them!

TOM. Wantee coat!

DICK. (*Standing up.*) Yes, yes, good Indian! Take it. (*Gives coat.* TOM *ties it round his neck by the sleeves.*)

BOB. Wantee shiney finger!

DICK. Oh, Susy, what is it?

SUSY. Your ring! But I would not be robbed in this way!

DICK. It is not *your* scalp they want! (*Takes off ring.*)

BOB. Wantee shiney finger, quickee!

DICK. (*Giving ring.*) Yes—yes! (*Gives ring.*)

TOM. Wantee red—redee!

SUSY. Your necktie is red.

DICK. Take it! (*Gives necktie.*)

TOM. Ugh! ugh! Injun fine! (*Ties necktie on his leg.*)

BOB. Wantee shootee!

DICK. What is it, Susy? Oh, cannot we persuade them to go?

SUSY. It must be your rifle! But you surely will not give them that! You said it cost so much!

DICK. It is not worth so much as my scalp! (*Gives* BOB *rifle.*)

TOM. Ugh! ugh! Wantee scalp!

BOB. Wantee scalp! (BOB *and* TOM *dance around* DICK, *flourishing their tomahawks. He drops into a chair, trembling with fear, and they rub his hair all up on end.*)

SUSY. Come into the kitchen and you shall have some food.

TOM. Wantee chokee! (*Points to* DICK'S *collar.*)

DICK. (*Giving collar.*) Yes, yes, good Indian!

BOB. Wantee bootee!

DICK. (*Giving his boots.*) Oh, good Indian, anything I've got! (TOM *puts the collar on his arm, like a bracelet. It should have a button.* BOB *fastens the boots together, and strings them round his neck.*)

TOM. Ugh! ugh! When Injun get scalp he be fine!

BOB. Wantee scalp! Me havee!

TOM. Me havee.

BOB. (*Very fiercely.*) Me havee white boy scalp!

TOM. (*Very savagely.*) Me takee! takee! (*They begin to jabber angrily and flourish their tomahawks.*)

DICK. Oh, Susy, if they would only murder each other!

TOM. Me takee! (*Rushes at* DICK, *who runs.*)

BOB. Me scalpee! (BOTH *chase* DICK, *who dodges here and there, finally running into closet again.*)

SUSY. (*Standing in front of closet.*) Stand back!

DICK. Oh, yes, Susy! Make them stand back!

TOM. Brave white boy! Gettee behind squaw

BOB. Hidee behind squaw gown!

SUSY. Hold the door, Dick. I will try to coax the Indians into the kitchen with me, if I can, to have some baked beans and coffee. (*Aside to* TOM.) You are carrying the joke too far. You will terrify the life out of him!

TOM. (*Aside to* SUSY.) It is such fun, after all his bombast! (*Aloud.*) Ugh! get bean!

SUSY. Come! (TOM *and* BOB *follow* SUSY *out of room.*)

DICK. (*Coming forward.*) Oh, what shall I do? What shall I do? They must have heard what I said, and they will come back and kill me! There is no way to get out of the house without going through the kitchen. My splendid rifle—my watch—my diamond ring! And all for nothing!

Enter DAISY.

DAISY. Cousin Dick!

DICK. I am here, Daisy!

DAISY. Cousin Dick, Susy says the Indians are going away.

DICK. Are you sure?

DAISY. Susy says so.

Enter SUSY.

DICK. Oh, Susy, are they really gone?

SUSY. Who?

DICK. The Indians!

SUSY. What Indians?

DICK. The Indians who were here just now!

SUSY. You must have been asleep, Dick. There have been no Indians here for months. The last were here long before you came. But they very often do stop here.

DICK. No Indians here?

DAISY. Where is your coat, Cousin Dick?

DICK. (*Bewildered.*) Sure enough. Where *is* my coat, if there were no Indians here?

DAISY. And you've lost your collar, too, and your necktie; and, oh, Cousin Dick, you look awfully funny! You've not got any boots! And your hair is all mussed!

SUSY. Cousin Dick has been asleep, and had the nightmare!

DICK. (*Aside.*) Can I have been asleep? It must be—and I came down-stairs without being dressed. I never knew anything so extraordinary! Cousin Susy, I hope you will pardon my disordered garments. I really scarcely know how to apologize. But I had a strange dream.

SUSY. About Indians, you said?

DICK. Yes; (*grandly*) and in my enthusiasm to conquer them, I must have thrown aside my coat and boots.

Enter TOM *and* BOB, *dressed as before, with the exception of their heads. Their faces are washed, and their hair parted and smooth.*

TOM. Certainly; you threw them aside!

BOB. And we picked them up!

BOTH. (*Dancing round* DICK.) Wantee scalpee! Brave boy, hidee behind squaw!

DICK. (*Timidly.*) It was no dream, then! *You* were the Indians! (*Boldly.*) It was a mean trick to play on me, and I don't thank you for it.

TOM. The meanness was not on our side. We suspected that your grand talk about bravery was not genuine, and we determined to try you. You can answer how you stood the test.

BOB. And we hope this will be a wholesome lesson to you in future. Your boasting might have led you into a far more serious scrape, and you should rather thank us for the friendly lesson which we have given you.

DICK. (*Looking at* SUSY, *who is smiling at him.*) Well, I suppose I must accept the situation, and take your masquerading in the way it was intended. I *do* thank you; I will lay this lesson to heart, and shall never forget the "INDIAN RAID."

CURTAIN.

GOING! GOING! GONE!

Characters.

JOHN.	STEPHEN SLIPPERTON.
HARRY.	MR. JONES.
WILL.	MRS. SMITH.
CHARLEY.	MRS. JOHNSON.

As many boys and ladies and gentlemen, dressed as customers, as the strength of the company and limits of the stage will allow.

SCENE.—*A large empty Room. In the background a large table, and behind this table black curtains that separate in the middle. There must be sufficient space back of these curtains for the table to be pulled back and hidden behind them. Attached to the table legs are strong ropes, and the part of pulling the table back should be carefully rehearsed, and work very smoothly. On the end of the table two candles, the wicks covered with flame-colored paper, as a real light would be dangerous. But when the table disappears, as will be described, the lights must be lowered suddenly, as the candles are supposed to light the scene. JOHN, HARRY, WILL, CHARLEY, and as many other boys as possible, assembled front of stage.*

JOHN. Now, boys, are we all of one mind with regard to Mr. Stephen Slipperton?

HARRY. I think we are.

ALL. We are! We are!

WILL. We are all of the opinion that he is a fraud, a swindler, a cheat, and that Eagle Hill has had about enough of him.

CHARLEY. Therefore we are going to gently hint to him this evening that his services are no longer required.

JOHN. We bore his cheats patiently while he confined them to thinly-washed brass for silver.

HARRY. Cloth that fell to pieces in the rain!

WILL. Caps that went into holes in a high wind!

CHARLEY. Boots with the soles gummed on !

JOHN. Emery bags stuffed with sand !

WILL. Shirts that disappeared in the first washing !

HARRY. Silk handkerchiefs nine-tenths cotton !

CHARLEY. Fire-works that wouldn't go off !

JOHN. But when he brought out that lot of Sheffield ware pen-knives at a great bargain, and imposed upon this community to a boy with a wretched cast-iron fraud, he—

WILL. Roused the American Eagle !

CHARLEY. Wakened the sleeping Yankee Doodle !

HARRY. And invited the vengeance of the boys of Eagle Hill !

JOHN. He will be here at eight o'clock to again offer his imitation jewelry and cast-iron cutlery to a confiding public. Are we resolved, to a boy, to stop his fraudulent career?

ALL. We are ! We are !

HARRY. See how the night is.

WILL. (*Looking out between the curtains.*) Raining fast.

JOHN. Is the mud thick behind there ?

WILL. Like a custard !

CHARLEY. Plenty of puddles ?

WILL. Hundreds !

JOHN. Man the ropes !

WILL. Boy the ropes, you mean !

JOHN. Run across to the shed, and huddle close until I give the signal. You all know it. (*All the boys, except* JOHN, *go behind the curtain.*) I think, Mr. Slipperton, Eagle Hill will convince you to-night that your room is preferable to your company. (*Clock strikes eight.*) Eight o'clock. It is time he was here !

Enter STEPHEN, *carrying a carpet-bag.*

STEPHEN. Oh, you are here, are you ?

JOHN. Of course I am. Didn't I tell you I would be ? (*Affects a half-stupid air.*)

STEPHEN. H'm ! Now I want you to understand your business. My assistant has met with an accident in the next town, and I must have some one in his place. You look like a smart boy.

JOHN. Thankye, sir !

STEPHEN. (*Putting carpet-bag on table and opening it.*) You see, when I am standing upon the table, I cannot well reach the goods.

You must stand here in front, and pass them to me, or to our customers. Understand?

JOHN. Yes, sir. Don't you want some more candles?

STEPHEN. Certainly not! certainly not! The less light the better.

JOHN. (*Aside.*) That's about the only thing he has ever said at Eagle Hill that wasn't a *lie*.

STEPHEN. Now, then, (*taking a bell out of bag*) ring that, while I get on the table. (JOHN *rings the bell loudly,* STEPHEN *climbs on table and stands to face audience.*)

Enter MRS. SMITH, MR. JONES, MRS. JOHNSON, *and others. The bids marked* VOICE *must be made by the customers and arranged at rehearsal. When all are in,* JOHN *stops ringing bell and stands beside table.*

STEPHEN. Ladies and gentlemen, I have this evening a splendid assortment of first-class goods and samples of goods that *must* be sold. The first lot is a magnificent cameo set. Pass up that cameo set—(JOHN *passes box*) breastpin and ear-rings! Classic heads—Titania, Babylon and Siberia!

JOHN. (*Aside.*) Shades of Homer defend us!

STEPHEN. Finest cameos, engraved by best Italian artists, and set in solid gold! I sold seven sets this morning for fifty dollars each! Who bids on this set? Fifty dollars—forty-five—forty—thirty-five! Oh, this is monstrous! They are *given* away at thirty dollars! Twenty-five! Come, gentlemen, give me a bid? Twenty—fifteen—start it yourselves! What is bid on this splendid cameo set, worth sixty dollars?

MR. JONES. Twenty-five cents.

STEPHEN. Thank you, sir. Twenty-five dollars bid on this—

MR. JONES. (*Loudly.*) Twenty-five *cents* !

STEPHEN. Oh, come now, you're joking! Well, I will start it, although really—you know—that is a little too absurd. Twenty-five cents is bid upon this cameo set—gold setting—twenty-five—five—five !

VOICE. Thirty !

STEPHEN. Thirty—thirty—going for thirty cents, this superb cameo set—thirty !

VOICE. Thirty-five!

STEPHEN. Thirty-five cents—it is positive stealing, really dreadful; why, the gold setting is worth twenty dollars alone, and each stone is a gem! Going for thirty-five!

VOICE. Forty!

VOICE. Forty-five!

VOICE. Fifty!

MR. JONES. One dollar! (*A pause.*)

STEPHEN. One dollar only am I bid for this superb cameo set! One dollar! Who'll make it a dollar five? One dollar! One dollar! One dollar! Come, gentlemen, I've a lot more goods to sell—one dollar! one dollar! Going! Going! Gone! to Mr.—

MR. JONES. Mr. Peter Jones!

STEPHEN. And I hope the robbery won't weigh upon your conscience, as it ought. One dollar! I shall not offer another set. It would ruin me! The next lot, ladies, is a shawl. Hand me that shawl. (JOHN *hands shawl.*) A real India shawl! (*The shawl shoud be conspicuously cheap-looking.*)

JOHN. (*Aside.*) Made in Lowell.

STEPHEN. Imported direct from Australia by our firm. All made of the finest camel's hair—our firm raise their own camels—dyed in the wool, ladies, can't fade! These shawls cost us two hundred dollars apiece in India!

MR. JONES. Thought you said Australia?

STEPHEN. Exactly! What am I bid for this superb camel's hair shawl? Dyed in the wool, soft as satin, warm as fur! Come, gentlemen, give me a bid.

MRS. JOHNSON. Two dollars!

STEPHEN. Do you think I am a lunatic? Two dollars! I never heard anything so preposterous!

MRS. SMITH. Two-fifty!

STEPHEN. Will no one give me a reasonable bid? (*Pause.*) Two-fifty for a real India shawl, finest camel's hair. Cost two hundred in Australia. Going for two-fifty, two-fifty—

VOICE. Three!

STEPHEN. For three dollars—three, three—who'll say three-fifty?

VOICE. Three-fifty!

STEPHEN. Thank ye! Three-fifty, for three-fifty.

VOICE. Three-seventy-five!

VOICE. Four! (*Pause.*)

STEPHEN. Four dollars! Come, ladies, you'll never have such a chance again—the only one left—look at it! (*Hands shawl to* JOHN, *who passes it to customers.*)

MRS. JOHNSON. Feels kinder cottony!

MRS. SMITH. Smells o' dye!

MR. JONES. Dear at twenty-five cents!

STEPHEN. Going at four dollars! At four! Four! (*Shawl handed back to* STEPHEN.) Who'll give me four-fifty?

VOICE. Four-fifty!

STEPHEN. It really is too ridiculous! A real India shawl! Why, the Sultan of Rhamajamboorahpoo has the exact counterpart of that shawl for his Sultaness. I've seen her with it on! Give me a respectable bid! Four-fifty!—fifty!

MRS. SMITH. Five!

STEPHEN. Five, five! Who'll give me five-fifty? Five! five! Going! going! (*Pause.*) Gone! to Mrs.—

MRS. SMITH. Mrs. Mirandy Smith!

STEPHEN. And a bargain you have, Mrs. Smith. You won't find such a shawl as that anywhere for less than three hundred dollars!

CHARLEY. (*Crawls out from behind curtain, under the table. Aside to* JOHN.) John!

JOHN. (*Aside to* CHARLEY.) In a minute!

CHARLEY. I'm a committee of one from outside.

JOHN. Somebody will see you. (CHARLEY *hides under table.*)

STEPHEN. The next lot, gentlemen, is a watch—a fine chronometer watch—pass that watch up here. (JOHN *passes watch.*) They set the city clock by that watch in London for five years! Solid gold, patent lever attachment! What am I bid for this magnificent watch, gentlemen? One hundred dollars—ninety—eighty—seventy—

CHARLEY. (*Loudly.*) Two hundred dollars!

STEPHEN. Thank you, sir! I am glad there is one gentleman here who can appreciate a bargain when he sees it! Two hundred dollars I am bid for this splendid gold watch—two hundred! Who will make it two hundred and ten? Two hundred—two hundred!

CHARLEY. Two hundred and fifty!

STEPHEN. Ah, this begins to look like business! Two hundred and fifty—two hundred and fifty—fifty—fifty! Who'll make it fifty-five? Fifty, fifty! Going—going! Gone! to— (*Profound silence.*)

STEPHEN. Who gets this magnificent watch for two hundred and fifty dollars? You, sir? You? You? (ALL *shake their heads.*)

MR. JONES. Come, whoever you are, don't keep us waiting here all night!

STEPHEN. (*To* JOHN.) Find that fellow!

JOHN. (*Pretending to look around.*) I think he must have run out, sir.

MR. JONES. Put the watch up again!

STEPHEN. Now I want no more fooling. An honest man can't get a living if he is to be made the victim of such jokes. (*To* JOHN.) You keep a sharp look out, and if there is any more such nonsense, just call in the police. (*Holds up watch.*) Who bids on this solid gold watch?

MR. JONES. One dollar!

STEPHEN. Oh, thank you! (*Sarcastically.*) One dollar, I think you said?

MR. JONES. One dollar!

STEPHEN. Well, any bid will do to start on! One dollar I am bid for this splendid watch, in prime order, set with jewels, solid gold! One dollar—one—one—

VOICE. One-fifty!

STEPHEN. One-fifty—fifty—who'll make it two? One-fifty—fifty—

VOICE. One-seventy-five!

STEPHEN. One-seventy-five—five—five—

VOICE. Two!

STEPHEN. Two dollars I am bid for the watch—two—two—

MRS. JOHNSON. Two-twenty-five!

STEPHEN. Two-twenty-five—five—five! (*Pause.*) Who bids two-fifty? Two-twenty-five! Going! Going! Gone!—to—

MRS. JOHNSON. Mrs. Johnson! (JOHN *takes watch.*)   .

STEPHEN. The next lot is a set of diamond studs. Pass me those studs! (JOHN *passes box.*) These, gentlemen, are handed to me by a gentleman in misfortune, who wishes to dispose of them. They were purchased in London, and cost five hundred dollars—pure diamonds, set in jet. Look at them! (JOHN *passes studs.*)

CHARLEY. (*Aside to* JOHN.) I say, John, it's getting awfully cold under that shed.

JOHN. Must have a little patience !

CHARLEY. And it rains cats and dogs !

JOHN. So much the better.   Huddle close !

CHARLEY. The fellows sent me in to tell you to hurry up.

JOHN. Some one will see you. Get back ! I won't be long now. Listen for the signal. (*Exit* CHARLEY. STEPHEN *fusses over the carpet-bag ; gives it back to* JOHN *during this conversation. Customers examine studs.*)

STEPHEN. (*Standing up.*) Well, gentlemen, what is offered for those genuine diamond studs ? (*Studs passed back.*) These are not made to sell ; but the property of a gentleman in temporary trouble, who entrusted them to my care.   Cost five hundred dollars !   What am I bid ?   Five hundred—five hundred—four hundred and fifty—four hundred—three hundred and fifty !   Come, gentlemen, you surely don't expect me to give these away !   Three hundred—three hundred dollars for a set of pure diamond studs, worth five hundred.

JOHN. (*Aside.*) Can't he pile it on !

STEPHEN. Three hundred—two-fifty—two hundred—oh, this is absurd !   If you haven't *any* money, what do you come to an auction sale for ?

VOICE. Never mind that !   Go on with the sale !

STEPHEN. Two hundred !   Who offers me two hundred dollars on this magnificent set of studs ?   (*Pause.*) Make a bid, gentlemen, make a bid.

VOICE. Five cents !

STEPHEN. Put that madman where the rain will cool his brain.

MR. JONES. Ten cents.

STEPHEN. There are two lunatics here.

VOICE. Fifteen cents !

STEPHEN. Go on, gentlemen—keep the farce up until you are tired !

VOICE. Twenty cents. (*Perfect silence.*)

STEPHEN. Oh, you've had enough *fun !*   Now make me a bid.

VOICE. I bid twenty cents !

STEPHEN. Twenty cents !   I'll not put up another lot to-night.

JOHN. (*Aside.*) I don't think you will !

STEPHEN. Twenty cents for three diamond studs !

JOHN. (*Aside.*) Warranted paste.

STEPHEN. In setting of jet and solid gold backs.

JOHN. (*Aside.*) So far back you can't find it.

STEPHEN. *Twenty cents !* I would never have believed such a bid *could* be made, if I had not heard it ! Twenty cents—going for twenty cents, a set of diamond studs, twenty—twenty—

VOICE. Twenty-five !

MR. JONES. Thirty !

STEPHEN. Thirty cents I'm bid ! thirty—thirty—who'll make it thirty-five ? Thirty ! thirty !

MRS. SMITH. Thirty-five !

STEPHEN. Thirty-five I'm bid—thirty-five cents—the gentleman who entrusted these studs to me will murder me outright ! Thirty-five !

VOICE. Forty !

STEPHEN. Forty ! Going for forty cents !

VOICE. Forty-five !

STEPHEN. For forty-five ! forty-five—

MR. JONES. Fifty !

STEPHEN. Fifty ! fifty ! Who'll make it fifty-five ? fifty, fifty, going ! (JOHN *gives a shrill whistle.*) Going ! Going !

BOYS. (*Behind curtain.*) Gone ! (*The table is pulled back suddenly, the curtain parting as it goes in, and falling instantly. STEPHEN holding on in a crouching position, as if thrown off his balance. Lights suddenly lowered.*)

CURTAIN.

THE BOOK-PEDDLER.

ℭharacters.

SIMON SMOOTHTONGUE—*A Book-peddler.*
JOHN.
HARRY.
MARY.
LOUISA.

SCENE.—*A Sitting-room.* JOHN *and* HARRY *reading ;* MARY *and* LOUISA *sewing.*

JOHN. (*Looking up from his book.*) Are we going rowing ?

LOUISA. Not until after tea. Mamma said that we must not go before sunset.

MARY. And I want to finish my pin-cushion.

HARRY. Oh, you girls don't think of anything else but that bothersome old fair. You are sewing all the time. (*Bell rings.*)

LOUISA. I wonder who that is ?

MARY. I hope it is not a visitor, when papa and mamma are both out.

Enter SIMON, *with a satchel.*

SIMON. Good afternoon, ladies and gentlemen !

HARRY. Good afternoon !

SIMON. I called in to see if I could not sell you a few books.

JOHN. Got any new ones ?

SIMON. All new ! I wouldn't think of offering old books to such an enlightened community as I find at Puddletown. Your mayor took several. (*Opens satchel.*)

MARY. I should like a new story-book.

SIMON. Here it is, then; " The Maniac of the Hills, or the Suicide's Revenge !"

MARY. Oh, I am quite sure mamma won't let me read that !

SIMON. (*Speaking volubly.*) I have a lovely history here—history of the world—beautiful pictures. (*Showing book.*) Here is Washington crossing the Nile—see the alligators! And this is

Nelson at Bunker Hill—a portrait, too! And this one represents the discovery of the Mississippi by Napoleon Bonaparte!

LOUISA. Did ever anybody hear such a tongue!

JOHN. What is this? (*Taking up book.*)

SIMON. Lectures on Astronomy—tells you all about the collapses of Mars, and the eclipses of Jupiter Apollo, and the tidal waves in the moon! Very interesting! All young people ought to read it. Illustrated, too! Got pictures of the comet Vesuvius and the planet of Oberon! Sold two copies to your seminary!

MARY. Is it possible! What is the blue-bound book?

SIMON. Tennyson! Got all his poetry—" Macbeth " and ". Thanatopsis " and " Rory O'More "—and all the rest of them; with a picture of the poet as he appeared at the Siege of Corinth.

HARRY. That must be interesting!

SIMON. Very. Most young ladies like poetry. Can't I sell you this volume, miss? Dirt cheap. Only one dollar. Bound in blue and gold—ten steel engravings, by Michael Angelo, designed expressly for this work.

LOUISA. (*Taking up book.*) You seem to have a great variety of works.

SIMON. Everything you can mention on my list. I only carry a few as specimens, but all orders will be filled with accuracy and dispatch. Neat thing you have there.

HARRY. What is it, Lou?

LOUISA. (*Reading title.*) " Selections from the Poets."

SIMON. Best collection ever published. All the great poets are there: Horace Greeley and Nicholas Nickleby and Dan Bryant.

JOHN. (*Very gravely.*) Anything from Tittlebat Titmouse's tragedy of " Cheese-cakes and Cider "?

SIMON. Certainly there is! No selection of poetry would be complete without that!

MARY. (*Looking at a book.*) " Stories from Homer." This looks interesting, Harry.

HARRY. (*Looking over* MARY's *shoulder.*) Very!

SIMON. Let me sell you that. Splendid edition! (*Aside.*) I wish I could read! It would be so much easier to find out what the books are about.

HARRY. I wonder if it is a reliable translation?

SIMON. (*Briskly.*) Oh, yes; I am sure it is! Translated from the French—(*aside*) it must be French!—(*aloud*) by a great scholar, employed by our firm, Mr. Ebenezer Scratchapen. Writes French and German, and can talk Portuguese as if he was a born Portugoose himself.

MARY. (*Doubtfully.*) I have half a mind to have this. I never expect to study Greek, and I should like to read some of the "Iliad."

SIMON. Better take it, miss, while you can. Whole edition sold in ten days, and only that one copy left. I couldn't get another if I tried.

LOUISA. (*Still looking over book.*) Here is "Thanatopsis," Mary.

SIMON. (*Aside.*) "Thanatopsis!" Oh, I know, "Uncle Tom's Cabin." (*Aloud.*) Yes, miss, you'll find several extracts from Uncle Tom's works. (*Aside.*) I declare, though, I never knew before that Topsy wrote poetry.

JOHN. Got any book about fishing and shooting?

SIMON. Of course I have. (*Tumbling over books.*) Here is one. H'm!—my eyes are not good.

JOHN. Why, that is a "Treatise on Needlework."

SIMON. (*Aside.*) So it is. I thought that knitting-needle was a fishing-pole. Very confusing not to be able to read. (*Finds another book.*) Will this do?

JOHN. Not exactly! That is a cook-book.

SIMON. The ladies will like that. Perhaps you will see if you can find something to suit you while I show the ladies this work.

JOHN. (*Turning over books.*) Very well. (*Aside to* HARRY.) His eyes must be very bad!

HARRY. (*Aside to* JOHN.) Or he doesn't know how to read.

SIMON. I would like you to look at this work on cookery, ladies. Written by a professional in the business, head cook to the Queen of England. (*Aside.*) What is his name? I was told especially to remember that. Maccaroni? No! It was a long name—Frangipanni! I do believe that is it. (*Aloud.*) Frangipanni's cook-book, ladies, full of plates. Cod's head on batter, illustrated.

HARRY. (*Aside to* JOHN.) I wonder if it has calf's head on literature?

MARY. (*Examining book.*) Mother would like this!

SIMON. Housekeepers cannot live without it! Children cry for it! The most popular book of the season—only four dollars!

LOUISA. Oh, Mary, I would not like to give that price, unless we were sure mother would care for it!

JOHN. Here's a tip-top book, Harry.

HARRY. What is it?

JOHN. "The American Boy's Own Book." (*Both* BOYS *examine book.*)

SIMON. (*Aside.*) I must get off some more of that stuff I learned by heart from the man who sold me his district. Let me think a minute—oh, yes! (*Aloud.*) I have a very fine work here: "The Ready Speaker," full of pieces to recite at exhibitions, all made up from first-class writers. Poetry, prose, dramatic and grammatic! Here's extracts from Shakespeare—everybody recites Shakespeare—and here are selections from his very last work, just published; on the Turco-Russian war—martial, you know. And here's the speech Virgil made at the Fourth of July celebration at Mount Vernon—every American boy ought to learn that!

MARY. (*Aside to* LOUISA.) Is he crazy, or does he think we are four first-class idiots?

LOUISA. (*Aside to* MARY.) Both, I guess.

SIMON. (*Aside.*) There was a whole lot more of it! I ought to remember it, when we went it over together about seventeen dozen times. (*Aloud.*) There is a splendid book about the fashions here; tells how to make everything ladies wear—button-hole stitch tarletan bonnets, Honiton lace, vinaigrettes, silver gilt ribbon gloves, chandelier lace, petticoats—everything! Why, the directions for embroidering palm leaf fans alone is worth the whole price of the book—only fifty cents! Tells you how to bias your apron strings, how to dove-tail your table-cloths, how to herring-bone your back hair. Everything a lady ought to know.

JOHN. (*Aside to* HARRY.) Wind him up again! He has run down!

HARRY. Did you ever hear anything like it?

JOHN. (*To* SIMON.) What have you in fiction?

SIMON. Everything! Here is the last edition of "The Lives of Great Heroes."

HARRY. Bless me! does he mean to be sarcastic?

SIMON. I assure you my stock comprises everything worth reading! It has been carefully selected for enlightened counties, such as this one; for talented boys, (*bowing to* JOHN) beautiful ladies, (*bowing to* MARY) rising genius, (*bowing to* HARRY) and graceful refinement (*bowing to* LOUISA). Do you want poetry? Here are all the poets! Smollet, Hume, Macaulay; all the historians! Horace, Virgil, Sidney Smith; all the astronomers! Dickens, Braddon, Collins! You cannot name any character of work not upon our list! (*Pauses, out of breath.*)

MARY. (*To* LOUISA.) I wish I had not ordered that new trimming on my dress. It makes my pocket-money very trifling this week.

LOUISA. (*To* MARY.) And I do not dare to break into mine until my bonnet comes home.

SIMON. There is a very pretty thing here, (*selects book*) all about pets—aviaries, ferneries, aquariums—every sort of recreation! Sold twenty copies just a little way from here, for a biographical society, looking for good authorities for their labors. (*To* MARY.) Can't I sell you this, ma'am?

MARY. I think not to-day.

SIMON. Great mistake not to take these opportunities. Very poor show of books in your store. I took a look at them as I passed. Their editions are all incomplete. Why, there is a whole volume missing of Waverley's "Hiawatha." (*Aside.*) I am sure that was the one the other peddler said was gone.

LOUISA. And have you the complete set?

SIMON. Can get it for you, miss, if you will just mark it on this list, (*takes catalogue from pocket*) and write your name and address on a card.

LOUISA. (*Gravely.*) When can I have it?

SIMON. By next week. (*Aside, sighing.*) Well, I've *one* order, anyhow!

MARY. (*Aside to* LOUISA.) What are you ordering?

LOUISA. (*Writing on card.*) What? Why, Waverley's "Hiawatha"!

MARY. (*Aside to* LOUISA.) That is too bad!

LOUISA. (*To* SIMON.) There is the card. I shall depend upon seeing the book next week.

SIMON. (*To* MARY.) Do let me have an order from you, miss.

MARY. Well, I don't mind. You can send me the volume you mentioned just now.

SIMON. Which one, miss?

MARY. Shakespeare's "Turco-Russian War."

SIMON. Perhaps you will just add it to the card?

MARY. (*Writing on card.*) Certainly!

SIMON. (*Aside.*) I'm getting on! I was afraid I would make a mess of it! (*Aloud.*) Can't you find anything to suit you, gentlemen?

HARRY. Well, as the ladies have given you an order, you may take mine for something on your list. Have you any good histories?

SIMON. (*Aside.*) Now I am sure I ought to remember *that.* History! Oh, yes! (*Aloud.*) Certainly, sir. We have Dickens' "Conquest of China," Thackeray's "Inundation of Persia," Coleridge's "Lives of the American Emperors." (*Aside.*) There were about fifty more. (*Aloud.*) The latest thing is "Rome on the Rampage," by Shelley.

HARRY. H'm! How about philosophy?

SIMON. Now if there is one thing above another upon which we *do* pride ourselves, it is our works on philosophy. We have everything, sir—everything!—from Plutarch's "Old Curiosity Shop" to Macbeth's "Astronomy."

HARRY. Have you any good biographies?

SIMON. (*Aside.*) Dear me, I'm afraid I'll forget some of it, after all! Biography! Oh, I know—that's countries, travels and things. (*Aloud.*) Oh, yes, sir; we have every kind of biography, with full-page maps.

HARRY. Maps!

SIMON. Yes; all the rivers and mountains, and the volcanic valleys, and—

HARRY. Oh, geography; but I said biography.

SIMON. Oh, excuse me, I'm a little hard of hearing.

HARRY. You may bring me the history you mentioned.

SIMON. "Barnaby Rudge"?

HARRY. No. The— (*Hesitates.*)

SIMON. John Wesley's "History of Patagonia"?

HARRY. No.

SIMON. Milton's "Discoveries in Japan"?

HARRY. Yes, that will do. I will put it on your card. (*Writes.*)

SIMON. I would like to sell you one of these. (*Begins to collect books.*)

JOHN. (*Aside.*) I declare, it is mean to send the poor fellow away with that absurd card. I wonder what my bank contains? (*Exit* JOHN.)

SIMON. (*Packing books.*) Heavy load to carry in this hot weather!

HARRY. It must be.

SIMON. I always hope to sell at least one book wherever I call. Can't I dispose of this gem of poetical selections to you? Why, the picture of Pickwick is worth the price of the volume.

HARRY. Not to-day.

SIMON. I'll attend to that order.

Enter JOHN.

JOHN. I see that "American Boy's Book" is marked two dollars?

SIMON. (*Looking over books.*) This?

JOHN. No; that is a Tennyson.

SIMON. Oh, my eyes are so bad.

JOHN. You have it there somewhere.

SIMON. (*Searching.*) Green cover?

JOHN. No; red.

SIMON. This?

JOHN. Yes. I'll take that. (*Gives money.*)

SIMON. Thanks! (*Packing satchel.*) I'll call in again next week with the ordered books, and new ones. Good morning.

ALL. Good morning. (*Exit* SIMON.)

HARRY. (*Laughing.*) I'd give a dollar to see the face of any bookseller who takes that order!

MARY. (*Laughing.*) So would I. Did you write your real name and address, Lou?

LOUISA. Of course not. Anybody could see he could not read.

JOHN. Well, it may be fun for you; but I have some sympathy for a poor fellow trying to earn an honest living, carrying that heavy satchel in the sun.

LOUISA. It was a little too bad.

MARY. Well, if he comes again, I'll tell mother about the Francatelli.

HARRY. Frangipanni, you mean! "Frangipanni's Cook-book."

CURTAIN.

THE BURGLAR-ALARM.

Characters.

MR. JOHN JONES—*A City Merchant residing in the country.*
MRS. JONES—*Very timid, and especially afraid of Burglars.*
MISS AMANDA JONES—*MR. JONES' Sister.*
MR. HENRY SMITH—*MRS. JONES' Brother.*
DINAH—*A colored Servant.*

SCENE.—*A Sitting-room, handsomely furnished. Centre of stage, a table with arm-chair beside it. Right of centre another arm-chair; left of centre a lounge. In the background a large window, that will open and shut.*

MRS. JONES *and* MISS AMANDA *discovered, seated.*

MRS. JONES. I can't imagine what keeps John so late!

Enter DINAH, *with a letter.*

DINAH. Boy jes' lef' dat 'ar, Miss Jones.

MRS. JONES. (*Opening letter.*) Oh, dear!

AMANDA. What is it, dear? No trouble, I hope!

MRS. JONES. Not exactly a *trouble.* John writes that he has been most unexpectedly called to Chicago, and must leave on the ten-thirty train this evening!

AMANDA. Mercy on me! He doesn't mean to leave us alone in this out-of-the-way place all night!

DINAH. Don't yer be skeered, honey—I'll take care o' yer!

MRS. JONES. No; he has sent a telegram to my brother, who always remains in his office until late, to come over here.

AMANDA. But suppose he does not come?

MRS. JONES. Oh, he will! But, candidly, dear Amanda, I feel very nervous! I wish Henry would come!

AMANDA. How can you help it? My heart is beating a regular tattoo!

MRS. JONES. Dinah, go fasten the house up. Shoot every bolt in as far as it will go, and check it.

DINAH. I will, fo' sure!

MRS. JONES. Put up all the chains!

DINAH. Yes, missee!

MRS. JONES. Double lock all the doors, and put a chair against every one.

DINAH. Ki! yi! I'll fix 'um burglar traps. (*Exit* DINAH.)

AMANDA. If I was married, *my* husband should stay at home and protect me!

MRS. JONES. Nonsense! A man must attend to his business.

AMANDA. A man's first business is to protect his family, and I shall take occasion to tell John so, you may be sure!

MRS. JONES. Very well.

AMANDA. The whole country is full of tramps! There were no less than four beggars at the gate this very afternoon, and one of them stared up at every window in the house.

MRS. JONES. Did you see him?

AMANDA. Of course I did!

MRS. JONES. Oh, Amanda, you frighten me nearly to death! You don't know anything about it, of course; but Amanda—(*in a low tone*) the catch of that window is broken.

AMANDA. Broken!

MRS. JONES. Hush! Nobody knows it but Mr. Jones and myself. There will be a man here to mend it to-morrow.

AMANDA. But suppose somebody gets in *to-night?*

MRS. JONES. (*Gloomily.*) I was just thinking of that very thing. Suppose anybody should!

Enter DINAH.

DINAH. Marse Smiff done come; jes' slammed de gate, he did! S'pose you ladies feel 'nuff sight better now! Ke! he! (*Exit* DINAH.)

MRS. JONES. I am so glad!

AMANDA. (*Simpering.*) Your dear brother is so brave!

Enter MR. SMITH.

MR. SMITH. How d'ye do, Jane? How are you, Miss Amanda? I just got John's telegram as I was leaving the office, and hurried over.

MRS. JONES. I am so glad.

MR. SMITH. But I can't stay.

BOTH LADIES. Can't stay!

MR. SMITH. Not now! I'll come back about—let me see—before midnight, I hope! But I must go over to Keenan's. I'll get back as soon as I can, and in the mean time—see here! (*Takes burglar-alarm from his pocket.*) I'm going to put this up.

MRS. JONES. What is it?

MR. SMITH. A burglar-alarm. (*Sets it off. Both* LADIES *cover their ears, and* DINAH *rushes in.*)

DINAH. De lawful sakes! what dat 'ar?

MR. SMITH. Dat 'ar's a burglar-alarm, Dinah, to let you know if there are thieves coming into the house.

DINAH. Jes' so! (*Aside.*) Done fought it was de ole Nick's rattle, 'deed did I!

MR. SMITH Now the easiest way to get into this house, when we except the doors, which you will bolt, of course, is at this window. I've come in this way many a time myself. So I am going to fasten this on here! I can hear it at Keenan's, and can run across the fields in five minutes.

AMANDA. Surely we shall not be afraid now!

MR. SMITH, (*Fastening alarm to window.*) There! Now if any one raises that window more than six inches, off that will go!

MRS. JONES. But I wish you could stay.

MR. SMITH. I wish so too; but I promised Mr. Keenan to see him this evening about the deed of those pasture lots. He's thinking of buying them for building purposes, and John is as anxious to sell as I am.

MRS. JONES. Yes. (*Sighing.*) Always business. Both you and John away, and we left alone in this great barn of a house, miles away from the city, for *business*.

MR. SMITH. Never mind, Jennie; when we are all rich we will hire a regiment of cavalry to protect the place. Good night!

MRS. JONES. Good night, if you must go!

MR. SMITH. The sooner I go, the sooner I will be back again. Good night, Miss Amanda.

AMANDA. (*Hysterically.*) Good night! Don't leave us unprotected long.

MR. SMITH. Not a minute longer than I can help. (*Exit* MR. SMITH.)

DINAH. It's done struck ten, Miss Jones, an' all de house am locked up.

MRS. JONES. Then we may as well retire.

AMANDA. I am sure I shall not sleep one wink.

MRS. JONES. Nor I. Come into my room, will you? Dinah, turn off the gas. (MRS. SMITH *and* AMANDA *go out.*)

DINAH. Specs Marse Smiff be comin' 'long in a little while, an' dis nigga neber hears nuffin after she goes asleep. He mighten ring de house down, an' I not hear him! I'll jes' turn down de gas an' sot here a spell. (*Turns out the gas. Stage in very dim light.*) Dar, I've done turned it out! Jes' like my clumsiness. (*Groping about.*) Can't find a match! Course I can't. (*Falls over a chair.*) Break my neck de fustus t'ing I knows. (*Yawns.*) Sakes alibe, but I'se sleepy! (*Sits down in arm-chair.*) Reckon Marse Smiff 'll be 'long presently, (*yawns*) an' I'll hear de bell (*very slowly*) here—for sure—guess I'll jes' wait here in de dark a spell, an' —an'— (*Yawns, and drops her head back on chair, asleep. Perfect silence for a moment.*)

Enter MISS AMANDA, *in a wrapper, with her hair loose.*

AMANDA. It is perfectly useless for me to try to sleep! I will just sit here until I hear Mr. Smith go up the stairs. Then I can feel secure and rest. (*Gropes her way to the sofa.*) I will just re-cline here and think of—of—well, Tennyson! There is nothing so soothing, (*yawns*) when one cannot rest, as to recall the beauties of a (*yawns*) favorite poet. I'll quote a few lines, (*very slowly*) to pass—the—time, from—from—(*rests her head on the sofa*) from —the—" Lotos-eaters "—and—(*yawns*) soothe myself—to—to— (*Sleeps. Perfect silence again for a moment.*)

Enter MRS. JONES, *with a wrapper on and her hair loose, stepping softly.*

MRS. JONES. I hope Amanda is asleep. For my part, I can't sleep! (*Gropes her way to chair near table.*) I will wait here un-til Henry comes and speak to him before he goes up-stairs. It is too bad for John to go off in this way. (*Yawns.*) He knows I never can sleep when I am nervous, and I am *so* afraid of burg-lars. (*Lets her head drop on the table.*) I wonder if Dinah really did see a suspicious-looking tramp? (*Yawns.*) There are so many now—and— (*speaking slowly*) they always seem to know when a house is unprotected. I wish Henry would come. (*Yawns.*) I think I'll take a nap while I wait. (*Sleeps. Silence again for a moment.*)

MR. JONES. (*Opening the window very little and putting his head in.*) I guess they're all gone to bed! Dear me, how tired I am! I had half a mind to go to a hotel when I missed the train; but I can't get off now till to-morrow evening, so I might as well be at home. Everybody must be asleep, so I'll not ring, for the door must be bolted, but just creep over to a sofa and take forty winks till daylight. (*Pushes up the window and starts the burglar-alarm. All three women jump up, screaming.*)

DINAH. (*Rushing to the window.*) I got him! I done got him! (*Puts her apron over MR. JONES' head, and drags him over the window-sill.*)

MRS. JONES. (*Running against AMANDA.*) Oh, you thieving wretch.

AMANDA. (*Seizing MRS. JONES.*) Murder! Fire! Murder! Thieves!

DINAH. I done cotched him! Come yere an' help me to hole onto him!

MRS. JONES. Amanda!

AMANDA. Jane!

MRS. JONES. Dinah's got the burglar! (*They rush over to DINAH.*)

DINAH. Hole on to his legs, Miss Jones! I done got his head tied up in de apron!

MR. JONES. Let me go! let me go! (*The longer the burglar-alarm can be made to ring in this conversation, the better. A small boy, with a watchman's rattle, behind the scenes, might keep up the noise.*)

AMANDA. Give me something to tie his legs!

MRS. JONES. Take my wrapper cord! (*Gives cord.*) I'll help you. (*They tie MR. JONES' legs, DINAH holding his head while he struggles and threshes his arms about.*)

AMANDA. There! (*Catches one arm.*) Hold his arms, Jane!

MRS. JONES. (*Catches the other arm.*) I've got one!

DINAH. Hole 'em fast! I'll get a clothes line!

MRS. JONES. No, no, don't go away! Take Miss Amanda's wrapper cord. (*They tie MR. JONES' hands. Bell rings noisily.*)

DINAH. Dars Marse Smiff! (*Exit* DINAH.)

MRS. JONES. My brother! Oh, how thankful I am!

AMANDA. (*Hysterically.*) Our protector comes!

Enter DINAH *and* MR. SMITH.

MR. SMITH. Did I hear the burglar-alarm?

MRS. JONES. Oh, yes! Oh, Henry, we've caught him!

MR. SMITH. (*Excitedly.*) A burglar! Why don't you have some light? (*Strikes a match and lights gas.*)

AMANDA. My preserver! (*Faints in* MR. SMITH's *arms.*)

MR. SMITH. Bless me! Here, Jane, Dinah, take her, can't you? The fellow may get away.

DINAH. I'll hole her! (*Takes* AMANDA.)

AMANDA. (*Recovering.*) Wretch!

DINAH. Sho' now, Miss 'Mandy, I ain't done nuffin to yer. (*All this time* MR. JONES *must struggle and make muffled sounds, as if smothering in the apron.*)

MR. SMITH. (*Touching* MR. JONES *with his foot.*) You're a nice specimen, now, ain't you?

MR. JONES. (*In a muffled voice.*) Untie me, you idiots!

DINAH. Poo' feller, s'pects he *is* half choked.

MRS. JONES. Oh, Henry, come away! He might have something that will go off.

MR. JONES. Can't you take this thing off?

MRS. JONES. What does he say?

AMANDA. I don't know! Oh, Jane! I'm going to have hysterics, I know I am! Oh! oh!

MR. SMITH. Take Miss Amanda up-stairs, Dinah, and give her some brandy.

AMANDA. Brandy! Oh, you brute! (*Sobs violently.*)

MRS. JONES. What ought we to do now, Henry?

MR. SMITH. Just let him lie there till morning, and I'll go for the police. You can all retire, and I will sit here and watch him!

MR. JONES. (*Struggling violently.*) I'm John Jones!

MRS. JONES. What does he say?

MR. SMITH. I can't distinguish the words, with all that cloth on his head. (*Stoops over* MR. JONES.) I guess we might take that off. I have my revolver, so he can't get away, and his hands and feet are tied.

AMANDA. Oh, don't! I'm sure I cannot bear the sight of the monster.

MRS. JONES. But he must be stifling, Amanda. We have no right to smother him, if he is a burglar.

MR. SMITH. Here, Dinah, sit him up. (*They lift* MR. JONES *from the floor to a chair.*)

MRS. JONES. You are sure he is securely tied?

MR. JONES. (*Roaring.*) Take this thing off my head!

MR. SMITH. Easy, now. Who tied it?

DINAH. Specs I done dat 'ar, Marse Smiff!

MR. SMITH. There are five hundred knots. Mercy on me, Jane, he must be half strangled! (MR. JONES *struggles and mutters.*)

DINAH. Easy, now. I'll help, Marse Smiff! You jes' hole him up, an' I'll untie him! (MR. SMITH *holds* MR. JONES *up*, DINAH *working at the knots in the apron.*)

AMANDA. Oh, Jane, what a guy you are!

MRS. JONES. Look in the mirror, my dear.

AMANDA. (*Trying to gather up her hair.*) I was never so agitated in all my life. Suppose we had not heard the alarm?

MRS. JONES. But I was here. I came down to speak to Henry before he went up-stairs.

AMANDA. Why, I was here too! I came down because I was too nervous to sleep. Oh, Jane, we might have all been murdered in our beds!

MRS. JONES. The wretch must have known Mr. Jones was away.

DINAH. Dar! Dey's all untied now, Marse Smiff.

MR. SMITH. Let's have a look at him, then. (*Gives the apron a twitch.*)

MRS. JONES. John!

AMANDA. My brother!

MR. SMITH. Jones!

DINAH. Marse Jones!

MR. JONES. Come and untie me! A nice set of idiots you are, ain't you, with your burglar-alarm!

CURTAIN.

[The characters should all be in attitudes of the utmost amazement at fall of curtain.]

MISSED HIS CHANCE.

Characters.

WALTER LEIGH.

NETTIE LEIGH.

PROF. WILCOX.

SAM BURTON.

TOM BATES.

JOHN JONES.

All the school children, boys and girls, the strength of the company will permit.

SCENE.—*A School-room, with children studying, talking in whispers, arranging desks, as if just before school-time.* WALTER *and* NETTIE *seated beside each other, right of foreground;* SAM *left of foreground;* JOHN *left of background. A teacher's desk centre of background.*

WALTER. (*Bending over a book.*) I think I have it now. I am not afraid of any part of the examination, excepting algebra, and (*sighing*) I am afraid I have not got a mathematical head, I do so hate mathematics. Now Latin is just splendid to study! (*Mutters over lesson.*)

SAM. (*Aside.*) I wonder where Tom is! I was dreadfully afraid he was hurt when he fell off the fence last night, but I did not dare wait to see.

JOHN. (*Arranging books.*) Forgotten my grammar! Of course I have. It wouldn't be me if I didn't forget something. I'd leave my head somewhere if it wasn't screwed on. Walt! Walt!

WALTER. What is it?

JOHN. Lend a fellow your grammar. I don't half know the lesson.

WALTER. (*Crossing the stage with book.*) Certainly!

JOHN. Thanks. I didn't mean to make you come to me though, Walt.

WALTER. That's no matter.

Enter PROF. WILCOX.

PROF. WILCOX. (*Taking seat at teacher's desk.*) Take your places! (ALL *seat themselves.*)

SAM. (*Aside*) He has found out. I see it in his eyes.

PROF. WILCOX. Attention! You are all aware, young ladies and gentlemen, that last week I threatened to expel from the school any boys again detected in orchard robbing.

SAM. (*Aside.*) I knew it!

PROF. WILCOX. I consider it a disgrace to the school to have had so many complaints already. This morning I hear that Mr. Green has lost the fruit of a very valuable imported plum tree, one raised with great expense and care. I have a clue to the culprit, but I will give him one chance to confess.

SAM. (*Aside.*) A clue! I am in a cold sweat! What can it be?

PROF. WILCOX. I am waiting to hear the confession! (*Perfect silence.*)

SAM. (*Aside.*) What can he have for a clue? If I only knew that! Oh, I wish the plums were back upon the tree!

PROF. WILCOX. (*Holding up a penknife.*) Since the culprit will not confess his fault, I must try to find him out. Do any of you recognize this penknife?

WALTER. (*Standing up.*) I do, sir! It is mine.

PROF. WILCOX. (*Amazed.*) Yours! Walter Leigh! I am surprised. If there was one boy in the school I considered entirely above the petty theft of orchard robbing, it was you.

WALTER. (*Proudly.*) You are right, sir. I do not covet stolen fruit.

PROF. WILCOX. But this penknife was found exactly under Mr. Green's pet plum tree. You must have dropped it there.

WALTER. I did not, sir. Appearances are certainly against me, but I was not in Mr. Green's orchard last night.

PROF. WILCOX. Ah! I begin to see! You had lent the knife?

WALTER. Yes, sir.

PROF. WILCOX. To whom?

WALTER. I cannot say, sir.

PROF. WILCOX. Do you mean that you do not know?

WALTER. No, sir.

PROF. WILCOX. That you will not betray a companion?

WALTER. Yes, sir.

PROF. WILCOX. You hear, boys! Walter will not expose the culprit; but unless he does so, I must accept the evidence before me, and conclude that the owner of the knife found under the tree

is the thief. I will give you ten minutes to consider. (*Exit* PROF.
WILCOX. *All the scholars begin to talk together in low tones, as if
greatly excited.*)

NETTIE. Oh, Walter, you will tell.

WALTER. I could not, Nettie! It would be too mean!

NETTIE. Not half so mean as to let you be punished for the
sneaking boy who borrowed the knife. Who was he, Walter?

WALTER. I am afraid if I tell such an ardent little champion as
you are, I might as well tell Prof. Wilcox. (NETTIE *coaxes in
dumb show.*)

SAM. (*Aside.*) Will he tell? He is sure to win the Latin prize
at next week's examination, and perhaps one of the others. He
certainly will tell! I—I had better confess. But I can't! Oh,
if I had only let those miserable plums alone!

JOHN. (*Aside.*) I wonder, now, if Tom knows anything about all
this! His mother told me he had broken his arm, and would not
be at school for a few days; but I was afraid of being late, and did
not wait to hear the particulars. It looks odd! Tom is not the
boy to let Walter miss his examination for his fault! I believe I
will go and tell him. (*Exit* JOHN.)

SAM. (*Aside, uneasily.*) I wonder where John has gone! Does
he suspect anything?

NETTIE. (*To* WALTER.) And mamma will be so grieved, Walter,
if you do not get even one prize.

WALTER. (*Firmly.*) There, Nettie, do not coax any more! I
will never be a traitor!

Enter PROF. WILCOX. ALL *sit silent.*

PROF. WILCOX. The ten minutes are over! (*Perfect silence.*)
Walter Leigh, stand out in the middle of the floor. (WALTER
stands centre of stage.) I ask you for the last time, do you know
who was in Mr. Green's orchard last night?

WALTER. (*Eagerly.*) No, sir, I do not, indeed.

PROF. WILCOX. Do you know who had this knife in his possession yesterday, and probably last night?

WALTER. Yes, sir.

PROF. WILCOX. Who was he?

WALTER. I cannot tell you, sir.

PROF. WILCOX. (*Sternly.*) You mean that you *will* not?

WALTER. Yes, sir.

PROF. WILCOX. Then you must pay the penalty of your obstinacy. You are expelled!

NETTIE. (*Sobbing.*) Oh, Walter, tell him! Oh, Walter! (*Sobs violently.*) Oh, why don't that dreadful mean boy tell the truth!

PROF. WILCOX. (*Very gravely.*) Take your cap, Walter, and go. You can return this afternoon for your books.

WALTER. Thank you, sir. (*Takes his cap and goes out.*)

NETTIE. He never stole the plums, never! Walter wouldn't touch a pin that wasn't his own.

PROF. WILCOX. I believe that, Nettie. I am forced to keep my word and expel the boy who appears to be the thief; but I respect Walter Leigh far more than the miserable sneak who retains his place by his cowardly silence. First class in reading. (*Several scholars stand up.*)

SAM. I am all in a shiver. Tom may confess when he is here, but I think he must be hurt.

Enter TOM, *with his arm in a sling,* JOHN *following him.*

TOM. (*Breathlessly.*) Oh, if you please, Professor Wilcox—(*Stops as if out of breath.*)

PROF. WILCOX. You are late, Bates! What is the matter with your arm?

TOM. (*Still panting.*) I broke it, sir, last night!

PROF. WILCOX. Are you able to be out?

TOM. The doctor told me to keep quiet, and I was not coming to school to-day; but John Jones came over to tell me Walter was in a scrape, because he would not tell who—who—(*Stops, confused.*)

PROF. WILCOX. Who robbed Mr. Green's plum tree. Is it possible *you* are the thief?

TOM. (*As if ashamed.*) I know it was stealing, sir, but I didn't think of anything but the fun. I don't want the plums much, and I am awfully sorry they were especially valuable—indeed I am! I thought they were just common plums.

PROF. WILCOX. But they were not *your* plums, if they had been common.

TOM. I know; and I won't ever steal another bit of fruit! But oh, please—about Walter! You won't punish him now?

PROF. WILCOX. Certainly not! John!

JOHN. Yes, sir.

PROF. WILCOX. Since you seem to like such errands, you may run after Walter and bring him back!

JOHN. Thank you, sir. Hurrah! (JOHN *runs out.*)

TOM. Thank you, sir. I—I suppose I am to be expelled, sir?

PROF. WILCOX. I will consider that. The promptness of your confession, and your coming forward with a broken arm, disposes me to be lenient this time.

TOM. Oh, if you will overlook it, there shall never be another time.

PROF. WILCOX. But, Bates, it appears to me to be very poor fun to get up in the night to steal fruit you do not care for, *alone!*

SAM. (*Aside.*) Oh, murder! I thought it was all over, and I was safe.

TOM. (*Confused.*) I—don't—think—it—is—very—very good fun, sir!

PROF. WILCOX. No. I generally detect *two* boys in all such expeditions.

TOM. (*Very much embarrassed.*) Do you, sir?

SAM. Oh, I am sure it is coming now.

PROF. WILCOX. Are you quite sure you were *alone* last night?

TOM. I—I left home alone.

PROF. WILCOX. Oh, you met your companion outside?

TOM. Please don't! I can't tell tales.

PROF. WILCOX. And, generally, I approve of such honorable silence. Once to-day I have made a mistake; for you were absent when Walter was expellled; but there is no one absent now but Walter and John. Both these were innocent?

TOM. Yes, sir.

PROF. WILCOX. Then your companion is here! Once more I give him a chance to speak. (*Perfect silence.*)

TOM. (*Aside.*) Why don't Sam confess?

PROF. WILCOX. I shall show no leniency now to this boy, who has twice refused to speak.

Enter WALTER *and* JOHN.

WALTER. Oh, Tom, thank you! Thank you, Sam!

ALL. Sam!

PROF. WILCOX. Sam! So, so—we have at last found the coward!

SAM. (*Aside.*) Oh, what shall I do?

WALTER. (*Surprised.*) Why, John, you said—

JOHN. The guilty party had confessed. But I meant Tom.

WALTER. But Tom would never have gone, if Sam— Oh, I did not mean—

PROF. WILCOX. You did not mean to betray Sam! We all understand that! Two honorable, truthful boys screen a cowardly thief! Stand up, Samuel Burton. (SAM *stands up, hanging his head.*)

TOM. (*Aside to* JOHN.) Don't he look mean?

JOHN. I bet he *feels* mean!

PROF. WILCOX. Burton, you are expelled, not only for this term, but for future ones. I have long thought your influence was a bad one. I will give you half an hour to collect your books. School will open again at ten o'clock. (*Exit* PROF. WILCOX.)

ALL THE BOYS. Three groans for Sam Burton! (*Three groans given.*)

NETTIE. Let's hiss him! (*All the* GIRLS *hiss.*)

JOHN. (*Singing. Tune—"When Johnny comes marching home."*)
      Oh, Sam-u-el, you're in a scrape!

ALL. (*In chorus.*)   Hurrah! hurrah!

JOHN.   And this time you will not escape!

ALL. (*In chorus.*)   Hurrah! hurrah!

JOHN.   We'll march you up, we'll march you down,
          We'll all parade you into the town,
          And we'll all feel gay when
               Sammy goes marching home!

ALL.   We'll all feel gay when
               Sammy goes marching home!

JOHN.   You've been a coward! you've been a sneak!

ALL.   Oh, dear! oh, dear!

JOHN.   You held your tongue, with a chance to speak!

ALL.   Oh, dear! oh, dear!

JOHN.   We think you've a terrible future to dread,
          And you'd better go home now, and bag your head!

ALL.   For we'll all feel gay when
               Sammy goes marching home

We'll all feel gay when
Sammy goes marching home !

(ALL *gather round* SAM, *two* BOYS *taking him by the arms, and making him lead a procession of all the others, who march after him slowly, singing the song given above.*)

CURTAIN.

THE GIRL OF THE PERIOD.

Characters.

HENRY LAWTON—*A young gentleman.*
LIZZIE LAWTON—*His sister.*
FANNY GRAVES—*A girl of the period.*
JANE—*A servant girl.*
OFFICER BATES—*A policeman.*

SCENE—*A Parlor, with modern furniture. Centre of background a window, with the curtains drawn back.* LIZZIE *seated, sewing upon a child's apron.* HENRY *standing up, as if about to leave the room.*

HENRY. Where is your friend, Lizzie ?

LIZZIE. She has gone out. I promised mother to finish this piece of work this morning, so I did not accompany her.

HENRY. I am afraid you do not enjoy this visit as much as you anticipated, sister.

LIZZIE. You are right. It sounds inhospitable to say so, but I heartily wish Fanny had never come, or would go home.

HENRY. I was very much surprised when I saw her, for I should have supposed your intimate friend as modest and lady-like as yourself.

LIZZIE. And so she was, Henry, when we were at boarding-school together. I never knew a sweeter girl ! But she is so changed, I can scarcely convince myself that it is my dear friend, Fanny Graves.

HENRY. She must indeed be changed if she was ever a lady-like girl. She is the most astounding specimen of that horrible species, the fast girl, it was ever my ill-fortune to meet.

LIZZIE. I am in terror every time she goes out, for fear she will be insulted. Our quiet town does not understand such dress and actions as hers.

HENRY. I hope she will not induce you to imitate her, Lizzie.

LIZZIE. No fear of that. Her daring really terrifies me!

HENRY. I believe in some city circles it is considered stylish to be fast; but certainly there is no charm in loud voices, vulgar manners and flashy dress, to a really refined person. A *fast lady!* Why, the very words are a contradiction to each other.

LIZZIE. I agree with you. Are you going out?

HENRY. Not just yet. I have a letter to write for the next mail, and just about time to finish it. (*Exit* HENRY.)

LIZZIE. I think Henry is quite right. I believe in my dear mother's teaching, that modesty is the greatest charm a young lady can possess. It makes me sad to see Fanny so altered!

Enter FANNY, *dressed in an exaggeration of the prevailing fashion, very high colors, very elaborate trimming, a dressy hat, kid gloves, and a great deal of jewelry. She carries a parasol and handkerchief.*

FANNY. (*Running to window, waves handkerchief.*) Dear fellow! I was sure he would follow me! He has gone now!

LIZZIE. (*Aside.*) What mischief is on foot now, I wonder!

FANNY. (*Coming forward.*) What are you doing, Lizzie?

LIZZIE. Making an apron for Pet.

FANNY. Before I would slave over a lot of brats, as you do! You are as bad as those horrid Paterson girls, who dress like perfect dowdies to help to educate their brothers!

LIZZIE. They are very much respected, Fanny, and they dress like ladies, in quiet good taste.

FANNY. Quiet good taste! All that sort of thing is quite out of date, I assure you! Girls now dress to attract attention—to please the beaux!

LIZZIE. It may be! Did you have a pleasant walk, Fanny?

FANNY. Perfectly delightful! (*Aside.*) Shall I tell her? She is such a horrid little nun, I'm half afraid!

LIZZIE. It is a pleasant day.

FANNY. Just lovely! Everybody was out, and my dress attracted a great deal of attention, I assure you.

LIZZIE. I am quite sure it did.

FANNY. Of course! It is in the very latest style. I expect pa made an awful row about the bills, after I left. Ma was really scared to death, thinking about it; but, as I tell her, I'll never get married if I shut myself up at home and dress like an old maid. I suppose ma has lots of rows about my bills; but I always run off when I hear pa raving.

LIZZIE. But does not your father tell you what you may spend?

FANNY. Of course he does! He allows us each two hundred a year, and there are three of us. But, of course, we know he must pay his bills or lose his credit, so we just buy what we please and have it charged. I did think Em went a little mite too far when she bought a diamond cross; but it was the sweetest thing, and as we all wear it in turn, it wasn't so dreadfully extravagant, after all. But I really did think pa'd scold the roof off. We had to hide it, or he'd have taken it back to the jeweler!

LIZZIE. I scarcely think I could enjoy finery obtained at such a cost.

FANNY. Oh, nonsense! Pa's got the money, only he's so horrid mean. Says he's being ruined by the extravagance of his family; and I'm sure ma does everything to *save*—won't even keep a girl, and slaves down in the kitchen all day to save the wages of a Biddy.

LIZZIE. But surely you all help her?

FANNY. Surely we don't! Nice looking objects we would be, washing dishes and ironing! Why, ma's face is as red as a boiled lobster all ironing day, and if we have more than two ruffled skirts apiece in the wash, you would think she was killed, she makes such a fuss!

LIZZIE. I should think you would at least do your own ironing!

FANNY. Well, we don't! I saw that horrid Jenny Green this morning.

LIZZIE. Horrid!

FANNY. Yes, goody, goody! She had on the same old green silk she wore at school, and a sacque as old as the hills.

LIZZIE. I presume she was visiting the poor. She is a district visitor, and we do not go amongst the poor and suffering in gay dresses.

FANNY. Then I wouldn't go at all; poking about in nasty little houses, all vermin and small-pox—ugh! I wouldn't do it for any money!

LIZZIE. Tastes differ!

FANNY. I should think so! I did have such a laugh this morning. You know Clara Moore?

LIZZIE. One of our belles!

FANNY. Well, she's got a new hat that is perfectly lovely, blue and white, the sweetest thing I ever saw. I wanted to pull it off her head and keep it. She came mincing up the street to me, with the sweetest smile, and I know she thought that hat would take all the conceit out of me. So I just thought to myself, "I'll take the starch out of you, my lady!" and I smiled as sweetly as she did, and said, "Why, how came you to get your new hat in last year's shape?" You should have seen her face come down. "Last year's shape!" said she. "Why, yes; we don't wear them in the city at all this year, and the milliner has put the trimming a great deal too low! And, don't be offended, but don't you think you're a little sallow to wear so trying a shade of blue?" and then I sailed on. She may be standing there yet, for all I know.

LIZZIE. But if the hat was really pretty and becoming, why did you want to mortify her?

FANNY. My dear, she looked so perfectly lovely, I wanted to tear her eyes out! I wish crimps were out of fashion!

LIZZIE. Why? I thought you must admire them, you are so particular about yours.

FANNY. But they make my head ache fit to split. It takes me an hour to put mine up, and I can't half sleep, they are so tight! (*Sitting down.*) And, talking of tight things, these boots nearly murder me!

LIZZIE. Why don't you take them off?

FANNY. I am going out.

LIZZIE. Again!

FANNY. (*Aside.*) Oh, I must tell her! (*Aloud.*) Yes, I've had an adventure!

LIZZIE. Indeed!

FANNY. (*Enthusiastically.*) Such a charming adventure! I

was walking down President Street, and I thought I would go into Smith and Brown's and price those cute little lockets in the window, when just as I was going in I saw, oh, such a love of a man! He had the most bewitching moustache! and the most magnificent black eyes; and he was looking at me! I just looked in the window again till he came quite near, and then I smiled.

LIZZIE. Fanny!

FANNY. And he smiled.

LIZZIE. Oh, Fanny—not a perfect stranger!

FANNY. Pshaw! don't be such an old maid! I dropped my glove and he picked it up, with such a bow!

LIZZIE. (*Aside.*) Oh, I didn't think she would go to such a length!

FANNY. Then I went into the store, and he looked in at the window! I knew he wanted to see *me*, so I went to the very front counter, and looked at lockets, and we had a regular handkerchief flirtation. He told me he was dying to know me, and adored me!

LIZZIE. Did he dare to *speak* to you?

FANNY. No; I told you it was a handkerchief flirtation; and when I left the store he followed me, and passed the house. I just waved my handkerchief to him, and he signaled me, " We shall meet again!"

LIZZIE. This is dreadful!

FANNY. I am going up to my room to put on another bracelet, and then I am going down town again. (*Exit* FANNY.)

LIZZIE. What shall I do! Mother and father are both out, and Fanny would never pay any attention to me!

Enter HENRY, *with a glove.*

HENRY. Can you mend my glove for me, Lizzie? (*Bell rings.*) Why, sister, what is the matter? You appear to be troubled.

LIZZIE. Don't question me, Henry, please; but do please help me to keep Fanny from going out again to-day.

Enter JANE.

JANE. There is a man at the door, sir, wants to see the gentleman of the house.

HENRY. Since father is out, I must go. Say I will be there in a moment, Jane.

JANE. Yes, sir. (*Exit* JANE.)

HENRY. Mend my glove for me, like a good little sister, while I am gone. (*Exit* HENRY.)

LIZZIE. I hope Fanny will not go out before he comes back. I cannot tell him my reason; but I know he will trust me enough to be sure there is some good one why I wish Fanny to stay at home.

Enter HENRY, *followed by* OFFICER BATES.

HENRY. You see, officer, there is no one here but my sister.

OFFICER BATES. (*Stepping to window.*) I am sure this is the house and the window.

HENRY. And I am sure you are mistaken.

OFFICER BATES. (*To* LIZZIE.) Didn't you have a visitor in here just now?

HENRY. (*Hotly.*) You shall not insult my sister by inquiring if she receives shop-lifters. I tell you you are mistaken, and over-stepping your duty.

OFFICER BATES. I'll offer every apology, sir, if I am; but I'd like to ask the young lady a question or two.

LIZZIE. Oh, Henry, what is the matter?

HENRY. Why, this man insists that he saw a shop-lifter at one of our windows, and has orders to arrest her.

LIZZIE. (*Haughtily.*) Oh, is that all! Of course he will be convinced of his mistake.

OFFICER BATES. Will you swear, miss, there wasn't no one at that window?

LIZZIE. There has been no one in this room to-day but the in-mates of our own house.

OFFICER BATES. Well, I am puzzled for once. I'm sure I don't want to make trouble, miss; but you see Smith and Brown have lost a great deal of valuable jewelry lately over the counter.

LIZZIE. (*Aside.*) Smith and Brown!

OFFICER BATES. And I was put on special duty to watch the store.

HENRY. (*Impatiently.*) Come, make a short story of it, if you please.

OFFICER BATES. I've got to satisfy myself, sir. As I said, I am on special duty to watch the store. Well, this morning when I was lounging on the other side of the street, I saw a young lady come sailing along, with just the flashy finery on that the city shop-lifters wear, all jewelry and ruffles, and I'll be blowed if she didn't stop right at Smith and Brown's window !

LIZZIE. (*Aside.*) Oh, I am afraid I shall faint !

OFFICER BATES. Just at that moment I spied one of the most slippery thieves in town coming down towards her—one of the swell fellows, that wear diamond studs, and give the police no end of trouble—and if he didn't smile at that girl, I'm a Dutchman !

HENRY. (*Aside to* LIZZIE.) Why do you tremble so ? The man has made a mistake—disagreeable, of course, but he cannot trouble us !

OFFICER BATES. So I just kept my eye on the pair of them, and the girl walked into the shop, asked to see a tray of lockets, and kept up a series of signals with her partner outside.

LIZZIE. (*Aside to* HENRY.) Keep Fanny out of the room. Don't stop to ask questions now.

HENRY. But she is out.

OFFICER BATES. Of course I followed them, and the girl came in here, and signalled her partner out of that window.

HENRY. You are entirely mistaken.

Enter FANNY.

OFFICER BATES. Why, there she is now ! (*To* FANNY.) You are my prisoner !

FANNY. How dare you !

OFFICER BATES. I arrest you on charge of Smith and Brown for shop-lifting !

FANNY. (*Screaming.*) Oh, what does he mean ?

HENRY. Officer, a word with you. (*Takes* OFFICER *to background.*)

FANNY. (*Sobbing.*) Oh, Lizzie, what does that horrid man mean ?

LIZZIE. He means that the Adonis with whom you were carrying on a handkerchief flirtation this morning was a notorious thief, and you were supposed to be stealing lockets for his benefit, while he watched your operations through the store window.

FANNY. (*Sobbing and clinging to* LIZZIE.) Oh, Lizzie, he cannot really arrest me, can he ?

LIZZIE. Don't sob so ! I hope Henry will persuade him that he is mistaken. (*Tries to comfort* FANNY.)

HENRY. (*Coming forward.*) Lizzie, can you give any explanation of this ?

LIZZIE. I think so ! (*Aside to* HENRY.) Do try to soothe her. (*Goes back and converses with* OFFICER BATES.)

HENRY. I am very sorry you have been subjected to such annoyance while visiting us, Miss Fanny.

FANNY. (*Sobbing.*) It is all my own folly. Oh, if I can only get out of this scrape, I will never, never do anything fast again as long as I live !

HENRY. You will certainly be the gainer, then, even by such a disagreeable experience as this.

FANNY. I shall die if he arrests me ! Oh, Mr. Lawton, can't I bribe him to go away? I know pa will pay any money to avoid such a disgrace !

HENRY. You may be sure we will do everything in our power to protect you !

OFFICER BATES. (*Coming forward.*) Well, miss, as I know Mr. Lawton, and can come in again if necessary, I won't do any more about it now. (*To* FANNY.) But I just want to give you a word of advice, miss. I've been fifteen years on the force, and I know what I'm talking about. If you want to keep out of trouble, you'd better take off some of them fallals you're wearing, and not be quite so ready to speak to strange men in the street.

Enter JANE.

JANE. There's a very fine gentleman at the door, Miss Lawton, with black hair on his lip, and he's asking if he can see the lady that lives here that wears—(*describes* FANNY'S *dress.*)

FANNY. Tell him no ! Tell him to go away !

OFFICER BATES. That's my man ! (*Exit* OFFICER BATES, *hurriedly.*)

HENRY. (*Looking out of window.*) There they go. The officer has arrested him !

FANNY. Oh, Lizzie, I shall never be able to look anybody in the face again ! (*Sobs.*)

LIZZIE. Oh, yes, you will ! (*Exit* JANE.)

HENRY. Be sure we will both keep your secret, Miss Fanny, and I think no one else knows it. I will call in at Smith and Brown's as I go down town. Mr. Smith is an old friend of father's, and will, I am sure, respect any confidential statement I make. (*Exit* HENRY.)

FANNY. How you must despise me!

LIZZIE. No. I think now my old friend, Fanny, I have loved so well, has come back to me, and I shall never again see—the girl of the period!

CURTAIN.

THE PHOTOGRAPH GALLERY.

𝕮𝖍𝖆𝖗𝖆𝖈𝖙𝖊𝖗𝖘.

JOHN DAUBUM, } *Photographers.*
ROBERT SITTUM, }

MISS SOPHONISBA PERKINS—*An Old Maid.*

CHLOE—*A Colored Woman.*

PAT—*An Irish Boy.*

MRS. MONTMORENCY HOWARD.

MONTMORENCY HOWARD—*Her Son, a boy of six or seven.*

SCENE.—*A Room, furnished like a Parlor in foreground. Centre of background, facing audience, a large chair upon a platform; opposite this a camera, covered with black cloth; left of background a door.* JOHN *reading a newspaper;* ROBERT *holding up a picture to the light.*

JOHN. (*Yawning.*) What are you doing?

ROBERT. Copying! Got to do something!

JOHN. Y-e-e-s. People down this way don't seem to care particularly about perpetuating their classic features.

ROBERT. As we've taken the room for a month, we're bound to stay, I suppose; but I imagine we shall not find ourselves millionaires when we leave.

JOHN. Luckily the month's rent is paid; but there is a fair and encouraging prospect of starving to death.

ROBERT. (*Suddenly and dramatically.*) I hear a step upon the stairs! (*Rushes to background, and into the doorway at left.*)

JOHN. If it should be a customer!

Enter MISS SOPHONISBA PERKINS, *very absurdly dressed. A very scraggy boy, with thin arms and shoulders, and big feet, dressed in a low-necked, short sleeved, short-skirted dress, is best suited to this part. Wears hat and shawl on entering.*
(JOHN *rises and bows.*) Good morning, madame !

SOPHONISBA. (*Severely.*) *Miss* Perkins, sir !

JOHN. Can I serve you, Miss Perkins ?

SOPHONISBA. Observing in the periodical appertaining to our municipality your advertisement concerning the delineation of the human physiognomy, I have called to ascertain the possibility of obtaining a representation of my features, for (*simpering*) a gift to a friend.

JOHN. (*Briskly.*) Ah, yes ! locket size ?

SOPHONISBA. (*As if confused.*) Well, yes. I think a locket would be an appropriate enclosure.

JOHN. Oh, decidedly ! We always take young ladies in vignette in a locket. (*Aside.*) Good chance to work off some of those lockets we've had so long.

SOPHONISBA. And the remuneration ?

JOHN. Very trifling ! Miniature style, gold locket, for—well, (*confidentially*) if you will allow us to retain a copy, (*winks aside*) we will say five dollars.

SOPHONISBA. Very satisfactory. Can I sit to-day ?

JOHN. H'm ! I must consult my partner. Our rush of business is so great—that—ahem ! Mr. Sittum !

ROBERT. (*Coming forward.*) Did you call me ?

JOHN. Will you be kind enough to consult our engagement book, and see if it will be *possible* for us to give Miss Perkins a sitting to-day ?

ROBERT. (*Doubtfully.*) To-day ! I am afraid—but I will see. (*Opens an enormous ledger on table.*) H'm ! Capt. Jones at ten, Judge Hopkins, ten-thirty, Mrs. General Smith, eleven— (*Mumbles, as if reading names.*) We might get one sitting in *now*, Mr. Daubum, but not later in the day.

SOPHONISBA. Apprehending such a possibility, I attired myself accordingly. (*Removes hat and shawl.*)

JOHN. (*Aside.*) What a fine anatomical study of the shoulders ! (*Aloud.*) Mr. Sittum, will you pose Miss Perkins ?

ROBERT. (*Bustling to background.*) This way, Miss Perkins.

JOHN. (*Going to camera.*) Full face, three-quarters, or profile?

SOPHONISBA. My profile has been frequently eulogized.

ROBERT. Three-quarter face, in my opinion, is most satisfactory. (*During dialogue* ROBERT *poses* MISS PERKINS, *standing off to observe effects, altering position, and imitating a photographer.* MISS PERKINS' *attitudes must be extremely affected, and her face simpering.*)

JOHN. (*Looking through camera.*) Perfect! Sit perfectly still! (ROBERT *brings frame from open doorway, which is slipped in.* JOHN *covers camera.*) Now, Miss Perkins, look at me.

SOPHONISBA. (*Dropping her eyes, affectedly.*) Oh, I couldn't!

JOHN. At this, then. (*Tapping curtain.*)

SOPHONISBA. I will raise my orbs heavenward! (*Rolls up her eyes.*)

JOHN. (*Taking out watch.*) Do not move! (*Twitches off cloth.*) So! that will do! (*Replaces cloth.*)

ROBERT. That should be a fine picture! (*Takes frame out, and through door, left.*)

SOPHONISBA. (*Languidly.*) It is very fatiguing!

JOHN. Delicate people often find it so. But there is no gift so valuable as the portrait of a beloved friend.

SOPHONISBA. (*Simpering.*) So I am assured—by—by—(*confusedly*) the friend who urged me to sit.

ROBERT. (*Calling from doorway.*) Very satisfactory! Miss Perkins can see a proof to-morrow.

SOPHONISBA. Oh! can I not see one now?

JOHN. Quite impossible! We never show a negative.

SOPHONISBA. (*Putting on hat and shawl.*) I will call, then, to-morrow. Good morning.

JOHN. Good morning. (*Exit* MISS PERKINS.)

ROBERT. (*Coming forward.*) Gone?

JOHN. Yes. What does the negative look like?

ROBERT. A dying duck in a thunderstorm! But we can touch it up with plenty of gold on the ear-rings and necklace. Wasn't she a dose?

Enter CHLOE.

CHLOE. Sarvint, massa. Is dis yere de place whar dey takes potumgraphses?

JOHN. This is the place.

CHLOE. Hi! yi! massa! Can yer take my potumgrap?

ROBERT. Certainly!

CHLOE. Fur a dollar?

JOHN. H'm—

CHLOE. Ain't got nudder red cint! 'Clar for gracious I ain't!

ROBERT. Well, we will oblige you this time; but you must promise not to mention how cheap we took the picture.

CHLOE. Keep my mouf close shet as a rat-trap!

JOHN. Come back here. (*Each sitting must include the regular motions of two photographers posing and taking the sitter, while the dialogue goes forward.*)

CHLOE. (*Taking off hat and shawl.*) De lawful sakes! What-ebber'll my ole man say, to see me a-grinnin' at him outen a pictur. Hi! dis yere's fun! (*Cuts a caper.*)

ROBERT. Sit here, if you please.

CHLOE. Sartin, marse! (*Looks at camera.*) Hi! What dat 'ar? (*Uneasily.*) Dat 'ar go off, marse?

JOHN. No. It looks like a cannon. You may look through it, if you wish!

CHLOE. (*Looking through camera.*) What dat gemman a-standin' on his head for? Better git down, marse. All yer brains run outen de top o' yer skull bone. (*Looks out.*) Hi! Got down a'ready. You'se a reg'lar circus fellow, you is, gettin' down offen yer head like dat.

ROBERT. Now, if you will sit here, we will take your picture.

CHLOE. (*Sitting down.*) Hi! Done specs I'll do dat 'ar. (*Stares forward with a broad grin.*)

JOHN. Don't smile so much.

CHLOE. (*Shutting mouth tightly.*) Jes 's you say, marse.

ROBERT. Oh, that is too glum. Put on a pleasant expression.

JOHN. Think of something you are fond of. Your husband.

CHLOE. De lawful sakes! Guess you don't know my ole man, marse!

JOHN. Well, your children.

CHLOE. Hi! yi! ain't got none!

ROBERT. Well, what are you fond of?

CHLOE. Well, dar's bacon, an' 'lasses, an' greens, an' lump sugar —awful fond o' lump sugar, marse.

ROBERT. Well, think of lump sugar, then.

CHLOE. Heap ruther see some.

JOHN. Come, I am waiting.

CHLOE. I'se all ready. (*Grins again.*)

JOHN. Guess that will do. (*Takes picture as before.*) There. Now you may get up.

CHLOE. Done froo a'ready?

JOHN. Yes; you can have the picture to-morrow.

CHLOE. You specs I'm gwine to pay you a dollar for jes dat 'ar? (ROBERT *takes picture to doorway, as before.*)

JOHN. Certainly.

CHLOE. You mus' tink dis nigga a fool! Whar's yer paint an fixin's?

JOHN. Oh, we'll paint it all for you.

CHLOE. Yaller gown, an' blue apron, an' red beads, and purple ear-rings?

JOHN. Yes—yes—come to-morrow.

CHLOE. (*Putting on hat and shawl.*) Now, you mine, I don't pay no dollar 'less dar's lots o' red an' blue on dat 'ar potumgrap.

JOHN. All right.

CHLOE. Good morning, marse! (*Raising voice.*) Good morning, t'udder marse, in de closet!

ROBERT. Good morning! (*Exit* CHLOE.)

JOHN. (*Calling.*) How is it, Bob?

ROBERT. (*Coming forward.*) First rate. You can see every tooth in her head.

JOHN. Be sure you put on plenty of paint.

ROBERT. Trust me for that!

Enter PAT.

PAT. Oh, be jabbers, is this where you got picthers took now?

JOHN. This is the place.

PAT. Fur a quarther?

ROBERT. Yes.

PAT. (*Fishing in his pocket.*) Ye'd betther take the quarther thin, now, for there's a pop-gun in the shop down-stairs that's moighty timpting intirely. I had to shut me eyes an' rush up sudden. But I promised me mither I'd have me picther took for the birthday of her, an' Pat Maloney 'll niver go back on his word. So you'd better take the quarther, as I was sayin'. (*Gives* JOHN *a handful of pennies.*)   Here's two more !   (*goes in another pocket*) an' one more !   (*In another pocket.*)   Och, here's three I'd clane forgot—(*in another pocket*) an' here's two I stowed away las' night.   Jest be a-countin' ov thim, will ye ?   (*Searching every pocket.*)

JOHN. (*Counting.*) Ten—twelve—fifteen—seventeen—nineteen —twenty-one—there are only twenty-two !

PAT. (*Scratching his head.*) Twinty-two, is it ?   There was twenty-foive !   Oh, me mimory's lavin' me !   There was a rapscallion of a three-pinny bit—jist the laistest mite of a piece—an' I was afraid I'd a hole to match it in one o' me pockets, so I put it in here. (*Takes off one shoe and looks in it.*) Oh, be jabbers, it's the ither one, now ! (*Takes off the other shoe and finds three cent piece.*) There you are, sir.

JOHN. (*Gravely.*) Quite correct.   Will you step back ?

PAT. Back !   Is it down-stairs again ?

ROBERT. No, no !   Come over here. (*Leads the way to sitter's chair.*)

PAT. Och !   Is that the place ?

JOHN. Do you want to be taken standing or sitting ?

PAT. Any way to suit.   Sitting's aisier !   I guess I'll sit here like a lord ! (*Sits bolt upright in chair.*)

ROBERT. Don't sit so stiffly !

PAT. (*Suddenly collapsing at every joint.*) So ?

JOHN. Bless me, no !   You look like a sack of meal.

ROBERT. (*Posing* PAT.) So, easily. (*Picture taken as before.*)

JOHN. That will do !

PAT. See the loike o' that !   Is it done ?

JOHN. It will be ready to-morrow.

PAT. Sure ?

JOHN. Sure !   Come about noon.

PAT. All right.   Good morning ! (*Exit* PAT.)

JOHN. Business is certainly looking up, Bob.

ROBERT. (*Coming forward.*) I guess that last advertisement did it.   I put in a pathetic appeal to relatives who must succumb to the dread destroyer, to leave their pictures to console their weeping friends—quoted a little poetry, too.

JOHN. Hark !   Was not that a carriage ?

ROBERT. (*Looking from window.*) A carriage it is !   Two horses, coachman, and footman in livery.   Lady and boy alighting, and—coming in here!

JOHN. Business certainly *is* looking up!

Enter MRS. HOWARD *and* MONTMORENCY; MONTMORENCY *hangs back, his mother pulling him.*

MRS. HOWARD. (*Who is very richly dressed.*) Come, my angel, come—have his picture taken for his dear mamma.

MONTMORENCY. (*Whining.*) Don't want to!

MRS. HOWARD. Mamma's own little popsey wopsey! He will come like a sweet little cherub.

MONTMORENCY. What'll you give me, if I do?

JOHN. (*Aside to* ROBERT.) Here's work for one day!

ROBERT. (*Aside to* JOHN.) Isn't he a nice cub?

JOHN. (*To* MRS. HOWARD.) Good morning, madame!

MRS. HOWARD. Good morning. I wish to obtain a picture of my darling boy. I am sure you never had a more beautiful subject!

JOHN. A fine little fellow. Come, my little man, take a seat over here.

MONTMORENCY. I won't!

MRS. HOWARD. Oh, my darling, that isn't a pretty way to speak to the gentleman!

MONTMORENCY. Don't care. Ain't going to have my picture taken!

MRS. HOWARD. Oh, my angel, do!

MONTMORENCY. What'll you give me?

MRS. HOWARD. Anything!

MONTMORENCY. A fairy book?

MRS. HOWARD. Yes, yes! a beautiful one!

MONTMORENCY. Won't have my picture taken for an old fairy book.   Give me a tool box?

MRS. HOWARD. Yes, dear, a lovely tool box!

MONTMORENCY. And a velocipede?

MRS. HOWARD. Yes, my lovey, a big velocipede.

MONTMORENCY. Don't want one! I want twenty pounds of cream candy.

MRS. HOWARD. But, my angel, it will make you sick.

MONTMORENCY. (*Howling.*) It won't!   I won't have my picture taken, then!

ROBERT. (*Aside to* JOHN.) I know what I would give him.

JOHN. (*Aside to* ROBERT.) My fingers are tingling to commence now!

MRS. HOWARD. Oh, mamma's lovesey dovesey, do sit for a picture. (*Pretends to cry.*) Mamma's crying for a picture of her own little toodleums.

MONTMORENCY. Don't care!

MRS. HOWARD. Mamma'll buy him two lovely tarts.

MONTMORENCY. (*Contemptuously.*) Two!

MRS. HOWARD. And some sour balls.

MONTMORENCY. I'll tell you what! Give me five dollars to spend just as I please, and I'll have my picture taken.

MRS. HOWARD. But, my pretty pet—

MONTMORENCY. Five dollars, or I won't sit!

MRS. HOWARD. Well, I will.

MONTMORENCY. Now I won't sit till you give it to me.

MRS. HOWARD. (*Opening purse.*) There! (*Gives money.*) Now he will sit like mamma's own precious angel.

MONTMORENCY. You've got to come too.

MRS. HOWARD. Very well. (ALL *go to background.* ROBERT *poses* MRS. HOWARD, *with* MONTMORENCY *standing beside her.*

JOHN. So! A lovely group. (*Removes cloth.*)

MONTMORENCY. (*Jumping up.*) Oh, there's a fly on you, ma!

JOHN. Another plate, if you please, Mr. Sittum. This one is spoiled. You must keep still, young gentleman.

MONTMORENCY. I won't if I don't choose.

MRS. HOWARD. Oh, my dear, the gentleman can't get a pretty picture of mamma's pet if he don't keep still. (ROBERT *arranges group.*)

JOHN. (*Removing cloth.*) Now, don't move.

MONTMORENCY. Atchoo! atchoo! (*Sneezes violently.*)

JOHN. (*Impatiently.*) We shall never obtain a likeness, at this rate!

MONTMORENCY. (*Whimpering.*) I can't help sneezing.

MRS. HOWARD. No, my darling, mamma knows he can't help it. (*To* JOHN.) Try again, if you please. You shall be amply remunerated for your time and trouble. (*Dramatically.*) No expense is too great, if only I can have a satisfactory likeness of my dear little angel.

JOHN. (*Politely.*) We are generally very successful with children, madame. But it is impossible to obtain a likeness unless the sitter keeps perfectly motionless.

MRS. HOWARD. I think he will keep still this time. You will be still—won't you, popsey wopsey?

MONTMORENCY. (*Sulkily.*) I s'pose so. (ROBERT *arranges group,* MONTMORENCY *scowls and frowns.*)

JOHN. Oh, that will never do! Put on a pleasant expression, my little man.

MONTMORENCY. I won't for you!

MRS. HOWARD. Oh, do smile, my love. (*To* JOHN.) His smile is so cherubic!

JOHN. Come, little man, look bright.

MONTMORENCY. (*Looking a little more cheerful.*) Well, do hurry up, then!

JOHN. That is better. (*Removes cloth.*)

MONTMORENCY. Oh! oh!

MRS. HOWARD. What is the matter, my pet?

JOHN. Another plate ruined.

MONTMORENCY. Oh, there's a pin running into my neck! Oh! oh!

MRS. HOWARD. (*Anxiously.*) Come here, love! (*Examines* MONTMORENCY'S *neck.*) There is no pin there, lovey—only a little starched end of your collar. There! that is all right, isn't it?

MONTMORENCY. (*Sulkily.*) Yes; you may just tell that Susan I'll stick a pin in her if she starches my collar that way again. (ROBERT *arranges group.*)

JOHN. (*Aside.*) If I could only have that imp alone for five minutes!

MRS. HOWARD. Lean upon me, Monty! There, put your head on my shoulder.

JOHN. Very effective! Now. (*Removes cloth*).

MONTMORENCY. Ah! (*Yawns very widely.*)

MRS. HOWARD. Oh, Monty! Monty!

JOHN. I'm afraid we will have to give it up, madame.

MONTMORENCY. (*Whining.*) Well, I can't help gaping. I'm most tired to death with the old picture.

MRS. HOWARD. Oh, do—do try once more! (ROBERT *arranges group.*)

JOHN. Now keep still one moment. (*Removes the cloth.* MONT-MORENCY *puts something in his mouth.*)

ROBERT. Ruined again.

MONTMORENCY. (*Chewing and swallowing hastily.*) It is only a bit of candy.

JOHN. But you must not eat candy when you are sitting for your picture.

MONTMORENCY. I guess I shan't ask you when I may eat candy!

MRS. HOWARD. Perhaps he will sit better alone! Won't you, treasure?

MONTMORENCY. I don't know.

MRS. HOWARD. Standing tires him. (*Rising.*) Here, poppet, sit down in this nice chair.

MONTMORENCY. (*Kicking his legs.*) Well, go ahead.

JOHN. Keep your legs still.

MONTMORENCY. (*Moving hands.*) All right.

JOHN. You must not move your hands.

MONTMORENCY. (*Sitting very erect and stiff.*) Oh, do hurry up! I'm tired to death.

JOHN. (*Removing cloth.*) That will do. (*Sound of music behind the scenes.*)

MONTMORENCY. Oh, there's the band! (*Rushes out.*)

MRS. HOWARD. Monty! Monty! Oh, he has gone!

JOHN. (*Drily.*) So it appears!

ROBERT. I am afraid you will never get his picture.

MRS. HOWARD. (*Haughtily.*) I am sure artists who understand their business would have no difficulty whatever in obtaining a beautiful picture, but I shall wait now until my next visit to the *city.* I might have known country photographers would not succeed! (*Sails out majestically.*)

JOHN. Whew!

ROBERT. I think if I could give that cub *one* good thrashing, I could die happy!

JOHN. (*Looking from window.*) There he is on a lamp-post, looking at the band, and his mother trying to coax him to come down.

ROBERT. Well, I'll just print off the pictures we have taken.

JOHN. And I will wait for customers.

CURTAIN.

THE ELOCUTION CLASS.

Characters.

PROF. LOUDVOICE—*Teacher of Elocution.*

JAMES,
THOMAS,
JOHN,   } *His Pupils.*
ROBERT,
HENRY,

SCENE.—*A Sitting-room, with the seats arranged to leave a space in the centre for the speaker during recitations.* JAMES *reading,* JOHN *looking out of window,* HENRY *drawing on a slate,* ROBERT *lounging on a chair, doing nothing.*

JAMES. Professor coming, John?

JOHN. (*Looking out.*) I don't see anything of him.

HENRY. It has struck three.

ROBERT. I hope he won't stay away to-day, of all days!

JAMES. I wish he never came. I hate elocution!

JOHN. So do I. A fellow feels awfully foolish standing up before a lot of strange people, swinging his arms about and shouting: (*Burlesquing.*)

    "Angels and ministers of grace defend us!
    Be thou a spirit of health or goblin damn'd,
    Bring with thee airs from heaven, or blasts from hell,
    Be thy intents wicked or charitable,
    Thou com'st in such a questionable shape
    That I will speak to thee!" (*Strikes attitude.*)

ROBERT. Bravo! That's not half so bad as doing the pathetic. (*Burlesquing.*)

    "Thou canst not speak of what thou dost not feel;
    Wert thou as young as I, Juliet, thy love
    An hour but married, Tybalt murdered,
    Doating like me, and like me banished,
    Then mightst thou speak, then mightst thou tear thy hair,
    And fall upon the ground, as I do now, (*Standing.*)
    Taking the measure of an unmade grave!"

HENRY. Why don't you fall?

ROBERT. Got my best clothes on, and the floor is dusty.

HENRY. I think the worst of all is the martial business. (*Burlesquing.*)

> "A thousand hearts are great within my bosom;
> Advance our standard, set upon our foes;
> Our ancient word of courage, fair Saint George,
> Inspire us with the spleen of fiery dragons!
> Upon them! Victory sits on our helms!"

THOMAS. Now I like that sort of thing. But I could never do the lackadaisical. (*Burlesquing.*)

> "She never told her love,
> But let concealment, like a worm i' the bud,
> Feed on her damask cheek; she pin'd in thought;
> And with a green and yellow melancholy
> She sat (like patience on a monument)
> Smiling at grief!"

JAMES. It is to be hoped she didn't grin like that!

THOMAS. I'll ask next time I see her.

JAMES. Well, I hate them all: pathetic, dramatic, lovelorn and patriotic. The only poetry I ever cared to learn was in a song. I like a real rattling one, like "The Bowld Soldier Boy." (*Singing.*)

> "Oh, there's not a trade that's going
>   Worth showing or knowing,
>   Like that from glory growing,
>   For a bowld sojer boy!
>   Where right or left we go,
>   Sure you know friend or foe
>   Will have the hand or toe
>   From the bowld sojer boy!
>   There's not a town we march thro',
>   But ladies, looking arch thro'
>   The window-panes, will sarch thro'
>   The ranks to find their joy.
>   While up the street each girl you meet,
>   With look so sly, will cry, 'My eye!
>   Oh, isn't he a darling, the bowld sojer boy!'"

ALL. Oh, isn't he a darling, the bowld sojer boy!

HENRY. But, like it or not, we've all got to recite something at the exhibition.

JAMES. And that will be next Wednesday.

JOHN. And we were all to select our recitations for the Professor to hear them to-day.

ROBERT. Oh, he will surely come.

THOMAS. He has a long walk, remember.

JAMES. What have you learned, Tom?

THOMAS. "Rienzi's Address to the Roman Citizens." I like something that gives a fellow a chance to air his dramatic talent.

HENRY. If he happens to have any. What are you going to recite, James?

JAMES. (*Lugubriously.*) "The Exile of Erin!"

JOHN. Hurrah for Jim! Erin go bragh! What is yours, Bob?

ROBERT. Tennyson's "Charge of the Light Brigade."

JOHN. Well, you *are* modest!

ROBERT. Might as well spread yourself on something tip-top!

JAMES. What's your choice, John?

JOHN. Oh, I like something funny! I'm going to recite one of Bon Gaultier's parodies.

JAMES. I suppose Henry has something touching and sentimental.

HENRY. Oh, I like what our old colored cook calls a mixtry. I'm going to give you pathos and humor stirred into one bowl.

JAMES. Where *can* the Professor be?

Enter PROF. LOUDVOICE.

PROF. LOUDVOICE. Good afternoon. Who is inquiring for me so pathetically?

JAMES. I was afraid you would not come, and we should have to bungle through our exhibition recitations as best we could.

PROF. LOUDVOICE. I should be very much disgusted, if, after a whole winter's tuition and study, you were to bungle, even if I had not come. Have you all made your selections for Wednesday evening?*

ALL. Yes, sir.

PROF. LOUDVOICE. Let me judge, then, how much you have

---

* As this dialogue is designed to give scholars a good opportunity for fine speaking, there is no burlesque introduced for the following recitations.

profited by my instructions. Take your seats. (ALL *take seats.*)
I shall leave all criticism until I close the class, as I wish to hear
each without interruption. Thomas, what is your selection?

THOMAS. "Rienzi's Address to the Roman Citizens."

PROF. LOUDVOICE. Remember, all of you, the directions of Ham-
let to the actors: "Suit the action to the word, the word to the
action, with this special observance, that you o'erstep not the
modesty of Nature; for anything so overdone is from the purpose
of playing, whose end, both at the first, and now, was, and is, to
hold, as 'twere, the mirror up to Nature." Now, Thomas, let us
hear your selection! Rise! (*Each, in turn, takes the centre of
stage, facing audience for his recitation.*)

THOMAS. (*Reciting.*) "Friends,
I come not here to talk. Ye know too well
The story of our thraldom. We are slaves!
The bright sun rises to his course, and lights
A race of slaves! He sets, and his last beam
Falls on a slave; not such as, swept along
By the full tide of power, the conqueror leads
To crimson glory and undying fame;
But base, ignoble slaves—slaves to a horde
Of petty tyrants, feudal despots; lords
Rich in some dozen paltry villages—
Strong in some hundred spearmen—only great
In that strange spell—a name. Each hour, dark fraud,
Or open rapine, or protected murder,
Cry out against them. But this very day,
An honest man, my neighbor—there he stands—
Was struck—struck like a dog, by one who wore
The badge of Ursini; because, forsooth,
He tossed not high his ready cap in air,
Nor lifted up his voice in servile shouts,
At sight of that great ruffian. Be we men,
And suffer such dishonor? Men, and wash not
The stain away in blood? Such shames are common.
I have known deeper wrongs! I, that speak to ye,
I had a brother once, a gracious boy,
Full of all gentleness, of calmest hope—
Of sweet and quiet joy—there was the look

Of heaven upon his face which limners give
To the beloved disciple. How I loved
That gracious boy! Younger by fifteen year
Brother at once and son! He left my side,
A summer bloom on his fair cheeks—a smile
Parting his innocent lips. In one short hour
The pretty, harmless boy was slain! I saw
The corse, the mangled corse, and then I cried
For vengeance! Rouse, ye Romans! Rouse, ye slaves!
Have ye brave sons? Look in the next fierce brawl
To see them die! And, if ye dare call for justice,
Be answered by the lash! Yet this is Rome,
That sate on her seven hills, and from her throne
Of beauty ruled the world! Yet we are Romans.
Why, in that elder day, to be a Roman
Was greater than a king! And once again—
Hear me, ye walls, that echoed to the tread
Of either Brutus!—once again, I swear,
The Eternal City shall be free! her sons
Shall walk with princes!" (*Resumes his seat.*)

PROF. LOUDVOICE. Very good, Thomas! John, what is your selection?

JOHN. Well, you know, Professor, I don't recite deep tragedy very well, so I have learned one of Aytoun's parodies, "Louis Napoleon's Address to his Army."

PROF. LOUDVOICE. Let us hear it.

JOHN. (*Taking centre of stage.*)

"Guards! who at Smolensko fled—
    No—I beg your pardon—bled!
For my Uncle blood you've shed,
        Do the same for me.
Now's the day and now's the hour,
Heads to split and streets to scour;
Strike for rank, promotion, power,
        Swag, and *eau de vie!*
Who's afraid a child to kill?
Who respects a shopman's till?
Who would pay a tailor's bill?
        Let him turn and flee.

Who would burst a goldsmith's door,
Shoot a dun, or sack a store?
Let him arm, and go before—
      That is, follow me!
See, the mob, to madness riled,
Up the barricades have piled;
In among them, man and child,
      Unrelentingly!
Shoot the men! there's scarcely one
In a dozen's got a gun;
Shoot them, if they try to run,
      With artillery!
Shoot the boys! each one may grow
Into—of the State—a foe.
(Meaning by the State, you know,
      My supremacy!)
Shoot the girls, and women old:
These may have sons, traitors bold,
Those may be inclined to scold
      Our severity!
Sweep the streets of all who may
Rashly venture in the way,
Warning for a future day
      Satisfactory.
Then, when still'd is every voice,
We, the nation's darling choice,
Calling on them to rejoice,
      Tell them—*France is free!*"

PROF. LOUDVOICE. Very well read, indeed. Just a shade less of energy and gesture, and you would recite tragedy very well, sir, in spite of your modest assertion to the contrary.

JOHN. (*Resuming seat.*) Thank you, sir.

PROF. LOUDVOICE. Robert, it is your turn now. What are we to have from you?

ROBERT. (*Rising.*) Tennyson's "Charge of the Light Brigade."

PROF. LOUDVOICE. Very good! Begin!

ROBERT. "Half a league, half a league,
     Half a league onward,
   All in the valley of death

Rode the six hundred.
'Forward, the Light Brigade!
Charge for the guns!' he said.
Into the valley of death
   Rode the six hundred!

'Forward, the Light Brigade!'
Was there a man dismayed?
Not though the soldiers knew
Some one had blundered;
Theirs not to make reply,
Theirs not to reason why,
Theirs but to do and die:
Into the valley of death
   Rode the six hundred

Cannon to right of them,
Cannon to left of them,
Cannon in front of them,
   Volleyed and thundered:
Stormed at with shot and shell,
Boldly they rode, and well:
Into the jaws of death,
Into the mouth of hell,
   Rode the six hundred!

Flashed all their sabres bare,
Flashed as they turned in air,
Sab'ring the gunners there,
Charging an army, while
   All the world wondered:
Plunged in the battery smoke,
Right through the line they broke
Cossack and Russian
Reeled from the sabre stroke,
   Shattered and sundered.
Then they rode back—but not,
Not the six hundred!

Cannon to right of them,
Cannon to left of them,

Cannon behind them,
  Volleyed and thundered :
Stormed at with shot and shell,
While horse and hero fell,
They that had fought so well
Came through the jaws of death,
Back from the mouth of hell,
All that was left of them,
  Left of six hundred !

When can their glory fade ?
Oh, the wild charge they made !
  All the world wondered !
Honor the charge they made !
Honor the Light Brigade !
  Noble six hundred !"

PROF. LOUDVOICE. Ah, that was very fine ! One never tires of such soul-stirring verse. (ROBERT *resumes his seat.*) Now, Henry !

HENRY. I studied something in an old volume of " Household Words," sir, " The Dirty Old Man."

PROF. LOUDVOICE. Never saw it. Let us hear what it is like.

HENRY. It is partly humorous, partly pathetic. (*Recites.*)

" In a dirty old house lived a Dirty Old Man,
  Soap, towels or brushes were not in his plan ;
  For forty long years, as the neighbors declared,
  His house never once had been cleaned or repaired.

'Twas a scandal and shame to the business-like street,
One terrible blot in a ledger so neat ;
The shop full of hardware, but black as a hearse,
And the rest of the mansion a thousand times worse.

Outside, the old plaster, all spatter and stain,
Looked spotty in sunshine, and streaky in rain ;
The window-sills sprouted with mildewy grass,
And the panes, from being broken, were known to be glass.

On the rickety sign-board no learning could spell
The merchant who sold, or the goods he'd to sell ;
But for house and for man a new title took growth
Like a fungus—the dirt gave its name to them both.

Within, there were carpets and cushions of dust,
The wood was half rot, and the metal half rust;
Old curtains—half cobwebs—hung grimly aloof;
'Twas a spider's Elysium from cellar to roof!

There, king of the spiders, that Dirty Old Man
Lives busy and dirty as ever he can;
With dirt on his fingers, and dirt on his face,
For the Dirty Old Man thinks the dirt no disgrace.

From his wig to his shoes, from his coat to his shirt,
His clothes are a proverb, a marvel of dirt;
The dirt is pervading, unfading, exceeding,
Yet the Dirty Old Man hath both learning and breeding.

Fine dames from their carriages, noble and fair,
Have entered his shop—less to buy than to stare;
And have afterwards said, though the dirt was so frightful,
The Dirty Man's manners were truly delightful.

But they pried not up-stairs through the dirt and the gloom,
Nor peeped at the door of the wonderful room
That gossips made much of, in accents subdued,
But whose inside no mortal might brag to have viewed.

That room—forty years since, folk settled and decked it—
The luncheon's prepared, and the guests are expected;
The handsome young host, he is gallant and gay,
For his love and her friends will be with him to-day.

With solid and dainty the table is drest,
The wine beams its brightest, the flowers bloom their best;
Yet the host need not smile, and no guest will appear,
For his sweetheart is dead, as he shortly shall hear.

Full forty years since turned the key in that door;
'Tis a room deaf and dumb 'mid the city's uproar.
The guests for whose joyance that table was spread
May now enter as ghosts, for they're every one dead.

Through a chink in the shutter dim lights come and go,
The seats are in order, the dishes in row;
But the luncheon was wealth to the rat and the mouse
Whose descendants have long left the dirty old house.

Cup and platter are masked in thick layers of dust,
The flowers fall'n to powder, the wines swath'd in crust;
A nosegay was laid before one special chair,
And the faded blue ribbon that bound it lies there.

The old man has played out his part in the scene—
Wherever he is now I hope he's more clean;
Yet give we a thought, free of scoffing or ban,
To that dirty old house and that Dirty Old Man."

PROF. LOUDVOICE. A very good selection, Henry. (HENRY *resumes his seat.*)

JAMES. (*Aside.*) My turn now. How I hate it!

PROF. LOUDVOICE. Now, James.

JAMES. My grandfather was Irish, sir, so I selected "The Exile of Erin."

PROF. LOUDVOICE. Very good.

JAMES. (*Rising to recite.*)

"There came to the beach a poor exile of Erin,
 The dew on his thin robe was heavy and chill;
For his country he sighed, when at twilight repairing
 To wander alone by the wind-beaten hill:
But the day-star attracted his eye's sad devotion,
For it rose o'er his own native isle of the ocean,
Where once, in the fire of his youthful emotion,
 He sang the bold anthem of Erin go bragh.

Sad is my fate! said the heart-broken stranger;
 The wild deer and wolf to a covert can flee,
But I have no refuge from famine and danger,
 A home and a country remain not to me.
Never again in the green sunny bowers,
Where my forefathers lived, shall I spend the sweet hours,
Or cover my harp with the wild woven flowers,
 And strike to the numbers of Erin go bragh!

Erin, my country! though sad and forsaken,
 In dreams I revisit thy sea-beaten shore;
But, alas! in a far foreign land I awaken,
 And sigh for the friends who can meet me no more!
Oh, cruel Fate! wilt thou never replace me

In a mansion of peace—where no perils can chase me?
Never again shall my brothers embrace me?
 They died to defend me, or lived to deplore!

Where is my cabin-door, fast by the wildwood?
 Sisters and sire, did ye weep for its fall?
Where is the mother that looked on my childhood?
 And where is the bosom friend, dearer than all?
Oh, my sad heart! long abandoned by pleasure,
Why did it dote on a fast-fading treasure?
Tears, like the rain-drops, may fall without measure,
 But beauty and rapture they cannot recall!

Yet all its sad recollections suppressing,
 One dying wish my lone bosom can draw,
Erin! an exile bequeaths thee his blessing!
 Land of my forefathers! Erin go bragh!
Buried and cold, when my heart stills her motion,
Green be thy fields, sweetest isle of the ocean!
And thy harp-striking bards sing aloud with devotion—
 Erin mavourneen! Erin go bragh!"

PROF. LOUDVOICE. Very well read! I am proud of my class, and quite sure you will all acquit yourselves well on Wednesday evening.

THOMAS. Won't you recite something for us, Professor, before you close the class?

PROF. LOUDVOICE. (*Smiling.*) I am afraid that is gross flattery, Thomas. You must have heard my voice to your heart's content.

HENRY. But you only recited in little snatches, to show us how to emphasize a word or a sentence.

JAMES. Do, Professor, give us one real recitation.

PROF. LOUDVOICE. What shall it be, then?

ROBERT. Shakspeare!

HENRY. Oh, yes—Mark Antony over Cæsar's body. The one you arranged for a recitation.

PROF. LOUDVOICE. (*Rising.*)
 "Friends, Romans, countrymen, lend me your ears:
 I come to bury Cæsar, not to praise him.
 The evil that men do lives after them,

The good is oft interred with their bones:
So let it be with Cæsar! The noble Brutus
Hath told you Cæsar was ambitious;
If it were so, it was a grievous fault,
And grievously hath Cæsar answer'd it.
Here, under leave of Brutus and the rest
(For Brutus is an honorable man—
So are they all, all honorable men),
Come I to speak in Cæsar's funeral.
He was my friend, faithful and just to me;
But Brutus says he was ambitious:
And Brutus is an honorable man.
He hath brought many captives home to Rome,
Whose ransoms did the general coffers fill.
Did this in Cæsar seem ambitious?
When that the poor have cried, Cæsar hath wept;
Ambition should be made of sterner stuff;
Yet Brutus says he was ambitious:
And Brutus is an honorable man.
You all did see, that on the Lupercal
I thrice presented him a kingly crown,
Which he did thrice refuse. Was this ambition?
Yet Brutus says he was ambitious:
And, sure, he is an honorable man.
I speak not to disprove what Brutus spoke,
But here I am to speak what I do know.
You all did love him once, not without cause:
What cause withholds you, then, to mourn for him?
Oh, judgment! thou art fled to brutish beasts,
And men have lost their reason!—bear with me;
My heart is in the coffin there with Cæsar,
And I must pause till it come back to me.

   *   *   *   *   *   *

But yesterday the word of Cæsar might
Have stood against the world: now he lies there,
And none so poor to do him reverence.
O masters! If I were dispos'd to stir
Your hearts and minds to mutiny and rage,
I should do Brutus wrong, and Cassius wrong:

Who, you all know, are honorable men.
I will not do them wrong : I rather choose
To wrong the dead, to wrong myself, and you,
Than I will wrong such honorable men."
Is not that about enough, boys?

THOMAS. Oh, you haven't come to the best part—the mantle.

PROF. LOUDVOICE. But I shall tire you.

ALL. No, no! We want to hear the rest.

PROF. LOUDVOICE.

"If you have tears, prepare to shed them now.
You all do know this mantle : I remember
The first time ever Cæsar put it on ;
'Twas on a summer's evening in his tent,
That day he overcame the Neroii.
Look! in this place ran Cassius' dagger through.
See what a rent the envious Casca made !
Through this the well-beloved Brutus stabbed ;
And as he pluck'd his cursed steel away,
Mark how the blood of Cæsar follow'd it,
As rushing out of doors, to be resolv'd
If Brutus so unkindly knocked, or no ;
For Brutus, as you know, was Cæsar's angel :
Judge, O you gods, how dearly Cæsar lov'd him !
This was the most unkindest cut of all ;
For when the noble Cæsar saw him stab,
Ingratitude, more strong than traitor's arms,
Quite vanquish'd him ; then burst his mighty heart ;
And in his mantle muffling up his face,
Even at the base of Pompey's statue,
Which all the while ran blood, great Cæsar fell.
Oh, what a fall was there, my countrymen !
Then I, and you, and all of us fell down,
Whilst bloody treason flourish'd over us.
Oh, now you weep : and I perceive you feel
The dint of pity ; these are gracious drops.
Kind souls ! what ! weep you, when you but behold
Our Cæsar's vesture wounded ? Look you here—
Here is himself, marr'd as you see, with traitors.

　　　*　　　　　*　　　　　　　　*　　　　*

Good friends, sweet friends, let me not stir you up
To such a sudden flood of mutiny !
They that have done this deed are honorable ;
What private griefs they have, alas! I know not,
That made them do it; they are wise and honorable,
And will, no doubt, with reasons answer you.
I come not, friends, to steal away your hearts ;
I am no orator, as Brutus is,
But, as you know me all, a plain, blunt man,
That love my friend ; and that they know full well,
That gave me public leave to speak of him.
For I have neither wit, nor words, nor worth,
Action, nor utterance, nor the power of speech
To stir men's blood ; I only speak right on ;
I tell you that which you yourselves do know,
Show you sweet Cæsar's wounds—poor, poor dumb mouths—
And bid them speak for me : but, were I Brutus,
And Brutus Antony, there were an Antony
Would ruffle up your spirits, and put a tongue
In every wound of Cæsar, that should move
The stones of Rome to rise and mutiny !"

ROBERT. Thank you, Professor.

HENRY. That's the best lesson we have had this term.

JAMES. You will come over Wednesday evening, won't you?

PROF. LOUDVOICE. I shall be here. Be sure you do me credit,
boys.

JOHN. We will try, sir.

THOMAS. That we will !

CURTAIN.

LOVE AND STRATAGEM.

Characters.

HARRY HAY.
KATE HAY—*His Sister.*
FLORENCE GATES—*A Young Heiress.*

SCENE I.—*A modern Parlor.*
SCENE II.—*A Parlor, differently furnished from that of first scene. Centre of background, a frame with a curtain easily raised and lowered. About the room some quaint, odd articles, seen in a rather dim light.*

SCENE I.—KATE *standing;* FLORENCE *seated, with disconsolate expression.*

KATE. (*Walking up and down, as if excited.*) It is the most ridiculous thing in the world, Flo!

FLORENCE. (*Sobbing.*) But a promise ought to be binding.

KATE. Not such a promise as that. The very idea of your aunt expecting you to live and die an old maid, because she hated, or pretended to hate, the very sight of a man! Hateful old thing!

FLORENCE. Oh, Kate! she was not hateful! She took me when I was a wee mite of a baby, and was as kind as a mother to me, and she has left me all her large fortune. I loved her dearly.

KATE. But she made a perfect nun of you; would never allow you to visit where you were likely to meet gentlemen, or have one of the sterner sex visit you. I am certain our intimacy would never have been countenanced if dear Harry had not been in Europe.

FLORENCE. (*Sighing.*) If she had only known him!

KATE. She must have liked him. Everybody does like Harry. (*Putting her arms around* FLORENCE, *coaxingly.*) Come, now, be reasonable. Harry loves you devotedly.

FLORENCE. (*Sadly.*) Yes, I am afraid he does.

KATE. And you love him?

FLORENCE. Y—e—e—s.

KATE. And if Miss Hannah Gates, your venerable aunt, had known him, she would never have exacted that promise that so worries you.

FLORENCE. But she did not know him, and she did exact the promise.

KATE. A promise to—what was it, exactly?

FLORENCE. She told me all the miseries of unhappy marriages—

KATE. (*Aside.*) Much she knew about it!

FLORENCE. And the happiness of perfect independence—

KATE. Well?

FLORENCE. And she made me promise never, *never* to marry any man without her cordial consent.

KATE. (*Starting up.*) What! I thought you promised never, *never* to marry any man, under any circumstances?

FLORENCE. It is just the same thing.

KATE. (*Aside.*) A glorious idea strikes me. A perfect inspiration!

FLORENCE. Of course she can never come from her grave to consent.

KATE. Why not? You say you are sure she will haunt you if you marry. She must come from her grave to do that.

FLORENCE. (*Starting up.*) Oh, Kate, Harry is coming!

KATE. (*Quietly.*) Well?

FLORENCE. (*In great agitation.*) I cannot see him; I will write to him.

KATE. (*Reproachfully.*) You are unkind.

FLORENCE. But—but—you see him to-day. I will be more composed to-morrow. (*Exit* FLORENCE.)

KATE. Poor Flo! It is easy to see how much she loves my brother. And yet her promise seems to be binding. Well, all is fair in love and war, and I think I can yet make a woman's wit bear upon this vexed question, and bring together this lovelorn pair.

HARRY. (*Behind the scenes.*) Where are you all? Flo! Kate!

Enter HARRY.

Halloo, Kitty! Alone?

KATE. As you see.

HARRY. (*Eagerly.*) But you have succeeded? You have per-

suaded Florence that the happiness of two lives is of more importance than humoring the absurd whims of a soured old maid ?

KATE. I wish I could say yes. Florence still persists in her
resolution to keep her promise at any cost. But—

HARRY. That sounds hopeful ! But ?

KATE. I think we may accomplish by stratagem what we will
never gain by argument.

HARRY. You little darling! How ?

KATE. Leave that to me. You never saw Miss Hannah ?

HARRY. Never; but I have heard her described. A little woman
who wore at seventy the dress of her young days.

KATE. Precisely. Her favorite dress was a brown silk, quite
short; prunella shoes ; a kerchief of white muslin; and of late
years a white cap, under the border of which were short curls of
gray hair. She had black eyes, and a very peculiar voice. I can
imitate it to perfection. (*Changing voice.*) Flo ! I'm really amazed
to hear you admiring a picture of a dreadful man !

HARRY. (*Laughing.*) Poor Flo ! I imagine she heard plenty of
that sort of stuff.

KATE. But now for my plan. You know all Snowden is excited
about the medium who pretends to raise spirits.

HARRY. Stuff and nonsense.

KATE. You may say that under your breath ; but just at present
I want you to be a devout believer in Professor—what is his name ?

HARRY. Professor Sylvester Jackson. You may see it placarded
on every fence in town in letters five feet long.

KATE. You must persuade Florence that it is a most wonderful
manifestation of ghostly power, and waken in her mind a profound
desire to witness his skill.

HARRY. What are you talking about ? I would not take Florence to one of his absurd pow-wows upon any consideration.

KATE. But he grants private interviews in his office.

HARRY. But—

KATE. You unreasonable man ! will you do as I direct ?

HARRY. Yes—what is it ?

KATE. Persuade Florence to go with me to visit Professor Jackson and witness his power of summoning departed spirits. I will
manage the rest.

HARRY. But cannot you explain—

KATE. I can explain nothing now. We may be interrupted; and, indeed, I hear Flo's step in the hall at this moment.

HARRY. I must work in the dark, then?

KATE. No; I will tell you my plan later. Here comes Florence!

Enter FLORENCE.

HARRY. (*Advancing to meet her.*) Good morning, Florence!

FLORENCE. (*Coldly.*) Good morning, Mr. Hay!

HARRY. *Mr.* Hay! (*Reproachfully.*) Am I, then, to consider myself a stranger where I have been at least a friend?

FLORENCE. (*Embarrassed.*) It—will—be—better.

HARRY. Better! I cannot so consider it.

KATE. (*Aside.*) I see a splendid opportunity to make a raid upon the wardrobe of the late Miss Hannah Gates, spinster, which I must improve. (*Aloud.*) I am going to your room, Flo, for the overskirt you promised to lend me for a pattern.

FLORENCE. (*Quickly.*) No, no, I will get it for you.

KATE. (*Going toward door.*) I know exactly where to find it. Take good care of Harry till I come down again. (*Exit* KATE.)

HARRY. (*Aside.*) As a sister, Kate is simply angelic. (*Aloud.*) I presume your new form of address is to inform me, without further explanation, that my proposal to you is rejected. You do not love me?

FLORENCE. Yes—no—I—I meant you to understand—it is impossible for me—to—to—

HARRY. Be my wife? And yet you are the last woman in the world I would have suspected of deliberate coquetry. Well, (*sighing*) live and learn!

FLORENCE. I—please do not have a bad opinion of me, Har—Mr. Hay. It is not best for us to keep up our old intimacy since—we—we must—be—only friends—and—and—

HARRY. (*Bitterly.*) And this forced formality is to extinguish my love for you, which I so foolishly hoped you returned. For I *was* idiot enough to think you loved me, Florence!

FLORENCE. (*Sobbing.*) I do—I do love you, Harry.

HARRY. (*Embracing her.*) My own love! My darling!

FLORENCE. (*Releasing herself.*) No, no, you must not! I dare not! I can never be your darling! Go away, and—(*sobbing*) never—come—again! My aunt's spirit will haunt me if I marry you! (*Sinks into a chair, weeping.*)

HARRY. (*Aside.*) H 'm! I begin to see Kate's idea. (*Aloud.*) Oh, speaking of spirits, you should see Professor Jackson's manifestations.

FLORENCE. (*Looking up, surprised.*) See what? (*Aside.*) I don't believe he cares one bit!

HARRY. Professor Jackson's spiritual manifestations. He calls up visible spirits.

FLORENCE. What nonsense!

HARRY. But it is not nonsense.

Enter KATE.

KATE. It would be refreshing to hear what you two can be talking about that is not nonsense.

HARRY. Don't be sarcastic, Catherine. Our *nonsense* is over; we are talking about Professor Jackson.

KATE. (*Clasping her hands.*) Oh, the dear old man! Florence, you must see him,

HARRY. Old! why he is—

KATE. (*Frowning at* HARRY.) Seventy, at least, though he is so tall and straight. His hair and beard are white as snow.

HARRY. Oh, yes! (*Aside.*) I'll wait for another hint before committing myself any further.

FLORENCE. But what does he do?

HARRY. Calls up spirits like the magicians in a fairy-tale book. Had the ghost of Tecumseh in the hall last evening.

KATE. You really must see him. We won't go to the hall, but to his office. Can't you go with us, Harry?

HARRY. Miss Gates has given me to understand, most distinctly, that my room is preferable to my company.

FLORENCE. Unkind! (*Aside.*) But he shall see that I can be as indifferent as he is. (*Aloud.*) Oh, we can go alone, Kate.

KATE. You will go, then? Can you meet me at noon, to-morrow, at the office, No.— Where is it, Harry?

HARRY. No. 227 Elm Place.

FLORENCE. But why cannot we go together?

HARRY. (*Aside.*) That's a poser for Miss Kate.

KATE. Oh, I have to go with mother to the dressmaker's! But I can meet you at noon.

HARRY. I know you will be delighted.

FLORENCE. (*Coldly.*) Undoubtedly.

KATE. Well, I must go! I'll meet you at the gate, Harry. I want to tie up my overskirt pattern. *Au revoir.* (*Exit* KATE.)

HARRY. Is it *au revoir* for me, too, Florence?

FLORENCE. I—I—certainly—I hope you will call again.

HARRY. (*Stiffly.*) Thank you! I shall certainly accept your most *cordial* invitation. Good morning, Miss Gates! (*Bows very formally, and exit.*)

FLORENCE. I cannot let him go away angry. Harry! Harry! He has gone! Oh, dear, my heart is broken!

SCENE II.—*Curtain rises, discovering* HARRY *pacing up and down.*

HARRY. Where can Kate be? We must be ready for our parts, and Florence may be here at any moment.

Enter KATE, *with a bundle.*

KATE. Well?

HARRY. All serene, arch conspirator. A ten-dollar note persuaded the professor to vanish much more quickly than his most lively ghost, and we have the field to ourselves. After Florence comes, all other visitors are to be told the medium is out of town.

KATE. (*Opening bundle.*) Array yourself, then. (*Passes articles as she names them.*) Here is your white wig and beard, your pointed cap—

HARRY. Wait a moment. (*Adjusts wig and cap.*) Now!

KATE. And your robe. (*Shakes out a long black robe, trimmed with grotesque embroidery.*)

HARRY. (*Putting on robe.*) And you?

KATE. As you see. (*Throws off bonnet and shawl. She wears a brown silk dress of antiquated pattern, prunella shoes, white kerchief pinned over her breast, white cap, gray curls, and black lace mittens.*) I need only my spectacles, and here they are. (*Puts on spectacles. Knocking outside.*)

HARRY. Here comes Florence. (*Pushes* KATE'S *bonnet and shawl under a table.*)

KATE. All right. (*Hides behind the curtain over frame.*) Can you see me?

HARRY. (*Adjusting curtain.*) No; keep quiet. (*Knock at door.*) Come in!

Enter FLORENCE.

HARRY. (*In disguised voice, which he must keep up.*) Good morning!

FLORENCE. I expected to meet friends here.

HARRY. Ah! You may perhaps desire to hold intercourse with some departed friend?

FLORENCE. I—no—yes. (*Aside.*) I must give some reason for coming.

HARRY. Allow me in that case to suggest that the spirits much prefer to meet their earthly friends alone; a crowd is offensive to them. Can you name any friend you wish to see? (*Aside.*) Now if she names anybody but her aunt I'm in a nice mess!

FLORENCE. No; I—oh, I wish I had not come!

HARRY. (*Aside.*) Poor little darling, she is half frightened to death. (*Aloud.*) Will you be seated? (*Places a chair to face frame.*) Perhaps some of your friends would manifest themselves. H'm! Is there any friend of this lady's here? (*Three raps behind curtain.*)

FLORENCE. (*Trembling.*) Oh, tell them to go away!

HARRY. Will the spirit rap out its name? (*A number of raps.*)

FLORENCE. Oh, I must go home! I am afraid!

HARRY. Hannah! Have you a friend called Hannah?

FLORENCE. Yes. (*Aside.*) I will be courageous, if it really is Aunt Hannah.

HARRY. Will the spirit manifest herself? (*Three raps.*)

HARRY. (*Drawing curtain, shows* KATE.) Do you recognize the spirit?

FLORENCE. Oh, it is Aunt Hannah! Will she speak to me?

KATE. (*In disguised voice.*) Florence!

HARRY. (*Aside.*) I'm afraid she will faint.

FLORENCE. Aunt Hannah, are—you—happy?

KATE. No—because you are not.

FLORENCE. You know that—

KATE. I know that my cruel wishes have nearly broken your heart. You love—

FLORENCE. (*Faintly.*) Yes.

KATE. And are beloved ?

FLORENCE. Yes.

KATE. But your promise to me keeps you from happiness ?

FLORENCE. Yes.

KATE. Be happy, then; I give my cordial consent to your marriage.

FLORENCE. (*rising.*) Aunt Hannah—I— (*Faints.*)

HARRY. (*Catching her.*) Kate, she has fainted; we have gone too far !

KATE. Get some water ! Take off that disguise; let her see a face she knows. (*Takes* FLORENCE.)

HARRY. (*Tearing off disguise, and getting water.*) Here !

KATE. Roll up the chair ! (*Places* FLORENCE *in chair.*) Now bathe her face; she must not see me. (*Bundles up* HARRY'S *disguise and exit.*)

HARRY. Oh, if we have really made her ill ! (*Bathing* FLORENCE'S *face.*)

FLORENCE. (*Faintly.*) Oh ! (*Opens her eyes.*) Harry ! I—where is—oh, what is it all ?

HARRY. You must have fainted, dear. I came to meet Kate, and found you insensible.

FLORENCE. (*Looking round.*) But the Professor ?

HARRY. I did not see him.

FLORENCE. Aunt Hannah ?

HARRY. Do not tremble so; you see there is no one here but ourselves.

FLORENCE. But the professor was here, and the spirit of my aunt.

HARRY. You are jesting.

FLORENCE. I speak only the truth. I saw her ! She spoke to me !

HARRY. (*Bitterly.*) To remind you, I presume, that her tyranny still holds you from happiness ?

FLORENCE. No. (*Blushing.*) She was kind and good—she—

HARRY. (*Eagerly.*) She released you ?

FLORENCE. Do you then care to hear ?

HARRY. Hurrah for Professor Jackson ! (*Embracing* FLORENCE.) Then there is still happiness for us.

FLORENCE. But, Harry, where can Kate be ?

Enter KATE, *as if in haste.*

KATE. Oh, I am so sorry to be late! But mamma was so long at the dressmaker's I could not get here one moment sooner. Now we can see if Professor Jackson can call up spirits.

FLORENCE. No, no, another time. I cannot bear any more.

HARRY. You are quite right. Who knows if she, the ghost, I mean, might not change her mind?

KATE. What ghost? Oh, Flo! did you really see anything?

FLORENCE. I will tell you when we get home. My carriage is here; will you not drive home with me—you—and— (*hesitating, and then extending her hand to* HARRY) Mr. Hay?

HENRY. Forbidden. You are never to use that name again, un-til—

KATE. When?

HARRY. I can retaliate by calling Florence *Mrs.* Hay. (*Leads* FLORENCE *to door, and exit.*)

KATE. There's gratitude! They've forgotten my existence. They will probably drive home without me. Shades of Professor Jackson's Indians, what barbarity!

Enter HARRY.

HARRY. What are you waiting for?

KATE. Oh, you have remembered me! I was just about to personate Miss Hannah again, in order to deliver my opinion of—a horrid man.

CURTAIN.

EXTREMES MEET.

ℭharacters.

MR. JOHN DUNCOMBE—*An Elderly Gentleman.*
MRS. JOHN DUNCOMBE—*His Wife.*
ALGERNON EASTBURN—*A Wealthy Young Gentleman, fashionable and fastidious.*
THOMAS BLAKE—*A Western Farmer, not wealthy.*
ESTELLE DUNCOMBE—MR. DUNCOMBE'S *Niece, an heiress.*
SUSAN HOLT—MRS. DUNCOMBE'S *Niece, a farmer's daughter.*

SCENE I.—*A handsomely furnished modern Parlor. Open piano, with music scattered upon it; sofas; table, with photograph-album and other books. Curtain rises, discovering* MR. *and* MRS. DUNCOMBE *playing backgammon.*

MR. DUNCOMBE. It is your throw, my dear.

MRS. DUNCOMBE. Oh, John, I can't play at all, I am so excited thinking about the dear girls! Wasn't it a splendid idea of mine to invite Mr. Eastburn and Mr. Blake to make us a little visit?

MR. DUNCOMBE. H'm—h'm! The fact is, my dear, that your Uncle James's money is developing some wonderful new traits in your character, and match-making is one of them.

MRS. DUNCOMBE. But, John, the poor, dear girls have no mother; and Estelle will certainly be the victim of some fortune-hunter, if we do not take care of her. And as for poor Susan, she has no chance at all, without one penny, unless Tom does take a fancy to her.

MR. DUNCOMBE. Oh, she is to marry *Tom.*

MRS. DUNCOMBE. Why, of course! They are exactly suited to each other. Tom won't care for a rich wife; but he must have a capable, useful one, and Susan is a capital housekeeper, a good seamstress—everything a farmer's wife ought to be.

MR. DUNCOMBE. Yes! yes! And I suppose Estelle is to marry Algernon.

MRS. DUNCOMBE. *Why, of course!* You know he is as rich as

she is, so he cannot be suspected of fortune-hunting.   And they are *exactly suited to each other*.   Both accomplished and refined, accustomed to society, graceful—

MR. DUNCOMBE. Useless and ornamental!

MRS. DUNCOMBE. Well, they are rich enough to be lazy.   Poor Susie, now, must be active; and Tom's farm would not flourish with an ornamental master.   But some one is coming! (*Throws dice.*)   Six and four!   I take your man up.

Enter ESTELLE, *very handsomely dressed in the height of the fashion, and* THOMAS BLAKE, *very plainly dressed in a gray suit.*

ESTELLE. (*As if continuing a conversation.*) And all these common vegetables really have such pretty blossoms?

MRS. DUNCOMBE. (*Aside.*) Dear! dear! Where is Algernon? The idea of Tom's boring Estelle with a conversation about *vegetables!*

TOM. Nature is a master-hand, Miss Estelle, in combining the useful and beautiful.   I assure you there is no prettier flower-bed than a bean-patch in blossom.   (*During all the conversation between the others,* MR. *and* MRS. DUNCOMBE *play backgammon, the lady in an absent-minded way, watching the others.*)

ESTELLE. (*Fanning herself languidly.*) Charming, I have no doubt.   (*Sits down;* TOM *standing, leaning over her chair, and appearing to converse.*)

MRS. DUNCOMBE. (*Rattling dice.*) Where can Algernon be?

Enter ALGERNON, *dressed in the height of the fashion, following* SUSAN, *who wears white, with no ornament but a few natural flowers.*

ALGERNON. You are cruel!   Pray let me have— (*Stops suddenly, as if just seeing the others.*)

MRS. DUNCOMBE. Susie! do be less boisterous.   You should enter a parlor quietly, as Estelle does.

SUSAN. Yes, auntie. (*Aside to* ALGERNON.)   But I never can be like Estelle, you know.

ALGERNON. (*Aside to* SUSAN.) It would be a burning shame if you were; she is all affectation.

MRS. DUNCOMBE. Estelle, dear, sing that new song for us.   Algernon will turn your music. Susan, did you show Tom the pictures we put in the album yesterday? (ALGERNON *and* ESTELLE *go to piano;* TOM *and* SUSAN *to table; all moving reluctantly.*)

ESTELLE. (*To* ALGERNON.) It is from the new opera.

ALGERNON. (*Selecting music.*) This?

ESTELLE. Yes. (*Sings some very showy selection. While she sings,* ALGERNON *looks at* SUSAN, *and* TOM *at* ESTELLE. TOM *rises and saunters to piano, while* ALGERNON *goes over to table, and converses in dumb show with* SUSAN.)

ESTELLE. (*Finishing the song.*) Something simpler would suit you better, perhaps, Mr. Blake?

TOM. Not at all. I have heard ballads murdered by untrained voices, till simplicity has quite lost its charm.

ESTELLE. High treason! I thought Nature was your closest friend?

TOM. So, indeed, she is. But one may— (*Sinks his voice to a confidential tone.*)

SUSAN. (*Sighing.*) I wish I could sing as Estelle does!

ALGERNON. A foolish wish. All those trills and cadenzas are perfectly meaningless. To me a simple ballad, sung as I heard the "Land of the Leal" sung this morning, is far sweeter.

SUSAN. (*Blushing.*) You heard! Why, it was scarcely sunrise!

ALGERNON. And you give me credit, I do not doubt, for sleeping till noon. But I am not quite a drone, though never such a busy bee as you are.

SUSAN. One must do something; and since I have no accomplishments, I patch and darn, bake and broil, like a housemaid.

ALGERNON. Would that some of our fine ladies— (*Sinks his voice to a confidential tone.*)

MRS. DUNCOMBE. (*Briskly.*) Dear me, we are all going to sleep. (*Pushes board aside.*) Come, young people, have a waltz. I will play for you. Algernon, take Estelle. Susan is waiting for you, Tom. (*She plays a waltz. The others pair off reluctantly as proposed, dance a few moments languidly, then stop.*)

ESTELLE. It is so warm to dance!

SUSAN. Yes, it is warm.

TOM. (*Aside to* ESTELLE.) But if you would take just one turn with *me.*

ESTELLE. (*With animation.*) Certainly! (*They waltz.*)

ALGERNON. Miss Susan, may I have the honor?

SUSAN. With pleasure! (*They all waltz with great animation.*)

MRS. DUNCOMBE. (*Looking up.*) Goodness me! (*Lets her hands fall with a crash on piano.*)

MR. DUNCOMBE. (*Aside.*) But, of course, Estelle and Algernon, Tom and Susie, are exactly suited to each other.

SCENE II.—*Same as before.*

Curtain rises, discovering TOM *pacing up and down, in a rage.*

TOM. Heartless coquette! I might have known that so dainty a darling would never care for a rough farmer like me! And yet— (*sighing*) I did think she might be won to love me. She seemed to admire our free Western life, and sometimes I fancied—pshaw! fancied, indeed! How could I imagine she loved me, with such a fine fop to contrast my manners with as Algernon Eastburn! Puppy! But Mrs. Duncombe says they are going to be married! I'll pack my trunk and start for Minnesota to-night! (*Exit.*)

Enter MRS. DUNCOMBE *and* ALGERNON.

ALGERNON. (*Gloomily.*) I am more than surprised—I am stunned!

MRS. DUNCOMBE. Pa and I are delighted with the match. Tom needs just such a wife as Susan, for he must make his own way, and she has lived on a farm all her life. She is not accomplished and brilliant like dear Estelle, but she is thoroughly well educated, and the most practical little thing.

ALGERNON. Yes. (*Aside.*) She's worth about ten dozen of such frivolous butterflies as Estelle.

MRS. DUNCOMBE. But I must go to give some orders to the servants. I will send Estelle to keep you company. (*Exit* MRS. DUNCOMBE.)

ALGERNON. Now, who would believe that sweet, artless girl such an arrant flirt? Going to marry that great, coarse Western fellow! Why, his neckties would throw me into convulsions. I thought Estelle was toning him down, but it was Susan. And she is going to marry him! Well, I'm not going to break my heart for *any* woman; but I think I'll go back to New York; I don't care to see this interesting couple after their engagement. Oh, Susie! Susie! Do you guess what a true love you have slighted? (*Exit.*)

Enter ESTELLE, *very slowly, with a piece of fancy work in her hand. She sits down and sighs. Enter* SUSAN, *with a piece of plain sewing. She sits down and sighs.*

ESTELLE. What are you making, dear?

SUSAN. Only hemming some handkerchiefs. I cannot embroider such lovely things as you do.

ESTELLE. They would be of very little use on a farm.

SUSAN. (*Sighing.*) Very little use. (*Aside.*) How did she know I meant to go home? (*Aloud.*) But they will be beautiful in your city rooms.

ESTELLE. I have so many. (*Aside.*) Who told her I was to return to the city? (*Aloud.*) Mr. Blake is a fine, noble fellow, Susie; I hope—

SUSAN. He is too blunt to please me! His manners have no polish, no refinement.

ESTELLE. But he has such a frank, winning address, and, if he is not dandified, I am sure he is never rude.

SUSAN. But Mr. Eastburn has perfect manners.

ESTELLE. He is too dandified! His whole heart is in his boots and neckties. I like a man to have a soul above dress.

SUSAN. And he has. It is custom, habit, that makes him fastidious. Under all his refined manners he has a true, manly nature.

ESTELLE. Perhaps he has. But, after all, you prefer Mr. Blake's honest, outspoken ways.

SUSAN. And you must admire Mr. Eastburn.

ESTELLE. I do not, then! What made you think so?

SUSAN. Why, Aunt Lizzie said you were engaged to him.

ESTELLE. I! Engaged to Algernon Eastburn! Aunt Lizzie said that?

SUSAN. Well, she said you were to be married very soon.

ESTELLE. When you marry Mr. Blake.

SUSAN. I! I marry Tom Blake! Never!

ESTELLE. But Aunt Lizzie told me you were to be married!

SUSAN. She dreamed it! Why, Estelle, I always thought he was desperately in love with you!

ESTELLE. (*Laughing.*) Oh, you darling! So did I.

SUSAN. And I am sure, certain, he never said one word of courting to me.

ESTELLE. But Algernon has. I am not blind, my dear.

SUSAN. (*Blushing.*) Did you think Mr. Eastburn—liked—me ?

ESTELLE. I am sure, positive, he loves you.

SUSAN. You dear girl! So am I.

Enter ALGERNON *and* TOM. ESTELLE *and* SUSAN *sew as if not seeing them.* ALGERNON *goes to* ESTELLE, TOM *to* SUSAN.

ALGERNON. What a lovely piece of embroidery, Miss Duncombe! (*Aside.*) Confound the fellow, he is taking her hand. (*Looking at* TOM *and* SUSAN.)

TOM. Industrious as usual, Miss Holt. (*Taking hold of* SUSAN'S *work, but looking at* ESTELLE.)

SUSAN. Only hemming a handkerchief.

TOM. (*Aside.*) How interested he is in her work!

ALGERNON. Have you any commissions for New York, Miss Duncombe?   I shall probably return to-morrow.

TOM. I must bid you all farewell, Miss Holt, I am going West to-night.

ESTELLE. To-morrow!

SUSAN. To-night!

ESTELLE. Susie, dear, did you know Mr. Eastburn talks of leaving us?

SUSAN. Estelle, did you know Mr. Blake is going home? (*They all rise.* SUSAN *bends her face over her work.* ESTELLE *walks to background.* TOM *follows* ESTELLE.)

ALGERNON. (*To* SUSAN.) You—you will permit me to offer my congratulations, Miss Holt.

SUSAN. (*Very low.*) Upon what?

ALGERNON. Blake is a fine fellow. (*Aside.*) Confound him!

SUSAN. Yes, he is a very nice man, and I—I hope Estelle will return his affection.

ALGERNON. Estelle! his affection!

SUSAN. (*Innocently.*) Why, surely you must have noticed how devoted he has been to her all summer.

ALGERNON. (*Rapturously.*) So he has! Oh, if you knew the load— (*Sinks his voice.*)

TOM. (*Coming forward with* ESTELLE.) And you are sure that Algernon loves Susan as, my darling, I love you?

ESTELLE. Look at them, Tom!

ALGERNON. (*Embracing* SUSAN.) You have made me the happiest man in the world !

TOM. (*Embracing* ESTELLE.) Always excepting me !

Enter MR. *and* MRS. DUNCOMBE.

MRS. DUNCOMBE. (*Aside.*) Dear, dear ! There is Tom pestering poor Estelle again. (*Aloud.*) Algernon, do show Estelle the new ferns. Tom, you have not taken Susie to see the carnations.

ALGERNON. Excuse me, Mrs. Duncombe, but I prefer to escort my promised wife myself. (*Offers arm to* SUSAN.)

ESTELLE. And I, dear auntie, can find the ferns with Tom.

MRS. DUNCOMBE. You don't mean that you are engaged to Tom, Estelle ?

ESTELLE. With your consent.

MRS. DUNCOMBE. And you to Algernon, Susie ?

SUSAN. If you are willing.

MRS. DUNCOMBE. But you don't suit each other at all.

MR. DUNCOMBE. Pardon me, my dear, but for a match-maker you seem to have forgotten one rule as old as the hills.

ALGERNON. And that is—

MR. DUNCOMBE. Extremes meet.

CURTAIN.

Graham's School Dialogues for Young People. A new and
original collection of Dialogues intended for Anniversaries and Exhibitions.
By George C. Graham. These dialogues have been written expressly to give
advanced scholars an opportunity for displaying their dramatic powers and
ingenuity; they are exceedingly amusing, and full of ludicrous and telling
stage-situations.

CONTENTS.	Males.	Females.	CONTENTS.	Males.	Females.
The Empty House	5	1	A Nightmare of India	7	
Turning the Tables	4		An Indian Raid	3	2
A Doctor by Proxy	6	1	Going ! Going ! Gone !	6	2
Strategy		4	The Book-Peddler	3	2
The Picnic Party	3	3	The Burglar-Alarm	2	3
An Aspirant for Fame	3		Missed His Chance	5	1
The New Boy	4		The Girl of the Period	2	3
Which was the Hero ?	3		The Photograph Gallery	4	3
Astonishing the Natives		3	The Elocution Class	6	
The Critics	6		Love and Stratagem	1	2
The Expected Visitor		6	Extremes Meet	3	3

16mo, 176 pages, illuminated paper cover. Price.................... 30 cts.
"   "   "   "   board "   "   ....50 cts.

Burbank's Recitations and Readings. A collection of Hu-
morous, Dramatic and Dialect Selections, edited and arranged for public
reading or recitation, by Alfred P. Burbank. Containing many choice selections never before in print, as well as some old favorites.

CONTENTS.

Conn's Description of the Fox Hunt.	Surly Tim's Trouble.
The Tailor's Thimble.	The Water Mill.
The O'Kelly Cabin.	The Fall of the Pemberton Mill.
The "Oolaghaun."	Death of Little Jo.
Rip Van Winkle.	The Soldier's Reprieve.
The Death of the Old Squire.	Brother Anderson.
Schneider's Description of " Leah."	A Basket of Flowers.
Love on the Half-Shell.	Mah'sr John.
Father Phil's Collection.	Daddy Flick's Spree.
A Literary Nightmare.	The Ballad of Babie Bell.
The Birth of Ireland.	Aux Italiens.
The Irishman's Panorama.	Breitmann in Maryland.
Money Musk.	" The Morning Argus " Obituary De-
The Ship of Faith.	partment.
Pup-pup-poetry.	Snyder's Nose.
A Senator Entangled.	Magdalena, or the Spanish Duel.
Christmas-Night in the Quarters.	" Bay Billy."
A Love Song.	Return of the Hillside Legion.
The Steamboat Race.	Cuddle Doon.
The Swell.	Sheridan's Ride.
The Little Stow-away.	The Power of Prayer.

16mo, 150 pp. Price.................................25 cts.

Frost's Dialogues for Young Folks. A Collection of Original, Moral and Humorous Dialogues. Adapted to the use of School and Church Exhibitions, Family Gatherings and Juvenile Celebrations on all Occasions. By S. A. Frost.

CONTENTS.	Boys.	Girls.	CONTENTS.	Boys.	Girls.
Novel Reading	1	1	A Place for Everything	2	2
The Bound Girl		4	I Want to be a Soldier	2	
Writing a Letter		2	Self-Denial	2	3
The Wonderful Scholar	1	2	The Traveler	3	
Slang	4		Idleness the Mother of Evil		4
The Language of Flowers		4	The French Lesson	5	
The Morning Call		4	Civility Never Lost	3	2
The Spoiled Child		4	Who Works the Hardest?	1	1
The Little Travelers	2	2	The Everlasting Talker		5
Little Things	1	1	The Epicure	3	
Generosity		2	True Charity	1	7
Country Cousins		4	Starting in Life	1	1
Winning the Prize		2	I Didn't Mean Anything	4	
The Unfortunate Scholar		4	Ambition	5	
The Day of Misfortunes	3		Choosing a Trade	9	
Jealousy	1	3	The Schoolmaster Abroad	7	
The May Queen		5	White Lies	3	
Temptation Resisted	3		The Hoyden	1	3

16mo, Paper Covers. Price..30 cts.
Bound in Boards..50 cts.

Frost's New Book of Dialogues. A series of entirely new and original humorous Dialogues, specially adapted for performance at School Anniversaries and Exhibitions, or other Festivals and Celebrations of the Young Folks.

CONTENTS.	Boys.	Girls.	CONTENTS.	Boys.	Girls.
Slang versus Dictionary	3		The Intelligence Office	4	3
Country or City		3	Cats	6	
Turning the Tables	3		Too Fine and Too Plain		3
The Force of Imagination		4	The Fourth of July Oration	5	
The Modern Robinson Crusoe	5		The Sewing Circle		7
The Threatened Visit		3	Fix	2	
The Dandy and the Boor	3		The Yankee Aunt	2	3
Nature versus Education		4	The Walking Encyclopedia	5	
The British Lion and Ameri-can Hoosier	3		The Novel Readers		3
			The Model Farmer	2	
Curing a Pedant		5	Buying a Sewing-Machine	4	2
Pursuit of Knowledge under Difficulties	2		Sam Weller's Valentine	2	
			The Hungry Traveler	2	
The Daily Governess		2	Deaf as a Post	1	2
The Army and Navy	2	2	The Rehearsal	6	
Economy is Wealth		3			

These Dialogues are admirably adapted for home performance, as they require no set scenery for their representation. By S. A. Frost. 180 pages, 16mo.

Paper covers. Price..30 cts.
Bound in boards, cloth back..50 cts.

Frost's Humorous and Exhibition Dialogues. This is a collection of sprightly, original Dialogues, in Prose and Verse, intended to be spoken at School Exhibitions. By S. A. Frost.

CONTENTS.	Boys.	Girls.	CONTENTS.	Boys.	Girls.
Bumps	4		The Chatterbox		4
Amateur Farming		2	Putting on Airs	3	
The Valentine	2		Writing a Tragedy	2	
Aunt Bethiah's Journey		4	Morning Calls		6
Will You Advertise?	2		When the Cat's Away the		
Sallie's Visit to the City		3	Mice will Play	6	9
Country Quiet	4		Very Bashful	1	3
Circumstances Alter Cases		4	It Never Rains but it Pours	2	
School or Work	4		A Slight Mistake	2	2
Bella's Visit to Camp		4	Munchausen Outdone	3	
The Hypochondriac	2		The Train to Mauro	2	1
Cross Purposes		4	The Unwilling Witness	2	
Rural Felicity	2		The Age of Progress	2	1

The Dialogues are all good, and will recommend themselves to those who desire to have innocent fun—the prevailing feature at a school celebration.
180 pages. Paper covers. Price ....30 cts.
Bound in boards ....50 cts.

Holmes' Very Little Dialogues for Very Little Folks. Containing forty-seven new and original dialogues, with short and easy parts, almost entirely in words of one syllable, suited to the capacity and comprehension of very young children.

CONTENTS.	Boys.	Girls.	CONTENTS.	Boys.	Girls.
The Bird's Nest	2	1	The Cow in the Garden	2	
All About Two Dolls		2	Our Verse	1	1
I'm a Man	2	1	Jack's Nap	4	
What are Little Boys Good			The Little Beggars	1	3
For?		2	The Doll's Sash		3
The Party		2	I Wish	2	4
The Rose Bush			The Cousin From the City	1	2
Which is Best?	1	1	Afraid of the Dark	2	1
The Drum		2	May's Five Dollar Note		3
Willie's Walk	1	1	The Snow	3	
The Parrot		2	Harry's Wish	2	
The Story		2	The Dead Bird		2
How Daisy Went to School	1	2	The Orange Tree	2	1
Clara's Gifts		2	Little by Little		2
What Tommy Found	2		Kitty's Bath		2
The Blind Man		2	A Stitch in Time Saves Nine		2
Poor Sick Lucy	1	1	Keeping Store	2	1
Josie's Fault		3	The Stolen Pets		2
The Rain Fairy		2	Lulu's Picture	1	2
Guess!	1	2	Mother Goose's Party	3	4
The Sick Doll	1	1	Oh, Dear!		3
Work or Play	1	1	That Echo	2	1
The Boat	2		The New Quarters	1	2
Little Mischief		1	Visit of Santa Claus	10	8

Paper covers. Price ....30 cts.
Bound in boards, cloth back ....50 cts.

McBride's Comic Dialogues for School Exhibitions and Literary Entertainments.

A collection of Original Humorous Dialogues, especially designed for the development and display of amateur dramatic talent, and introducing a variety of sentimental, sprightly, comic and genuine Yankee characters, and other ingeniously developed eccentricities. By H. Elliott McBride.

CONTENTS.	Boys.	Girls.	CONTENTS.	Boys.	Girls.
From Punkin Ridge	6	3	Something to our Advantage	4	1
Arabella's Poor Relations	2	2	Jimtown Lyceum	5	3
A Row in the Kitchen	1	2	United at Last	3	1
The Gumtown Woman's Association	2	6	Scene in a Backwoods School	8	
			Trouble in a Mormon Family	1	5
Advertising for a Husband	3	1	Josiah's Proposal	3	1
Ivery Inch a Gintleman	3	2	The Stage-Struck Blacksmith	4	2
Goose Hollow Farmer's Club	9		A Rumpus in a Shoemaker's		
Reunion of Peter and Jane	2	2	Shop	2	1
Awful Boots	3	1	Recess Speeches	5	5
A Pain in the Side	1	2			

16mo, illuminated paper covers. Price ....30 cts.

Bound in boards ....50 cts.

McBride's All Kinds of Dialogues.

A collection of Original Humorous and Domestic Dialogues, introducing Yankee, French, Irish, Dutch, and other characters. Excellently adapted for Amateur performances. By H. Elliott McBride.

CONTENTS.	Boys.	Girls.	CONTENTS.	Boys.	Girls.
Jeduthan and Jane	5	4	Personating Olders		2
Cured	4	1	Peleg and Patience	3	3
Out All Around	1	2	Snarl's Children	3	1
The Pine Valley Boys	5		Woman's Rights	1	4
Marrying a Poetess	5	4	A Boys' Meeting	6	
The Old Aunt	3	1	Mr. Worth's Farm Hands	5	2
Rejected	1	2	Charlie's Speech	2	1
An Evening at Home	1	3	Mrs. Thompson's Nephew	2	1
John Robb and Anna Cobb	3	3	An Anti-Railroad Meeting	8	
A Reconstructed Man	1	2	Saved	4	
An Interrupted Proposal	1	2	The Bungtown Lyceum	5	4
A Visit from the Smiths	4	4			

This book constitutes a second series of McBride's Comic Dialogues, and affords an additional variety f the spirited dialogues and short dramatic scenes contained in the latter book. They are all entirely original, and develop in a marked degree the eccentricities and peculiarities of the various ideal, but genuine characters which are represented in them. They are specially adapted for School Exhibitions and all other celebrations where the success of the entertainment is partly or entirely dependent on the efforts of the young folks.

Illuminated paper covers. Price............................30 cts.

Bound in boards..50 cts.

MARTINE'S DROLL DIALOGUES

AND

LAUGHABLE RECITATIONS.

By Arthur Martine, author of "Martine's Letter-Writer," etc., etc. A collection of Humorous Dialogues, Comic Recitations, Brilliant Burlesque, Spirited Stump Speeches and Ludicrous Farces, adapted for School and other Celebrations and for Home Amusement.

CONTENTS.

188 pages. Paper covers. Price.......................................**30 cts.**

Bound in boards, cloth back... ....**50 cts.**

BARTON'S COMIC RECITATIONS

AND

HUMOROUS DIALOGUES.

Containing a variety of Comic Recitations in Prose and Poetry, Amusing Dialogues, Burlesque Scenes, Eccentric Orations, Humorous Interludes and Laughable Farces. Designed for School Commencements and Amateur Theatricals. Edited by Jerome Barton.

CONTENTS.

This is one of the best collection of Humorous Pieces especially adapted to the Parlor Stage that has ever been published. 16 mo. 180 pages.

Paper covers. Price ....30 cts.

Bound in boards, cloth back.............................. • ....50 cts.

BRUDDER BONES' BOOK OF STUMP SPEECHES

AND

BURLESQUE ORATIONS.

Also containing Humorous Lectures, Ethiopian Dialogues, Plantation Scenes, Negro Farces and Burlesques, Laughable interludes and Comic Recitations. Compiled and edited by John F. Scott.

CONTENTS.

16 mo. 188 pages. Paper covers. Price ....**30 cts.**

Bound in boards, illuminated..**50 cts.**

Kavanaugh's Juvenile Speaker. For very little boys and

girls. Containing short and easily-learned Speeches and Dialogues, expressly adapted for School Celebrations, May-Day Festivals and other Children's Entertainments. By Mrs. Russell Kavanaugh. This book is just the thing for Teachers, as it gives a great number of short pieces for very young children, with directions for appropriate dresses.

It includes a complete programme for a May-Day Festival, with opening chorus and appropriate speeches for nineteen boys and girls, including nearly forty additional speeches for young and very small children.

It introduces the May-Pole Dance, plainly described in every detail, and forming a very attractive and pleasing exhibition.

Besides the above, it contains the following Dialogues and Recitations, for two, three or more boys and girls of various ages:

	Boys.	Girls.		Boys.	Girls.
Salutatory	1		Balance Due	1	
Salutatory	1		Recitation	1	
Opening Song		13	The Coming Woman	1	
Opening Recitation	1	12	Speech		1
An Interrupted Recitation	1	1	The Power of Temper	1	
An Imaginative Invention	1		Truth and Falsehood	1	
Speech		1	Recitation		1
A Joyful Surprise	3	2	Recitation	1	
An Oration	1		Recitation	1	
How He Had Him	2	1	Christmas Forty Years Ago	1	
The Old Maid		1	Speech		1
The Old Bachelor	1		Trying Hard	1	
Poetry, Prose and Fact	1	2	The School-Boy	1	
The Dumb Wife	1		Recitation		1
To Inconsistent Husbands	1		"I Told You So"	1	
Small Pitchers have Large Ears		2	Speech	1	
Sour Grapes	1		Speech		1
Not Worth While to Hate	1		Speech		1
A Strike Among the Flowers		1	Choosing a Name		1
A Witty Retort	1		Baby Bye		4
The Young Critic	2		Dialogue	2	
"They Say"		1	Little Puss		1
Speech	1		Poor Men vs. Rich Men	1	
"Angels Can Do No More."	1		Helping Papa and Mamma	2	2
Recitation	1		Annabel's First Party		1
Dialogue	1	1	The Spendthrift Doll		1
Holiday Speech	1		The Little Mushrooms		3
The Love-Scrape	2	1	Valedictory	1	
An Old Ballad	1	1	Riding in the Cars		1
The Milkmaid	1	1	Riding in the Cars	1	
Billy Grimes, the Drover		2	Speech	1	
Grandmother's Beau		1	The Cobbler's Secret	1	
Speech	1		Dialogue	1	1
Honesty the Best Policy	4		Valedictory	1	

The whole embraces a hundred and twenty-three easy and very effective pieces, from which selections can be made to suit the capacities of boys and girls of from two to sixteen years of age.

16mo, illuminated paper cover. Price...................................30 cts.
  "   Boards..50 cts.

The Young Debater and Chairman's Assistant. By an ex-Member of the Philadelphia Bar. Containing instructions how to Form and Conduct Societies; how to Form and Conduct Clubs and other organized Associations; Rules of Order for the Government of their Business and Debates; how to Compose Resolutions, Reports and Petitions; how to Organize and Manage Public Meetings, Celebrations, Dinners, Pic-Nics and Conventions; Duties of the President and other Officers of a Club or Society, with Official Forms; Hints on Debate and Public Speaking; Forms for Constitutions and By-Laws. To any one who desires to become familiar with the duties of an Officer or Committee-man in a Society or Association this work will be invaluable, as it contains the most minute instructions in everything that pertains to the routine of Society Business. 152 pages, paper covers...30 cts. Bound in boards, with cloth back.............. ....50 cts.

How to Conduct a Debate. A Series of Complete Debates, Outlines of Debates and Questions for Discussion. In the complete debates, the questions for discussion are defined, the debate formally opened, an array of brilliant arguments adduced on either side, and the debate closed according to parliamentary usages. The second part consists of questions for debate, with heads of arguments, for and against, given in a condensed form, for the speakers to enlarge upon to suit their own fancy. In addition to these are a large collection of debatable questions. The authorities to be referred to for information being given at the close of every debate throughout the work. By Frederic Rowton. 232 pages, 16mo. Paper covers...50 cts. Bound in boards, cloth back..75 cts.

The Vegetable Garden. Containing thorough instructions for Sowing, Planting and Cultivating all kinds of Vegetables, with plain directions for preparing, manuring and tilling the soil to suit each plant; including, also, a summary of the work to be done in a Vegetable Garden during each month of the year. This work embraces, in a condensed but thoroughly practical form, all the information that either an amateur or a practical gardener can require in connection with the successful raising of Vegetables and Herbs. It also gives separate directions for the cultivation of some seventy different Vegetables, including all the varieties of esculents that form the ordinary stock of a kitchen garden or truck farm. By James Hogg. 140 pages, paper covers................................ ....30 cts. Full cloth.................. ....50 cts.

The Amateur Trapper and Trap-Maker's Guide. A complete and carefully prepared treatise on the art of Trapping, Snaring and Netting. This comprehensive work is embellished with fifty engraved illustrations; and these, together with the clear explanations which accompany them, will enable anybody of moderate comprehension to make and set any of the traps described. It also gives the baits usually employed by the most successful Hunters and Trappers, and exposes their secret methods of attracting and catching animals, birds, etc., with scarcely a possibility of failure. Large 16mo, paper covers.... ....50 cts. Bound in boards, cloth back..75 cts.

How to Write a Composition. The use of this excellent handbook will save the student the many hours of labor too often wasted in trying to write a plain composition. It affords a perfect skeleton of one hundred and seventeen different subjects, with their headings or divisions clearly defined, and each heading filled in with the ideas which the subject suggests; so that all the writer has to do, in order to produce a good composition, is to enlarge on them to suit his taste and inclination. 178 pages, paper covers...30 cts. Bound in boards, cloth back.......................................50 cts.

BEECHER'S RECITATIONS

AND

READINGS.

Humorous, Serious, Dramatic, including Prose and Poetical Selections in Dutch, French, Yankee, Irish, Backwoods, Negro and other Dialects. Edited by Alvah C. Beecher. This excellent selection has been compiled to meet a growing demand for Public Readings, and contains a number of the favorite pieces that have been rendered with telling effect by the most popular Public Readers of the present time. It includes, also, choice selections for Recitations, and is, therefore, admirably adapted for use at Evening Entertainments, School Celebrations, and other Festival occasions.

CONTENTS.

Paper covers. Price..30 cts.
Bound in boards, cloth back.......................................50 cts.

·HOWARD'S RECITATIONS.

Comic, Serious and Pathetic. Being a carefully selected collection of fresh Recitations in Prose and Poetry, suitable for Anniversaries, Exhibitions, Social Gatherings, and Evening Parties; affording, also, an abundance of excellent material for practice and declamation. Edited by Clarence J. Howard.

CONTENTS.

16mo. 180 pages. Paper covers. Price.............................**30 cts.**
Bound in boards, cloth back...**50 cts.**

CHECKERS AND CHESS.

Spayth's American Draught Player; or, The Theory and Practice of the Scientific Game of Checkers. Simplified and Illustrated with Practical Diagrams. Containing upwards of 1,700 Games and Positions. By Henry Spayth. Sixth edition, with over three hundred Corrections and Improvements. Containing: The Standard Laws of the Game—Full instructions—Draught Board Numbered—Names of the Games, and how formed—The "Theory of the Move and its Changes" practically explained and illustrated with Diagrams—Playing Tables for Draught Clubs—New Systems of numbering the Board—Prefixing signs to the Variations—List of Draught Treatises and Publications chronologically arranged. Bound in cloth, gilt side and back..$3.00

Spayth's Game of Draughts. By Henry Spayth. This book is designed as a supplement to the author's first work, "The American Draught Player"; but it is complete in itself. It contains lucid instructions for beginners, laws of the game, diagrams, the score of 3 4 games, together with 34 novel, instructive and ingenious "critical positions." Cloth, gilt back and side..$1.50

Spayth's Draughts or Checkers for Beginners. This treatise was written by Henry Spayth, the celebrated player, and is by far the most complete and instructive elementary work on Draughts ever published. It is profusely illustrated with diagrams of ingenious stratagems, curious positions and perplexing problems, and contains a great variety of interesting and instructive Games, progressively arranged and clearly explained with notes, so that the learner may easily comprehend them. With the aid of this Manual a beginner may soon become a proficient in the game. Cloth, gilt side..75 cts.

Scattergood's Game of Draughts, or Checkers, Simplified and Explained. With practical Diagrams and Illustrations, together with a Checker-Board, numbered and printed in red. Containing the Eighteen Standard Games, with over 200 of the best variations, selected from various authors, with some never before published. By D. Scattergood. Bound in cloth, with flexible covers..50 cts.

Marache's Manual of Chess. Containing a description of the Board and Pieces, Chess Notation, Technical Terms, with diagrams illustrating them, Laws of the Game. Relative Value of Pieces. Preliminary Games for Beginners, Fifty Openings of Games, giving all the latest discoveries of Modern Masters, with the best games and copious notes. Twenty Endings of Games, showing easiest ways of effecting Checkmate, Thirty-six ingenious Diagram Problems, and sixteen curious Chess Stratagems, being one of the best Books for Beginners ever published. By N. Marache. Bound in boards, cloth back..50 cts.
Bound in cloth, gilt side..75 cts.

DICK & FITZGERALD, Publishers,

Box 2975.   NEW YORK.

DIALOGUE BOOKS.

The Dialogues contained in these books are all entirely original; some of them being arranged for one sex only, and others for both sexes combined. They develop in a marked degree the eccentricities and peculiarities of the various characters which are represented in them; and are specially adapted for School Exhibitions and other celebrations, which mainly depend upon the efforts of the young folks.

McBride's Comic Dialogues. A collection of twenty-three Original Humorous Dialogues, especially designed for the display of Amateur dramatic talent, and introducing a variety of sentimental, sprightly, comic and genuine Yankee characters, and other ingeniously developed eccentricities. By H. Elliott McBride. 180 pages, illuminated paper covers..30 cts. Bound in boards... ....50 cts.

McBride's All Kinds of Dialogues. A collection of twenty-five Original, Humorous and Domestic Dialogues, introducing Yankee, Irish, Dutch and other characters. Excellently adapted for Amateur Performances. 180 pages, illuminated paper covers...................30 cts. Bound in boards...50 cts.

Holmes' Very Little Dialogues for Very Little Folks. Containing forty-seven New and Original Dialogues, with short and easy parts, almost entirely in words of one syllable, suited to the capacity and comprehension of very young children. Paper covers.....................30 cts. Bound in boards, cloth back...50 cts.

Frost's Dialogues for Young Folks. A collection of thirty-six Original, Moral and Humorous Dialogues. Adapted for boys and girls between the ages of ten and fourteen years. By S. A. Frost. 176 pages. paper covers...30 cts. Bound in boards...................... ....50 cts.

Frost's New Book of Dialogues. Containing twenty-nine entirely New and Original Humorous Dialogues for boys and girls between the ages of twelve and fifteen years. 180 pages, paper covers.........30 cts. Bound in boards, cloth back............. ....50 cts.

Frost's Humorous and Exhibition Dialogues. This is a collection of twenty-five Sprightly Original Dialogues, in Prose and Verse, intended to be spoken at School Exhibitions. 178 pages, paper covers.30 cts. Bound in boards..50 cts.

WE WILL SEND A CATALOGUE free to any address. containing a list of all the Dialogues in each of the above books, together with the number of boys and girls required to perform them.

DICK & FITZGERALD, Publishers,

Box 2975.   **NEW YORK.**

AMATEUR THEATRICALS.

All the plays in the following excellent books are especially designed for Amateur performance. The majority of them are in one act and one scene, and may be represented in any moderate-sized parlor, without much preparation of costume or scenery.

Burton's Amateur Actor. A complete guide to Private Theatricals; giving plain directions for arranging, decorating and lighting the Stage; with rules and suggestions for mounting, rehearsing and performing all kinds of Plays, Parlor Pantomimes and Shadow Pantomimes. Illustrated with numerous engravings, and including a selection of original Plays, with Prologues, Epilogues, etc. .6mo, illuminated paper cover.....30 cts.
Bound in boards, with cloth back...............................50 cts.

Parlor Theatricals; or, Winter Evenings' Entertainment. Containing Acting Proverbs, Dramatic Charades, Drawing-Room Pantomimes, a Musical Burlesque and an amusing Farce, with instructions for Amateurs. Illustrated with engravings. Paper covers.........30 cts.
Bound in boards, cloth back....... ....50 cts.

Howard's Book of Drawing-Room Theatricals. A collection of twelve short and amusing plays. Some of the plays are adapted for performers of one sex only. 180 pages, paper covers.............30 cts.
Bound in boards, with cloth back...............................50 cts.

Hudson's Private Theatricals. A collection of fourteen humorous plays. Four of these plays are adapted for performance by males only, and three are for females. 180 pages, paper covers.................30 cts.
Bound in boards, with cloth back.. ....50 cts.

Nugent's Burlesque and Musical Acting Charades. Containing ten Charades, all in different styles, two of which are easy and effective Comic Parlor Operas, with Music and Piano-forte Accompaniments. 176 pages, paper covers......................................30 cts.
Bound in boards, cloth back...............................:50 cts.

Frost's Dramatic Proverbs and Charades. Containing eleven Proverbs and fifteen Charades, some of which are for Dramatic Performance, and others arranged for Tableaux Vivants. 176 pages, paper covers.30 cts.
Bound in boards, with cloth back... ....50 cts.

Frost's Parlor Acting Charades. These twelve excellent and original Charades are arranged as short parlor Comedies and Farces, full of brilliant repartee and amusing situations. 182 pages, paper covers..30 cts.
Illuminated boards................................... 50 cts.

Frost's Book of Tableaux and Shadow Pantomimes. A collection of Tableaux Vivants and Shadow Pantomimes, with stage instructions for Costuming. Grouping, etc. 180 pages, paper covers..30 cts.
Bound in boards, with cloth back...............................50 cts.

Frost's Amateur Theatricals. A collection of eight original plays: all short, amusing and new. 180 pages, paper covers......30 cts.
Bound in boards, with cloth back...............................50 cts.

WE WILL SEND A CATALOGUE containing a complete list of all the pieces in each of the above books, together with the number of male and female characters in each play, to any person who will send us their address. Send for one.

DICK & FITZGERALD, Publishers,
Box 2975. NEW YORK.

Mrs. Partington's Carpet-Bag of Fun. A collection of over 1,000 of the most Comical Stories, Amusing Adventures, Side-Splitting Jokes, Cheek-extending Poetry, Funny Conundrums, Queer Sayings of Mrs. Partington, Heart-Rending Puns, Witty Repartees, etc. The whole illustrated by about 150 comic wood-cuts. 12mo, 300 pages, ornamented paper covers......................75 cts.

Harp of a Thousand Strings; or, Laughter for a Life-time. A book of nearly 400 pages ; bound in a handsome gilt cover; crowded full of funny stories, besides being illustrated with over 200 comic engravings, by Darley, McLennan, Bellew, etc............ ....$1.50

Chips from Uncle Sam's Jack-Knife. Illustrated with over 100 Comical Engravings, and comprising a collection of over 500 Laughable Stories, Funny Adventures. Comic Poetry, Queer Conundrums, Terrific Puns and Sentimental Sentences. Large octavo...................25 cts.

Fox's Ethiopian Comicalities. Containing Strange Sayings, Eccentric Doings, Burlesque Speeches, Laughable Drolleries and Funny Stories, as recited by the celebrated Ethiopian Comedian............10 cts.

Ned Turner's Circus Joke Book. A collection of the best Jokes, Bon Mots, Repartees, Gems of Wit and Funny Sayings and Doings of the celebrated Equestrian Clown and Ethiopian Comedian, Ned Turner...10 cts.

Ned Turner's Black Jokes. A collection of Funny Stories, Jokes and Conundrums, interspersed with Witty Sayings and Humorous Dialogues, as given by Ned Turner, the celebrated Ethiopian Delineator..10 cts.

Ned Turner's Clown Joke Book. Containing the best Jokes and Gems of Wit, composed and delivered by the favorite Equestrian Clown, Ned Turner. Selected and arranged by G. E. G...................10 cts.

Charley White's Joke Book. Containing a full exposé of all the most laughable Jokes. Witticisms, etc., as told by the celebrated Ethiopian Comedian, Charles White..............................10 cts.

Black Wit and Darky Conversations. By Charles White. Containing a large collection of laughable Anecdotes, Jokes, Stories. Witticisms and Darky Conversations......................................10 cts.

Yale College Scrapes; or, How the Boys Go It at New Haven. This is a book of 114 pages, containing accounts of all the famous "Scrapes" and "Sprees" of which students of Old Yale have been guilty for the last quarter of a century ....25 cts.

Laughing Gas. An Encyclopedia of Wit, Wisdom and Wind. By Sam Slick, Jr. Comically illustrated with 100 original and laughable Engravings, and nearly 500 side-extending Jokes.................30 cts.

The Knapsack Full of Fun; or, 1,000 Rations of Laughter. Illustrated with over 100 comical engravings, and containing Jokes and Funny Stories. By Doesticks and other witty writers. Large quarto..30 cts.

The Comical Adventures of David Dufficks. Illustrated with over one hundred Funny Engravings. This is a book full of fun....25 cts.

The Plate of Chowder. A Dish for Funny Fellows. Appropriately illustrated with 100 comic engravings. 12mo, paper covers...25 cts

The Young Debater and Chairman's Assistant. By an ex-

Member of the Philadelphia Bar. Containing instructions how to Form and Conduct Societies; how to Form and Conduct Clubs and other organized Associations; Rules of Order for the Government of their Business and Debates; how to Compose Resolutions, Reports and Petitions; how to Organize and Manage Public Meetings, Celebrations, Dinners, Pic-Nics and Conventions; Duties of the President and other Officers of a Club or Society, with Official Forms; Hints on Debate and Public Speaking; Forms for Constitutions and By-Laws. To any one who desires to become familiar with the duties of an Officer or Committee-man in a Society or Association this work will be invaluable, as it contains the most minute instructions in everything that pertains to the routine of Society Business.
152 pages, paper covers...30 cts.
Bound in boards, with cloth back.......... ....50 cts.

How to Conduct a Debate. A Series of Complete Debates,

Outlines of Debates and Questions for Discussion. In the complete debates, the questions for discussion are defined, the debate formally opened, an array of brilliant arguments adduced on either side, and the debate closed according to parliamentary usages. The second part consists of questions for debate, with heads of arguments, for and against, given in a condensed form, for the speakers to enlarge upon to suit their own fancy. In addition to these are a large collection of debatable questions. The authorities to be referred to for information being given at the close of every debate throughout the work. By Frederic Rowton. 232 pages, 16mo.
Paper covers..50 cts.
Bound in boards, cloth back......................................75 cts.

The Vegetable Garden. Containing thorough instructions for

Sowing, Planting and Cultivating all kinds of Vegetables, with plain directions for preparing, manuring and tilling the soil to suit each plant; including, also, a summary of the work to be done in a Vegetable Garden during each month of the year. This work embraces, in a condensed but thoroughly practical form, all the information that either an amateur or a practical gardener can require in connection with the successful raising of Vegetables and Herbs. It also gives separate directions for the cultivation of some seventy different Vegetables, including all the varieties of esculents that form the ordinary stock of a kitchen garden or truck farm. By James Hogg.
140 pages, paper covers..30 cts.
Full cloth..50 cts.

The Amateur Trapper and Trap-Maker's Guide. A com-

plete and carefully prepared treatise on the art of Trapping, Snaring and Netting. This comprehensive work is embellished with fifty engraved illustrations; and these, together with the clear explanations which accompany them, will enable anybody of moderate comprehension to make and set any of the traps described. It also gives the baits usually employed by the most successful Hunters and Trappers, and exposes their secret methods of attracting and catching animals, birds, etc., with scarcely a possibility of failure. Large 16mo, paper covers..............................50 cts.
Bound in boards, cloth back....................................75 cts.

How to Write a Composition. The use of this excellent hand-

book will save the student the many hours of labor too often wasted in trying to write a plain composition. It affords a perfect skeleton of one hundred and seventeen different subjects, with their headings or divisions clearly defined, and each heading filled in with the ideas which the subject suggests; so that all the writer has to do, in order to produce a good composition, is to enlarge on them to suit his taste and inclination.
178 pages, paper covers..30 cts.
Bound in boards, cloth back....................................50 cts.

Barber's American Book of Ready-Made Speeches.

Containing 159 original examples of Humorous and Serious Speeches, suitable for every possible occasion where a speech may be called for, together with appropriate replies to each. Including:

Presentation Speeches.	*Off-Hand Speeches on a Variety of Subjects.*
Convivial Speeches.	
Festival Speeches.	*Miscellaneous Speeches.*
Addresses of Congratulation.	*Toasts and Sentiments for Public and Private Entertainments.*
Addresses of Welcome.	
Addresses of Compliment.	*Preambles and Resolutions of Congratulation, Compliment and Condolence.*
Political Speeches.	
Dinner and Supper Speeches for Clubs, etc.	

With this book any person may prepare himself to make a neat little speech, or reply to one when called upon to do so. They are all short, appropriate and witty, and even ready speakers may profit by them. Paper....5U cts.
Bound in boards, cloth back................................75 cts.

Day's American Ready-Reckoner. By B. H. Day. This

Ready-Reckoner is composed of Original Tables, which are positively correct, having been revised in the most careful manner. It is a book of 192 pages, and embraces more matter than 500 pages of any other Reckoner. It contains: Tables for Rapid Calculations of Aggregate Values, Wages, Salaries, Board, Interest Money, etc.; Tables of Timber and Plank Measurement; Tables of Board and Log Measurement, and a great variety of Tables and useful calculations which it would be impossible to enumerate in an advertisement of this limited space. All the information in this valuable book is given in a simple manner, and is made so plain, that any person can use it at once without any previous study or loss of time.
Bound in boards, with cloth back....................................50 cts.
Bound in cloth, gilt back..75 cts.

The Art and Etiquette of Making Love. A Manual of Love,

Courtship and Matrimony. It tells

How to cure bashfulness,	*How to break off an engagement,*
How to commence a courtship,	*How to act after an engagement,*
How to please a sweetheart or lover,	*How to act as bridesmaid or groomsman.*
How to write a love-letter,	
How to "pop the question,"	*How the etiquette of a wedding and the after reception should be observed,*
How to act before and after a proposal,	
How to accept or reject a proposal,	

And, in fact, how to fulfill every duty and meet every contingency connected with courtship and matrimony. 175 pages. Paper covers ....30 cts.
Bound in boards, cloth back..50 cts.

Frank Converse's Complete Banjo Instructor Without a

Master. Containing a choice collection of Banjo Solos and Hornpipes, Walk Arounds, Reels and Jigs, Songs and Banjo Stories, progressively arranged and plainly explained. enabling the learner to become a proficient banjoist without the aid of a teacher. The necessary explanations accompany each tune, and are placed under the notes on each page, plainly showing the string required, the finger to be used for stopping it, the manner of striking, and the number of times it must be sounded. The Instructor is illustrated with diagrams and explanatory symbols. 100 pages. Bound in boards, cloth back..50 cts.

Hard Words Made Easy. Rules for Pronunciation and Accent;

with instructions how to pronounce French, Italian, German, Spanish, and other foreign names ....12 cts.

Rarey & Knowlson's Complete Horse Tamer and Farrier.

A New and Improved Edition, containing: Mr. Rarey's Whole Secret of Subduing and Breaking Vicious Horses; His Improved Plan of Managing Young Colts, and Breaking them to the Saddle, to Harness and the Sulky. Rules for Selecting a Good Horse, and for Feeding Horses. Also the Complete Farrier or Horse Doctor; being the result of fifty years' extensive practice of the author, John C. Knowlson, during his life an English Farrier of high popularity; containing the latest discoveries in the cure of Spavin. Illustrated with descriptive engravings. Bound in boards, cloth back .50 cts.

How to Amuse an Evening Party. A Complete collection of

Home Recreations. Profusely Illustrated with over Two Hundred fine wood-cuts, containing Round Games and Forfeit Games, Parlor Magic and Curious Puzzles, Comic Diversions and Parlor Tricks, Scientific Recreations and Evening Amusements. A young man with this volume may render himself the *beau ideal* of a delightful companion at every party, and win the hearts of all the ladies, by his powers of entertainment. Bound in ornamental paper covers.. 30 cts.
Bound in boards, with cloth back................................... 50 cts.

Frost's Laws and By-Laws of American Society. A Com-

plete Treatise on Etiquette. Containing plain and Reliable Directions for Deportment in every Situation in Life, by S. A. Frost, author of "Frost's Letter-Writer," etc. This is a book of ready reference on the usages of Society at all times and on all occasions, and also a reliable guide in the details of deportment and polite behavior. Paper covers................... 30 cts.
Bound in boards, with cloth back................................... 50 cts.

Frost's Original Letter-Writer. A complete collection of Orig-

inal Letters and Notes, upon every imaginable subject of Every-Day Life, with plain directions about everything connected with writing a letter. By S. A. Frost. To which is added a comprehensive Table of Synonyms, alone worth double the price asked for the book. We assure our readers that it is the best collection of letters ever published in this country; they are written in plain and natural language, and elegant in style without being high-flown. Bound in boards, cloth back, with illuminated sides................. 50 cts.

North's Book of Love-Letters. With directions how to write

and when to use them, and 120 Specimen Letters, suitable for Lovers of any age and condition, and under all circumstances. Interspersed with the author's comments thereon. The whole forming a convenient Hand-book of valuable information and counsel for the use of those who need friendly guidance and advice in matters of Love, Courtship and Marriage. By Ingoldsby North. Bound in boards...................................... 50 cts.
Bound in cloth... 75 cts.

How to Shine in Society; or, The Science of Conversation.

Containing the principles, laws and general usages of polite society, including easily applied hints and directions for commencing and sustaining an agreeable conversation, and for choosing topics appropriate to the time, place and company, thus affording immense assistance to the bashful and diffident. 16mo. Paper covers..................................... 25 cts.

The Poet's Companion. A Dictionary of all Allowable Rhymes

in the English Language. This gives the Perfect, the Imperfect and Allowable Rhymes, and will enable you to ascertain to a certainty whether any word can be mated. It is invaluable to any one who desires to court the Muses, and is used by some of the best writers in the country...... 25 cts.

Mind Your Stops. Punctuation made plain, and Composition

simplified for Readers, Writers and Talkers........................ 12 cts.

Five Hundred French Phrases. A book giving all the French

words and maxims in general use in writing the English language... 12 cts.

Sut Lovingood. Yarns spun by "A Nat'ral Born Durn'd Fool."

Warped and Wove for Public Wear, by George W. Harris. Illustrated with eight fine full page engravings, from designs by Howard. It would be difficult, we think, to cram a larger amount of pungent humor into 300 pages than will be found in this really funny book. The Preface and Dedication are models of sly simplicity, and the 24 Sketches which follow are among the best specimens of broad burlesque to which the genius of the ludicrous, for which the Southwest is so distinguished, has yet given birth. 12mo, tinted paper, cloth, gilt edges..... ....$1.50

Uncle Josh's Trunkful of Fun. Containing a rich collection of

Comical Stories, Cruel Sells,	*New Conundrums, Mirth-Provoking*
Side-Splitting Jokes, Humorous Poetry,	*Speeches,*
	Curious Puzzles, Amusing Card
Quaint Parodies, Burlesque Sermons,	*Tricks, and*
	Astonishing Feats of Parlor-Magic.

This book is illustrated with nearly 200 funny engravings, and contains, in 64 large octavo double-column pages, at least three times as much reading matter and real fun as any other book of the price.................. 15 cts.

The Strange and Wonderful Adventures of Bachelor

Butterfly. Showing how his passion for Natural History completely eradicated the tender passion implanted in his breast—also detailing his Extraordinary Travels, both by sea and land—his Hair-breadth Escapes from fire and cold—his being come over by a Widow with nine small children—his wonderful Adventures with the Doctor and the Fiddler, and other Perils of a most extraordinary nature. The whole illustrated by about 200 engravings...30 cts.

The Laughable Adventures of Messrs. Brown, Jones and

Robinson. Showing where they went, and how they went, what they did, and how they did it. Here is a book which will make you split your sides laughing. It shows the comical adventures of three jolly young greenhorns, who went traveling, and got into all manner of scrapes and funny adventures. Illustrated with nearly 200 thrillingly-comic engravings.....30 cts.

The Mishaps and Adventures of Obadiah Oldbuck. This

humorous and curious book sets forth, with 188 comic drawings, the misfortunes which befell Mr. Oldbuck; and also his five unsuccessful attempts to commit suicide—his hair-breadth escapes from fire, water and famine—his affection for his poor dog, etc. To look over this book will make you laugh, and you can't help it..... ....30 cts.

Jack Johnson's Jokes for the Jolly. A collection of Funny

Stories, Droll Incidents, Queer Conceits and Apt Repartees. Illustrating the Drolleries of Border Life in the West, Yankee Peculiarities, Dutch Blunders, French Sarcasms, Irish Wit and Humor, etc., with short Ludicrous Narratives; making altogether a Medley of Mirthful Morsels for the Melancholy that will drive away the blues, and cause the most misanthropic mortal to laugh. Illustrated paper covers.......................25 cts.

Snipsnaps and Snickerings of Simon Snodgrass. A collec-

tion of Droll and Laughable Stories, illustrative of Irish Drolleries and Blarney, Ludicrous Dutch Blunders, Queer Yankee Tricks and Dodges, Backwoods Boasting, Humors of Horse-trading, Negro Comicalities, Perilous Pranks of Fighting Men, Frenchmen's Queer Mistakes, Scotch Shrewdness, and other phases of eccentric character, that go to make up a perfect and complete Medley of Wit and Humor. It is also full of funny engravings...25 cts.

Madame Le Normand's Fortune Teller. An entertaining book, said to have been written by Madame Le Normand, the celebrated French Fortune Teller, who was frequently consulted by the Emperor Napoleon. A party of ladies and gentlemen may amuse themselves for hours with this curious book. It tells fortunes by "The Chart of Fate" (a large lithographic chart), and gives 624 answers to questions on every imaginable subject that may happen in the future. It explains a variety of ways for telling fortunes by Cards and Dice; gives a list of 79 curious old superstitions and omens, and 187 weather omens, and winds up with the celebrated Oraculum of Napoleon. We will not endorse this book as infallible; but we assure our readers that it is the source of much mirth whenever introduced at a gathering of ladies and gentlemen. Bound in boards. **40 cts.**

The Fireside Magician; or, The Art of Natural Magic Made Easy. Being a scientific explanation of Legerdemain, Physical Amusement, Recreative Chemistry, Diversion with Cards, and of all the mysteries of Mechanical Magic, with feats as performed by Herr Alexander, Robert Heller, Robert Houdin, "The Wizard of the North," and distinguished conjurors—comprising two hundred and fifty interesting mental and physical recreations, with explanatory engravings. 132 pages, paper. **30 cts.** Bound in boards, cloth back...................................**50 cts.**

Howard's Book of Conundrums and Riddles. Containing over 1,200 of the best Conundrums, Riddles, Enigmas, Ingenious Catches and Amusing Sells ever invented. This splendid collection of curious paradoxes will afford the material for a never-ending feast of fun and amusement. Any person, with the assistance of this book, may take the lead in entertaining a company, and keep them in roars of laughter for hours together. Paper covers...... ....**30 cts.** Bound in boards, cloth back...................................**50 cts.**

The Parlor Magician; or, One Hundred Tricks for the Drawing-Room. Containing an extensive and miscellaneous collection of Conjuring and Legerdemain, embracing: Tricks with Dice, Dominoes and Cards; Tricks with Ribbons, Rings and Fruit; Tricks with Coin, Handkerchiefs and Balls, etc. The whole illustrated and clearly explained with 121 engravings. Paper covers.............................**30 cts.** Bound in boards, with cloth back.............................**50 cts.**

Book of Riddles and 500 Home Amusements. Containing a curious collection of Riddles, Charades and Enigmas; Rebuses, Anagrams and Transpositions; Conundrums and Amusing Puzzles; Recreations in Arithmetic, and Queer Sleights, and numerous other Entertaining Amusements. Illustrated with 60 engravings. Paper covers...............**30 cts.** Bound in boards, with cloth back......   ....**50 cts.**

The Book of Fireside Games. Containing an explanation of a variety of Witty, Rollicking. Entertaining and Innocent Games and Amusing Forfeits, suited to the Family Circle as a Recreation. This book is just the thing for social gatherings, parties and pic-nics. Paper covers .**30 cts.** Bound in boards, cloth back...................................**50 cts.**

The Book of 500 Curious Puzzles. Containing a large collection of Curious Puzzles, Entertaining Paradoxes, Perplexing Deceptions in Numbers, Amusing Tricks in Geometry; illustrated with a great variety of Engravings. Paper covers......................................**30 cts.** Bound in boards, with cloth back.............................**50 cts.**

Parlor Tricks with Cards. Containing explanations of all the Tricks and Deceptions with Playing Cards ever invented. The whole illustrated and made plain and easy with 70 engravings. Paper covers..**30 cts.** Bound in boards, with cloth back.............................**50 cts.**

Day's Book-Keeping Without a Master. Containing the Rudiments of Book-keeping in Single and Double Entry, together with the proper Forms and Rules for opening and keeping condensed and general Book Accounts. This work is printed in a beautiful script type, and hence combines the advantages of a handsome style of writing with its very simple and easily understood lessons in Book-keeping. The several pages have explanations at the bottom to assist the learner, in small type. As a pattern for opening book accounts it is especially valuable—particularly for those who are not well posted in the art. DAY'S BOOK-KEEPING is the size of a regular quarto Account Book, and is made to lie flat open for convenience in use..50 cts.

Blank Books for Day's Book-Keeping. We have for sale Books of 96 pages each, ruled according to the patterns mentioned on page 3 of DAY'S BOOK-KEEPING, suitable for practice of the learner, viz.: No. 1—For General Book-keeping, pages 4 and 5; for Cash Account on page 13; for Day-Book in Single Entry, pages 15 to 25. No. 2—For Condensed Accounts, pages 9 and 10; for Cash Account, page 12; for Journal in Double Entry, pages 34 to 43. No. 3—For Ledgers in Double or Single Entry, pages 26 to 44. Each Number ....50 cts.

How to Learn the Sense of 3,000 French Words in one Hour. This ingenious little book actually accomplishes all that its title claims. It is a fact that there are at least three thousand words in the French language, forming a large proportion of those used in ordinary conversation, which are spelled exactly the same as in English, or become the same by very slight and easily understood changes in their termination. 16mo, illuminated paper covers......................................25 cts.

How to Speak in Public; or, The Art of Extempore Oratory. A valuable manual for those who desire to become ready off-hand speakers; containing clear directions how to arrange ideas logically and quickly, including illustrations, by the analysis of speeches delivered by some of the greatest orators, exemplifying the importance of correct emphasis, clearness of articulation, and appropriate gesture. Paper covers............25 cts.

Live and Learn. A guide for all those who wish to speak and write correctly; particularly intended as a Book of Reference for the solution of difficulties connected with Grammar, Composition, Punctuation, &c., &c., containing examples of 1,000 mistakes of daily occurrence in speaking, writing and pronunciation. Cloth, 16mo, 216 pages................75 cts.

The Art of Dressing Well. By Miss S. A. Frost. This book is designed for ladies and gentlemen who desire to make a favorable impression upon society. Paper covers....................................30 cts.
Bound in boards, cloth back...50 cts.

Thimm's French Self-Taught. A new system, on the most simple principles, for Universal Self-Tuition, with English pronunciation of every word. By this system the acquirement of the French Language is rendered less laborious and more thorough than by any of the old methods. By Franz Thimm ....25 cts.

Thimm's German Self-Taught. Uniform with "French Self-Taught," and arranged in accordance with the same principles of thoroughness and simplicity. By Franz Thimm............................25 cts.

Thimm's Spanish Self-Taught. A book of self-instruction in the Spanish Language, arranged according to the same method as the "French" and "German," by the same author, and uniform with them in size. By Franz Thimm..25 cts.

Thimm's Italian Self-Taught. Uniform in style and size with the three foregoing books. By Franz Thimm......................25 cts.

CARD AND OTHER GAMES.

"Trump's" American Hoyle; or, Gentleman's Hand-Book of Games. This work contains an exhaustive treatise on Whist, by William Pole, F.R.S., and the rules for playing that game as laid down by the Hon. James Clay. It also contains clear descriptions of all the games played in the United States, with the American rules for playing them: including Euchre, Bézique, Cribbage, All Fours, Loo, Poker, Brag, Piquet, Pedro Sancho, Penuchle, Railroad Euchre, Jack Pots, Ecarté, Boston, Cassino, Chess, Checkers, Backgammon, Billiards, Dominoes, and a hundred other games. This work is designed as an American authority in all games of skill and chance, and will settle any disputed point. It has been prepared with great care, and is not a re-hash of English games, but a live American book, expressly prepared for American players. THE AMERICAN HOYLE contains 525 pages, is printed on fine white paper, bound in cloth, with extra gilt side and beveled boards, and is profusely illustrated............$2.00

The Modern Pocket Hoyle. By "Trumps." Containing all the games of skill and chance, as played in this country at the present time, being an "authority on all disputed points." This valuable manual is all original, or thoroughly revised from the best and latest authorities, and includes the laws and complete directions for playing one hundred and eleven different games. 388 pages, paper covers.............................50 cts.
Bound in boards, with cloth back.........................75 cts.
Bound in cloth, gilt side and back............................$1.25

Hoyle's Games. A complete Manual of the laws that govern all games of skill and chance, including Card Games, Chess, Checkers, Dominoes, Backgammon, Dice, Billiards (as played in this country at the present time), and all Field Games. Entirely original, or thoroughly revised from the latest and best American authorities. Paper covers............50 cts.
Boards...75 cts.
Cloth, gilt side....................................$1.25

Walker's Cribbage Made Easy. Being a new and complete Treatise on the Game in all varieties. By George Walker, Esq. A very comprehensive work on this Game. It contains over 500 examples of how to discard for your own and your adversary's crib.
142 pages, bound in boards..............................50 cts.

100 Tricks With Cards Exposed and Explained. By J. H. Green, the Reformed Gambler. This book exposes and explains all the Mysteries of the Gambling Tables. It is interesting not only to those who play, but to those who do not. Paper covers.....................30 cts.
Bound in boards, with cloth back...........................50 cts.

How Gamblers Win; or, The Secrets of Advantage Playing Exposed. Being a complete and scientific exposé of the manner of playing all the various advantages in the various Card Games, as practiced by professional gamblers. This work is designed as a warning to self-confident card-players. Bound in boards, with cloth back..............50 cts.

DICK & FITZGERALD, Publishers,

Box 2975.   NEW YORK.

Martine's Sensible Letter-Writer.

Being a comprehensive and complete Guide and Assistant for those who desire to carry on Epistolary Correspondence; containing a large collection of model letters on the simplest matters of life, adapted to all ages and conditions—

EMBRACING,

Business Letters ; Applications for Employment, with Letters of Recommendation and Answers to Advertisements ; Letters between Parents and Children ; Letters of Friendly Counsel and Remonstrance ; Letters soliciting Advice, Assistance and Friendly Favors ;

Letters of Courtesy, Friendship and Affection ; Letters of Condolence and Sympathy ; A Choice Collection of Love-Letters, for Every Situation in a Courtship ; Notes of Ceremony, Familiar Invitations. etc., together with Notes of Acceptance and Regret.

The whole containing 300 Sensible Letters and Notes. This is an invaluable book for those persons who have not had sufficient practice to enable them to write letters without great effort. It contains such a variety of letters, that models may be found to suit every subject.

207 pages, bound in boards, cloth back....................................50 cts.
Bound in cloth..75 cts.

Martine's Hand-Book of Etiquette and Guide to True

Politeness. A complete Manual for all those who desire to understand good breeding, the customs of good society. and to avoid incorrect and vulgar habits. Containing clear and comprehensive directions for correct manners, conversation, dress, introductions, rules for good behavior at Dinner Parties and the Table. with hints on carving and wine at table ; together with the Etiquette of the Ball and Assembly Room, Evening Parties, and the usages to be observed when visiting or receiving calls ; Deportment in the street and when traveling. To which is added the Etiquette of Courtship, Marriage, Domestic Duties and fifty-six rules to be observed in general society. By Arthur Martine. Bound in boards ..50 cts.
Bound in cloth, gilt sides...75 cts.

Dick's Quadrille Call-Book and Ball-Room Prompter.

Containing clear directions how to call out the figures of every dance, with the quantity of music necessary for each figure, and simple explanations of all the figures which occur in Plain and Fancy Quadrilles. This book gives plain and comprehensive instructions how to dance all the new and popular dances, fully describing

The Opening March or Polonaise, Various Plain and Fancy Quadrilles, Waltz and Glide Quadrilles, Plain Lancers and Caledonians, Glide Lancers and Caledonians, Saratoga Lancers. The Parisian Varieties, The Prince Imperial Set. Social and Basket Quadrilles, Nine-Pin and Star Quadrilles, Gavotte and Minuet Quadrilles,

March and Cheat Quadrilles, Favorite Jigs and Contra-Dances, Polka and Polka Redowa, Redowa and Redowa Waltz, Polka Mazourka and Old Style Waltz, Modern Plain Waltz and Glide, Boston Dip and Hop Waltz, Five-Step Waltz and Schottische, Varsovienne and Zulma L'Orientale, Galop and Deux Temps, Esmeralda, Sicilienne, Danish Dance,

AND OVER ONE HUNDRED FIGURES FOR THE "GERMAN;"

To which is added a Sensible Guide to Etiquette and Proper Deportment in the Ball and Assembly Room, besides seventy pages of dance music for the piano.

Paper covers..50 cts.
Bound in boards...75 cts.

Lola Montez' Arts of Beauty; or, Secrets of a Lady's Toilet.

With hints to Gentlemen on the Art of Fascinating. Lola Montez here explains all the Arts employed by the celebrated beauties and fashionable ladies in Paris and other cities of Europe, for the purpose of preserving their beauty and improving and developing their charms. The recipes are all clearly given, so that any person can understand them, and the work embraces the following subjects:

How to obtain such desirable and indispensable attractions as A Handsome Form ;	*A Soft and Abundant Head of Hair; Also, How to Remedy Gray Hair;*
A Bright and Smooth Skin ;	*And harmless but effectual methods of removing Superfluous Hair and*
A Beautiful Complexion ;	*other blemishes, with interesting in-*
Attractive Eyes, Mouth and Lips ;	*formation on these and kindred*
A Beautiful Hand, Foot and Ankle ;	*matters.*
A Well-trained Voice ;	

Illuminated paper cover..25 cts.

Hillgrove's Ball-Room Guide and Complete Dancing-Master.

Containing a plain treatise on Etiquette and Deportment at Balls and Parties, with valuable hints on Dress and the Toilet, together with

Full Explanations of the Rudiments, Terms, Figures and Steps used in Dancing;	*Reels, Round, Plain and Fancy Dances, so that any person may learn them without the aid of a*
Including Clear and Precise Instructions how to dance all kinds of Quadrilles, Waltzes, Polkas, Redowas,	*Teacher; To which is added easy directions how to call out the Figures*

of every dance, and the amount of music required for each. Illustrated with 176 descriptive engravings. By T. Hillgrove, Professor of Dancing.
Bound in cloth, with gilt side and back.............................$1.00
Bound in boards, with cloth back..................................75 cts.

The Banjo, and How to Play it.

Containing, in addition to the elementary studies, a choice collection of Polkas, Waltzes, Solos, Schottisches, Songs, Hornpipes, Jigs, Reels, etc., with full explanations of both the "Banjo" and "Guitar" styles of execution, and designed to impart a complete knowledge of the art of playing the Banjo practically, without the aid of a teacher. This work is arranged on the progressive system, showing the learner how to play the first few notes of a tune, then the next notes, and so on, a small portion at a time, until he has mastered the entire piece, every detail being as clearly and thoroughly explained as if he had a teacher at his elbow all the time. By Frank B. Converse, author of the "Banjo without a Master." 16mo, bound in boards, cloth back..50 cts.

Row's National Wages Tables.

Showing at a glance the amount of wages from half an hour to sixty hours, at from $1 to $37 per week. Also from one-quarter of a day to four weeks, at $1 to $37 per week. By Nelson Row. By this book, which is particularly useful when part of a week, day or hour is lost, a large pay-roll can be made out in a few minutes, thus saving more time in making out one pay-roll than the cost of the book. Every employer hiring help by the hour, day or week, and every employee, should obtain one, as it will enable him to know exactly the amount of money he is entitled to on pay-day. Half bound....................50 cts.

Row's Complete Fractional Ready-Reckoner.

For buying and selling any kind of merchandise, giving the fractional parts of a pound, yard, etc., from one-quarter to one thousand, at any price from one-quarter of a cent to five dollars. By Nelson Row. 36mo, 232 pages, boards..50 cts.

Blunders in Behavior Corrected.

A book of Deportment for both Ladies and Gentlemen. By means of this book you can learn the most difficult phases in Etiquette, or behavior in good society............12 cts.

Delisser's Horseman's Guide. Comprising the Laws on Warranty, and the Rules in purchasing and selling horses, with the decisions and reports of various courts in Europe and the United States ; to which is added a detailed account of what constitutes soundness and unsoundness, and a precise method, simply laid down, for the examination of horses, showing their age to thirty years old ; together with an exposure of the various tricks and impositions practiced by low horse-dealers (jockeys) on inexperienced persons ; also, a valuable Table of each and every bone in the structure of the Horse. By George P. Delisser, Veterinary Surgeon.
Bound in boards, cloth back..75 cts.
Bound in cloth..$1.00

Brisbane's Golden Ready-Reckoner. Calculated in Dollars and Cents. Showing at once the amount or value of any number of articles or quantity of goods, or any merchandise, either by the gallon, quart, pint, ounce, pound, quarter, hundred, yard, foot, inch, bushel, etc., in an easy and plain manner. To which are added Interest Tables, calculated in dollars and cents, for days and for months, at six per cent. and at seven per cent. per annum, alternately ; and a great number of other Tables and Rules for calculation never before in print. Bound in boards................35 cts.

How to Cook Potatoes, Apples, Eggs and Fish, Four Hundred Different Ways. Our lady friends will be surprised when they examine this book, and find the great variety of ways that the same article may be prepared and cooked. The work especially recommends itself to those who are often embarrassed for want of variety in dishes suitable for the breakfast-table, or on occasions where the necessity arises for preparing a meal at short notice. Paper covers.............................30 cts.
Bound in boards, with cloth back..................................50 cts.

The American Housewife and Kitchen Directory. This valuable book embraces three hundred and seventy-eight recipes for cooking all sorts of American dishes in the most economical manner : it also contains a variety of important secrets for washing, cleaning, scouring and extracting grease, paint, stains and iron-mould from cloth, muslin and linen. Bound in ornamental paper covers...30 cts.
Bound in boards, with cloth back...................................50 cts.

How to Cook and How to Carve. Giving plain and easily understood directions for preparing and cooking, with the greatest economy, every kind of dish, with complete instructions for serving the same. This book is just the thing for a young Housekeeper. It is worth a dozen of expensive French books. Paper covers.............................30 cts.
Bound in boards, with cloth back...................................50 cts.

The American Home Cook Book. Containing several hundred excellent recipes. The whole based on many years' experience of an American Housewife. Illustrated with engravings. All the Recipes in this book are written from actual experience in Cooking. Paper....30 cts.
Bound in boards, cloth back...50 cts.

The Yankee Cook Book. A new system of Cookery. Containing hundreds of excellent recipes from actual experience in Cooking ; also, full explanations in the art of Carving. 126 pages, paper covers.30 cts.
Bound in boards, with cloth back....................................50 cts.

How to Mix all Kinds of Fancy Drinks. Containing clear and reliable directions for mixing all the beverages used in the United States. Embracing Punches, Juleps, Cobblers, Cocktails, etc., etc., in endless variety. By Jerry Thomas. Illuminated paper covers.....................50 cts.
Bound in full cloth...75 cts.

What Shall We Do To-Night? or, Social Amusements for

Evening Parties. This elegant book affords an almost inexhaustible fund of amusement for evening parties, social gatherings and all festive occasions, ingeniously grouped together so as to furnish complete and ever-varying entertainment for Twenty-six evenings. Its repertoire embraces all the best round and forfeit games, clearly described and rendered perfectly plain by original and amusing examples, interspersed with a great variety of ingenious puzzles, entertaining tricks and innocent sells; new and original Musical and Poetical pastimes, startling illusions and mirth-provoking exhibitions; including complete directions and text for performing Charades, Tableaux, Parlor Pantomimes, the world-renowned Punch and Judy, Gallanty Shows and original Shadow-pantomimes; also, full information for the successful performance of Dramatic Dialogues and Parlor Theatricals, with a selection of Original Plays, etc., written expressly for this work. It is embellished with over one hundred descriptive and explanatory engravings, and contains 366 pages, printed on fine toned paper. Extra cloth...$2.00

The Secret Out; or, 1,000 Tricks with Cards, and Other

Recreations. Illustrated with over 300 engravings. A book which explains all the Tricks and Deceptions with Playing Cards ever known, and gives, besides, a great many new ones. The whole being described so carefully, with engravings to illustrate them, that anybody can easily learn how to perform them. This work also contains 240 of the best Tricks of Legerdemain, in addition to the Card Tricks. Such is the unerring process of instruction adopted in this volume, that no reader can fail to succeed in executing every Trick, Experiment, Game, etc., set down, if he will at all devote his attention, in his leisure hours, to the subject; and, as almost every trick with cards known will be found in this collection, it may be considered the only complete work on the subject ever published.
12mo, 400 pages, bound in cloth, gilt side and back................$1.50

The Magician's Own Book; or, The Whole Art of Con-

juring. A complete hand-book of Parlor Magic, containing over a thousand Optical, Chemical, Mechanical, Magnetic and Magical Experiments, Amusing Transmutations, Astonishing Sleights and Subtleties, Celebrated Card Deceptions, Ingenious Tricks with Numbers, curious and entertaining Puzzles, the Art of Secret Writing, together with all the most noted tricks of modern performers. Illustrated with over 500 wood-cuts, the whole forming a comprehensive guide for amateurs. 12mo, cloth, gilt... ..$1.50

The Sociable; or, One Thousand and One Home Amuse-

ments. Containing Acting Proverbs, Dramatic Charades, Acting Charades or Drawing-room Pantomimes, Musical Burlesques, Tableaux Vivants, Parlor Games, Games of Action, Forfeits, Science in Sport and Parlor Magic, and a choice collection of curious Mental and Mechanical Puzzles, etc. Illustrated with numerous engravings and diagrams. The whole being a fund of never-ending entertainment. 376 pages, cloth, gilt......$1.50

Athletic Sports for Boys. A Repository of Graceful Recrea-

tions for Youth, containing clear and complete instructions in Gymnastics, Limb Exercises, Jumping, Pole-Leaping, Dumb Bells, Indian Clubs, Parallel Bars, the Horizontal Bar, the Trapeze, the Suspended Ropes, and the manly accomplishments of Skating, Swimming, Rowing, Sailing, Horsemanship, Riding, Driving, Angling, Fencing and Broadsword. Illustrated with 194 wood-cuts. Bound in boards............................75 cts.

The Young Reporter; or, How to Write Short-Hand. A

Complete Phonographic Teacher, intended as a School-book, to afford thorough instructions to those who have not the assistance of an Oral Teacher. By the aid of this work, any person of the most ordinary intelligence may learn to write Short-Hand, and report Speeches and Sermons in a short time. Bound in boards, with cloth back........... ....50 cts.

What Shall We Do To-Night? or, Social

Amusements for Evening Parties. This elegant book affords an almost inexhaustible fund of amusement for Evening Parties, Social Gatherings and all Festive Occasions, ingeniously grouped together so as to furnish complete and ever-varying entertainment for Twenty-six evenings. Its repertoire embraces all the

Best Round and Forfeit Games, clearly described and rendered perfectly plain by original and amusing examples, interspersed with a great variety of Ingenious Puzzles, Entertaining T. and Innocent Sells; new and original Musical and Poetical pastimes, Startling Illusions and Mirth-provoking Exhibitions; including complete directions and *for performing Charades, Tableaux, Parlor Pantomimes, the world-renowned Punch and Judy, Gallanty Shows and original Shadow-pantomimes; also, full information for the successful performance of Dramatic Dialogues and Parlor Theatricals, with a selection of Original Plays, etc.,*

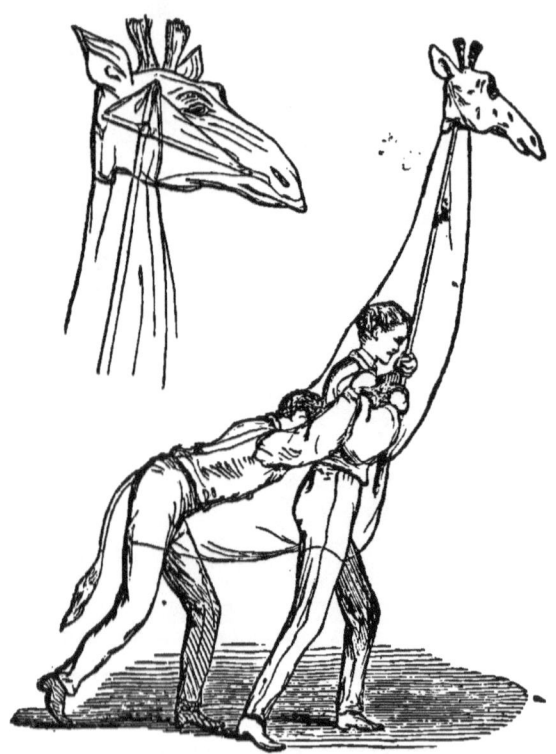

written expressly for this work. It is embellished with over ONE HUNDRED DESCRIPTIVE AND EXPLANATORY ENGRAVINGS, and contains 366 pages, printed on fine toned paper. 12mo, bound in extra cloth, beveled....................$2.00

The Art and Etiquette of Making Love. A

Manual of Love, Courtship and Matrimony. It tells

How to Cure Bashfulness;
How to Commence a Courtship;
How to Please a Sweetheart or Lover;
How to Write a Love-Letter;
How to "Pop the Question";
How to Act Before and After a Proposal;
How to Accept or Reject a Proposal;
How to Break off an Engagement;
How to Act After an Engagement;
How to Act as Bridesmaid or Grooms-man;
How the Etiquette of a Wedding and the After-Reception Should be Observed;

And, in fact, how to fulfill every duty and meet every contingency connected with courtship and matrimony. It includes also a choice collection of sensible Letters suitable for all the contingencies of Love and Courtship.
176 pages, paper covers..............................**30 cts.**
Bound in boards, cloth back.......................**50 cts.**

Dick's Quadrille Call-Book and Ball-Room

Prompter. Containing clear directions how to call out the figures of every dance, with the quantity of music necessary for each figure, and simple explanations of all the figures and steps which occur in Plain and Fancy Quadrilles. Also, a plain analysis and description of all the steps employed in the favorite round dances, fully describing:

The Opening March or Polonaise,
Various Plain and Fancy Quadrilles,
Waltz and Glide Quadrilles,
Plain Lancers and Caledonians,
Glide Lancers and Caledonians,
Saratoga Lancers,
The Parisian Varieties,
The Prince Imperial Set.
Social and Basket Quadrilles,
Nine-Pin and Star Quadrilles,
Gavotte and Minuet Quadrilles,

March and Cheat Quadrilles,
Favorite Jigs and Contra-Dances,
Polka and Polka Redowa,
Redowa and Redowa Waltz,
Polka Mazourka and Old Style Waltz,
Modern Plain Waltz and Glide,
Boston Dip and Hop Waltz,
Five-Step Waltz and Schottische,
Varsovienne, and Zulma L'Orientale,
Galop and Deux Temps,
Esmeralda, Sicilienne, Danish Dance,

AND OVER ONE HUNDRED FIGURES FOR THE "GERMAN;"

To which is added a Sensible Guide to Etiquette and Proper Deportment in the Ball and Assembly Room, besides seventy pages of dance music for the piano.
Paper covers...................................**50 cts.**
Bound in boards................................**75 cts.**

Uncle Josh's Trunkful of Fun. A portfolio of
first-class Wit and Humor, and never-ending source of Jollity.

CONTAINING A RICH COLLECTION OF

Oomical Stories. Cruel Sells,
Side-Splitting Jokes,
Humorous Poetry,
Quaint Parodies,
Burlesque Sermons,

New Conundrums,
Mirth-Provoking Speeches,
Curious Puzzles,
Amusing Card Tricks, and
Astonishing Feats of Parlor-Magic.

This book is illustrated with nearly 200 Funny Engravings, and contains 64 large octavo double-column pages... ....**15 cts.**

Barber's American Book of Ready-Made
Speeches. Containing 159 original examples of Humorous and Serious Speeches, suitable for every possible occasion where a speech may be called for, with appropriate replies to each.

INCLUDING

Presentation Speeches.
Convivial Speeches.
Festival Speeches.
Addresses of Congratulation.
Addresses of Welcome.
Addresses of Compliment.
Political Speeches.
Dinner and Supper Speeches for Clubs, etc.

Off-Hand Speeches on a Variety of Subjects.
Miscellaneous Speeches.
Toasts and Sentiments for Public and Private Entertainments.
Preambles and Resolutions of Congratulation, Compliment and Condolence.

With this book any person may prepare himself to make a neat little speech, or reply to one when called upon to do so. They are all short, appropriate and witty, and even ready speakers may profit by them. Paper..........................**50 cts.**
Bound in boards, cloth back........................**75 cts.**

The Amateur Trapper and Trap-Maker's Guide.

A complete and carefully prepared treatise on the art of Trapping, Snaring and Netting; containing plain directions for constructing the most approved Traps, Snares, Nets and Dead-Falls; the best methods of applying them to their various purposes; and the most successful Baits for attracting all kinds of Animals, Birds, etc., with their special uses in each case; introducing receipts for preparing Skins and Furs for Market.

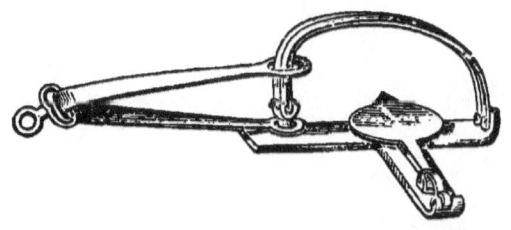

The entire work is based on the experience of the most successful Trappers, and on information derived from other authentic professional sources. By Stanley Harding. This comprehensive work is embellished with fifty well drawn and engraved illustrations; and these, together with the clear explanations which accompany them, will enable anybody of moderate comprehension to make and set any of the traps described. IT TELLS

How to make all kinds of Traps;
How to make all kinds of Snares;
How to Set and Secure Traps;
How to Attract Animals from a Distance;
How to Prepare Baits;
How to Bait a Trap;

How to Trap or Snare all kinds of Animals;
How to Trap or Snare Birds of every description;
How to Cure and Tan Skins;
How to Skin and Stuff Birds or Animals.

It also gives the baits usually employed by the most successful Hunters and Trappers, and exposes their secret methods of attracting and catching Animals, Birds, etc., with scarcely a possibility of failure. Large 16mo, paper covers.........**50 cts.**
Bound in boards, cloth back.........................**75 cts.**

How to Write a Composition.

This original work will be found a valuable aid in writing a composition on any topic. It lays down plain directions for the division of a subject into its appropriate heads, and for arranging them in their natural order, commencing with the simplest theme, and advancing progressively to more complicated subjects. Paper..**30 cts.**
Bound in boards, cloth back........................ **50 cts.**

The Magician's Own Book.

One of the most extraordinary and interesting volumes ever printed—containing the Whole Art of Conjuring, and all the Discoveries in Magic ever made, either by ancient or modern philosophers. IT EXPLAINS

All Sleight of Hand Tricks;
Tricks and Deceptions with Cards;
The Magic of Chemistry;
Mysterious Experiments in Electricity and Galvanism;
The Magic of Pneumatics, Aerostatics, Optics, etc.;
The Magic of Numbers;

Curious Tricks in Geometry;
Mysterious and Amusing Puzzles, and answers thereto;
The Magic of Art;
Miscellaneous Tricks and Experiments;
Curious Fancies, etc., etc.

 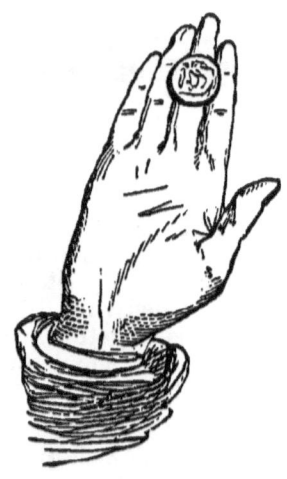

The tricks are all illustrated by Engravings and Tables, so as to make them easily understood and practiced. As a volume for the amusement of an evening party, this book cannot be surpassed. Gilt binding, 362 pages.....................**$1.50**

East Lynne; or, The Earl's Daughter.

Library edition, complete and unabridged. This novel is Mrs. Henry Wood's masterpiece, and stands in the very front ank of all the works of fiction ever written; it has scarcely a riv ' as a brilliant creation of literary genius, and is prominent among the very few works of its class that have stood the test of time, and achieved a lasting reputation. In originality of design, and masterly and dramatic development of the subject, East Lynne stands unrivaled; it will be read and re-read long after the majority of the ephemeral romances of to-day have passed out of existence and been forgotten. A handsome 12mo volume of 598 pages, from new electrotype plates, printed on fine toned paper, and elegantly bound in cloth, in black and gold...**$1.50**

The Biblical Reason Why.

A Hand-Book for Biblical Students, and a guide to family Scripture reading. This work gives REASONS founded upon the Bible, and assigned by the most eminent Divines and Christian Philosophers, for the great and all-absorbing events recorded in the History of the Bible, the Life of our Saviour and the Acts of His Apostles.

EXAMPLE.

Why did the first patriarchs attain such extreme longevity.
Why was the term of life afterwards shortened?
Why are there several manifest variations in names, facts and dates, between the books of Kings and Chronicles?

Why is the book of the prophecies of Isaiah a strong proof of the authenticity of the whole Bible?
Why did our Saviour receive the name of Jesus?
Why did John the Baptist hesitate to administer the rite of Baptism to Jesus?

This volume answers 1,493 similar questions. Beautifully illustrated. Large 12mo, cloth, gilt side and back...........$1.50

The Reason Why: General Science.

A careful collection of reasons for some thousands of things which, though generally known, are imperfectly understood. A book for the million. This work assigns reasons for the thousands of things that daily fall under the eye of the intelligent observer, and of which he seeks a simple and clear explanation.

EXAMPLE.

Why does silver tarnish when exposed to light?
Why do some colors fade, and others darken, when exposed to the sun?
Why is the sky blue?

What develops electricity in the clouds?
Why does dew form round drops upon the leaves of plants?

This volume answers 1,325 similar questions. 356 pages, bound in cloth, gilt, and embellished with a large number of woodcuts, illustrating the various subjects treated of.........$1.50

The Reason Why: Natural History.

Giving reasons for hundreds of interesting facts in connection with Zoology, and throwing a light upon the peculiar habits and instincts of the various orders of the Animal Kingdom.

EXAMPLE.

Why has the lion such a large mane?
Why does the otter, when hunting for fish, swim against the stream?
Why do dogs turn around two or three times before they lie down?
Why have flat fishes their upper sides dark, and their under sides white?

Why do sporting dogs make what is termed "a point"?
Why do birds often roost upon one leg?
Why do frogs keep their mouths closed while breathing?
Why does the wren build several nests, but occupy only one?

This volume answers about 1,500 similar questions.
Illustrated, cloth, gilt side and back...................$1.50

The American Boy's Book of Sports and

Games. A Repository of In and Out-door Amusements for Boys and Youths. Containing 600 large 12mo pages. Illustrated with nearly 700 engravings, designed by White, Herrick, Weir and Harvey, and engraved by N. Orr. This is unquestionably the most attractive and valuable book of its kind ever issued in this or any other country. It was three years in preparation, and embraces all the sports and games that tend to develop the physical constitution, improve the mind and heart, and relieve the tedium of leisure hours, both in the parlor and the field.

The engravings are in the first style of the art, and embrace eight full-page ornamental titles, and two large colored chromos, illustrating the several departments of the work, beautifully printed on tinted paper. The book is issued in the best style, being printed on fine sized paper, and handsomely bound. Extra cloth, gilt side and back, extra gold, beveled boards.....**$2.00**

Jack Johnson's Jokes for the Jolly. A collection of Funny Stories, illustrating the Drolleries of Border Life in the West, Yankee Peculiarities, Dutch Blunders, French Sarcasms, Irish Wit and Humor, etc.

Illustrated paper covers...........................**25 cts.**

"Trump's" American Hoyle; or, Gentleman's Hand-Book of Games.

This work contains an exhaustive treatise on Whist, by William Pole, F.R.S., and the rules for playing that game as laid down by the Hon. James Clay. It also contains clear descriptions of all the games played in the United States, with the American rules for playing them; including

Euchre, Bezique, Cribbage, Baccara, All Fours, Loo, Poker, Brag, Piquet, Pedro Sancho, Penuchle, Railroad Euchre, Jack Pots, Ecarté, Boston, | *California Jack, Cassino, Chess, Checkers, Backgammon, Billiards, Dominoes, and a hundred other games.*

 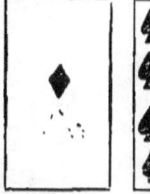 

This work is designed as an American authority in all games of skill and chance, and will settle any disputed point. It has been prepared with great care, and is not a re-hash of English games, but a live American book, expressly prepared for American players. THE AMERICAN HOYLE contains 525 pages, is printed on fine white paper, bound in cloth, with extra-gilt side and beveled boards, and is profusely illustrated.........**$2.00**

Spayth's American Draught Player; or, The Theory and Practice of the Scientific Game of Checkers.

Simplified and Illustrated with Practical Diagrams. Containing upwards of 1,700 Games and Positions. By Henry Spayth. Fifth edition, with over two hundred Corrections and Im-

provements. Containing: The Standard Laws of the Game— Full Instructions—Draught Board Numbered—Names of the Games, and how formed—The "Theory of the Move and its Changes" practically explained and illustrated with Diagrams— Playing Tables for Draught Clubs—New Systems of Numbering the Board—Prefixing Signs to the Variations—List of Draught Treatises and Publications chronologically arranged.
Bound in cloth, gilt side and back....................**$3.00**

Sut Lovingood. Yarns spun by "A Nat'ral Born Durn'd Fool."

Warped and Wove for Public Wear by George W. Harris. Illustrated with eight fine full page engravings,

from designs by Howard. It would be difficult, we think, to cram a larger amount of pungent humor into 300 pages than will be found in this really funny book. The Preface and Dedication are models of sly simplicity, and the 24 Sketches which follow are among the best specimens of broad burlesque to which the genius of the ludicrous, for which the Southwest is so distinguished, has yet given birth. Cloth, gilt edges.........$1.50

How to Conduct a Debate. A Series of

Complete Debates,

Outlines of Debates, and

Questions for Discussion.

In the complete debates, the questions for discussion are defined, the debate formally opened, an array of brilliant arguments adduced on either side, and the debate closed according to parliamentary usages. The second part consists of questions for debate, with heads of arguments, for and against, given in a condensed form for the speakers to enlarge upon to suit their own fancy. In addition to these are

A Large Collection of Debatable Questions.

The authorities to be referred to for information are given at the close of every debate. By Frederic Rowton.

232 pages, paper ....**50 cts.**

Bound in boards, cloth back....................**75 cts.**

The Secret Out; or, 1,000 Tricks with Cards,

and Other Recreations. Illustrated with over 300 engravings.

A book which explains all the Tricks and Deceptions with Playing Cards ever known, and gives, besides, a great many new ones. The whole being described so carefully, with engravings to illustrate them, that anybody can easily learn how to perform them. This work also contains 240 of the best Tricks of Legerdemain, in addition to the Card Tricks.

SYNOPSIS OF CONTENTS.

PART I.—*Tricks with Cards performed by skillful Manipulation and Sleight of Hand.*

PART II.—*Tricks performed by the aid of Memory, Mental Calculation and the Peculiar Arrangement of the Cards.*

PART III.—*Tricks with Cards performed by the aid of Confederacy and sheer Audacity.*

PART IV.—*Tricks performed by the aid of Ingenious Apparatus and Prepared Cards.*

PART V.—*Tricks of Legerdemain, Conjuring, Sleight of Hand and other Fancies, commonly called White Magic.*

PART VI.—*Tricks in White Magic, performed by the aid of Ingenious Contrivance and Simple Apparatus.*

PART VII.—*Natural Magic, or Recreations in Science, embracing Curious Amusements in Magnetism, Mechanics, Acoustics, Chemistry, Hydraulics and Optics.*

PART VIII.—*A Curious Collection of Entertaining Experiments, Amusing Puzzles, Queer Sleights, Including the Celebrated Science of Second Sight, Recreations in Arithmetic, and Fireside Games for Family Pastime, and other Astonishing Scientific Paradoxes and Attractive Amusements.*

THE SECRET OUT is, by all odds, the most curious book that has been published in many years, and lays bare the whole machinery of magic, and with a simplicity so perfect that nobody can fail to become a domestic magician in a week, with very little study and practice. Such is the unerring process of instruction adopted in this volume, that no reader can fail to succeed in executing every Trick, Experiment, Game, etc., set down, if he will at all devote his attention, in his leisure hours, to the subject; and., as every trick with cards known will be found in this collection. it may be considered the only complete work on the subject ever published. 400 pages, bound in cloth, gilt..............$1.50